You Can't
Hit a Woman

and other stories

PETER CHEYNEY

COLLINS

fontana books

First published 1937
First issued in Fontana Books 1958
Second Impression, June 1966

To
Roanne

Printed in Great Britain
Collins Clear-Type Press
London and Glasgow

CONTENTS

YOU CAN'T HIT A WOMAN

I MET Alexis Fengler-Nichoelavitch in Paris towards the end of 1926 a year samous for the General Strike and a fatuous dance called the Black Bottom.

I suppose it was the Black Bottom that was responsible for the Fengler-Nichoelavitch episode, because if an unwholesome negro had not attempted to dance it with a woman who had dined not wisely but too well, and if I had not tried to tell the black brother just where he got off the tram it would have been quite unnecessary for Alexis to crown him with a bottle of Dubonnet, in which case I should never have been subjected to the inconveniences which have fallen to my lot ever since.

After the negro had been removed—we were at one of those innumerable bars with the usual "Cossack" appurtenances on the Rue Clichy—and I had realised that Alexis' pull was sufficiently strong in those parts to annul any possibility of trouble with *gardiens de la paix*—he and I and the woman, who was also Russian, sat at a table and became very sentimental about everything.

She told us how she had escaped from the revolution; what exorbitant payments "in kind" to bearded *commissars* her escape had necessitated; how she yearned after the "best kind of love" and how like her brother Nicky—the one who was hung out of a window on a piece of telephone wire by the Bolsheviki—I was.

She said Alexis reminded her of her fiancé, an officer in the Imperial Regiment of Sharpshooters, who, as a true loyalist, attempted to blow up a revolutionary train, but made an unfortunate mistake with the time fuse on the home-made bomb, necessitating his collection afterwards in an old sack.

She then began to cry and we were all very sorrowful and sympathetic, after which she cheered up considerably and kissed us both with great passion and a vague suggestion of garlic and said that we ought to buy champagne. Then she went peaceably to sleep.

Alexis was—and still is—tall and slim, persuasive and distinguished. He had a very white face and most charming manners. He was graceful and very strong—his skill with an épee was amazing. To my own knowledge he speaks five languages perfectly, and for all I know he may speak half a dozen more just as well. He was twenty-six years old in those days, and would therefore have been sixteen at the time of his escape from Russia during the revolution, a fact which would account for his extraordinary mentality.

During the ten days following this episode—in which time I adventured generally about Paris with Alexis—finishing up in the Seine from which I was dragged half unconscious with a brick in each pocket, and later in a polite interview at the Sûreté Générale, which I discovered that even the powers that were in those days had a certain respect for Alexis, I learned a great deal about him.

Women adored him. He had one of those flexible and vibrant noses that twitched at the end when he talked, and I have never yet met a woman of any age who remained entirely unaffected by this phenomenal attribute. I once suggested to him that he hypnotised them by causing them to concentrate on his quivering proboscis and that afterwards they had forgotten how not to agree with anything he suggested. His reply was characteristically modest. He said that possibly there was some truth in what I said but that he did not believe it really mattered very much, and that in any event he thought that the eventual result would have been very much the same.

He was probably right. In any event he was certainly one of those people who have a decided flair for producing acquiescence in others to such an extent that when I

8

eventually decided to return to England it was not until I was half-way to Newhaven that I realised sadly that I had guaranteed his overdraft on a Paris bank, given him a letter of introduction to a lady in Vienna to whom I had been careful to present no one before, and allowed him to "borrow" two suits and six very good silk shirts from my wardrobe, without so much as a murmur.

By profession Alexis was an *agent*. I suppose he was some sort of spy, but the word does not somehow suit him. Also I have reason to believe he worked more or less indiscriminately for any one who paid him well enough. When I first met him he was doing *contre-espionage* against the Soviets, although since then he has, I believe, worked for them on at least two occasions, and has also been employed by very nearly every European Power that boasts—in these days of Mr. Eden and "open diplomacy"—of good Intelligence Services.

It was not until the summer of 1928 that I next heard from him. One evening I received a letter, though I have yet to discover how he knew my address. In it he said that he was shortly coming to England and that he was very much looking forward to seeing me; that business would take him immediately on his arrival to a farm some forty miles from London.* He suggested that it would be a very good idea if I went directly down to the farm and awaited his arrival, because he thought I would have an amusing time.

"I am asking you to go down to the farm, Pierre," he wrote, "because first of all I know that any excuse to stop work is good enough for you, and secondly because I am certain that down there you will have some excellent opportunities for studying the somewhat peculiar sides of feminine human nature, in fact I think if you don't go you will be missing a great deal. Anyhow, I shall take it that you will go, and look forward to seeing you.

*This farm was the Sepach Farm in "*Le Rayon Qui Tue*,"—published by Firenze et Fils in France.

9

"Life has been rather dull. I had three weeks in prison in Lithuania owing to an extraordinary case of mistaken identity, but at the end of that time I managed to persuade the authorities that I was not me, so they let me out."

My first reaction to this letter was one of annoyance. I rather disliked Alexis taking me for granted and thinking that I should go down to the farm just because he had endeavoured to pique my curiosity about some woman. I was even more annoyed because I knew that he was right and that I should go.

I walked about my sitting-room for ten minutes thinking about Roberta. Roberta, I should point out, was a very charming woman of thirty-two years of age to whom I was then engaged, and she had very decided ideas about my not " getting mixed up with women," as she invariably called the process. Just then I had just finished a right royal row with Roberta over the fact that she had paid me a sudden visit when I was entertaining a Georgian lady (one of the most supreme ash blondes it has ever been my lot to encounter) and refused to believe that I was simply taking notes from the fair Georgian for a series of articles which I intended at some time, possibly, to write.

However, I did not see how Roberta could be annoyed, providing she was kept in that ignorance which is bliss, so I put a call through to the farm, told them who I was and asked if it were possible for me to come down and stay for a bit. I said I was a little nervous and that the doctor had ordered quiet.

The woman at the other end, who spoke with a decided country accent, said it would be quite all right, and we arranged that I should go down the next day.

I arrived at eight o'clock in the evening. The farm was an interesting place, rather old and rambling, perched on the side of a gently sloping hill. Down in the valley was a splash of colour caused by a profusion of flowers, and on the hillside across the valley a little wood completed a charming pastoral scene.

I began to feel rather pleased with myself, and to look forward to an adventure of some kind, because I knew that Alexis would not be coming to this place merely for the purpose of viewing the scenery.

The farm was a fairly desolate place. It was surrounded by a fence and fronted on to a third-class country road which wound over the hills to the nearest town which was some eight miles away. Beyond the town was the sea.

I met three people on arrival. They were the farmer, a broad-shouldered man of about forty-five years of age, his wife, who had spoken to me on the telephone, and her father, a villainous-looking old curmudgeon who wore a smock and had only one tooth right in the middle of his upper jaw. When I arrived I went into the kitchen and the old man was seated at a wooden table, eating bread and cheese and pickled onions. I remember wondering what would happen if he managed to spear one of the onions on his single tooth.

Mrs. Garrage showed me to a large and well-furnished bedroom on the first floor at the end of a long passage on the east side of the house, and I arranged that I would have a meal brought up there. After I had eaten it I lit a pipe and hung out of the window.

After a bit I gave this up and began to read, a process in which I was interrupted by a certain amount of noise from below. I got up, went to the window and looked out. Some people had arrived by car, and apparently an argument was going on between them and the father as to whether there was room enough in the outhouse, which was used as a garage, for their car as well as my own.

Eventually, after a certain amount of talk, the man driving the car managed to back it in the shed. While he was doing this I had an opportunity to inspect the woman who was with him and who had got out of the car and was standing in the courtyard. I wondered if this were the "feminine interest" which Alexis had mentioned.

She certainly appeared beautiful. I could not see her face distinctly, but her hair was quite charming and she had an excellent figure, and when she walked she gave evidence of that indefinable quality of sex which some women possess and which is so attractive.

After he had put the car away, the man came out of the shed. I thought he was a horrible-looking fellow. He was about five feet eleven, very broad-shouldered and wore one of those funny velour hats with a narrow brim and a very high crown, the type of hat which one often sees in Germany. He had a large brown face with a bulbous nose and little eyes, and when he took his hat off to wipe his brow, I saw that he had black hair and a bald spot. I felt that I didn't like him a bit and wondered what he was doing driving around the country with such a charming woman. There and then I christened him "Pig-face."

After a bit I went back to my chair and took up my book again, but I could not settle down to read. Whether it was the arrival of these two people or whether my mind had already begun to wonder about the woman and Pig-face, I don't know.

Outside, from down the passage, I could hear rumblings and footsteps and voices, and I gathered that the new arrivals were to occupy rooms on this floor and that their bags were being moved in.

I put down my book and went to the window. I could see that there was going to be a charming sunset and I thought that I might as well go and look at it—at least this is what I told myself. Really, I suppose, I wanted to have another look at the woman.

When I stepped out into the long passage I saw her. She was standing with her back to me whilst the old granddad in the smock was trying to push a fairly large steamer trunk round from the passage into the room. He seemed to be having difficulty, and pushed and pulled and cursed darkly to himself.

I took a couple of steps along the passage and then waited until the old boy had got the trunk into the room. Then I began to walk again and she turned round to look at me.

She was quite lovely. I have already said that she was fairly tall and willowy. She had pretty curves and was a true—as apart from a peroxide—blonde. She had large and surprisingly turquoise eyes set in a face that would have stirred even a casting director. As she stood there, casually turning away from me after one quick glance and preparing to enter the bedroom, I was able to see that her hands were very beautiful, with long tapering fingers and nails nicely pink and free from those fearful daubs that some modern women use on their finger-nails, and—I am told—sometimes their toe-nails.

I walked along the passage and down the stairs. Half-way down I met Pig-face. His eyes were very little and dark, and he was stumping up the stairs and looking very bad-tempered about something. He was red in the face and I imagined that he had been sweating a bit over getting his car into the shed beside mine, which must have been a rather difficult process to say the least of it.

I stood on one side to let him pass. He was level with me on the stairs when he half-turned and said in a surly voice :

"I suppose that was your car in the garage outside. You had it right across the place. I think you might have put it in properly. I had a great deal of trouble in getting my car in at all. Hein?"

He seemed to become more bad-tempered with every word. He annoyed me. Although he spoke without any really obvious accent it seemed to me that he was a foreigner speaking rather good English. I felt annoyed at his rudeness and said nothing at all, which I thought might annoy him still more.

13

It did.

"You'll have some trouble getting your car out if you want to use it," he said. "I've put it at the back and my own car is heavy and I object to anybody driving it except myself, so if you want to get your car you'll have to let me know and I'll have to come down and move mine, which, when you come to think of it, is a damn trouble—don't you think?"

I was furious. I said the thing which I thought would annoy him most. His little red eyes were almost blazing and the idea came into my head that he was fearfully angry with the woman about something. I hoped, maliciously, that she was being difficult and not letting him have his own way about things. This thought gave me a certain amount of pleasure. I smiled at him and said:

"So what?"

He turned a bright pink colour with rage and looked for a moment as if he was going to break into a torrent of bad language. Then he evidently thought better of it and turned and stumped up the stairs and heavily along the passage.

I went down the stairs and out by the side door. I walked round the side of the farm—the western end—through the little shrubbery, and stood looking at the sunset. Far away down on the white ribbon of road I could see a boy riding towards the farm on a bicycle. I promptly divided my attention between the sunset and the boy, who after a few minutes resolved himself into a telegraph boy on a bicycle.

When he arrived at the farm gate I walked over to meet him. He had a telegram in his hand, and I told him who I was and asked if it were for me.

It was, and as I had expected, it was from Roberta. Roberta, as I have already said, had very definite ideas about the way in which she considered I ought to behave. Whilst possessing charm and a great many truly feminine qualities, she was entirely unable to comprehend the artistic temperament, especially in its relationships with members of the opposite sex. The hours that I have spent trying to make it adequately clear to Roberta that any man following any creative profession must, of necessity, take an interest in women *en masse,* was, as the Americans say, "nobody's business," but she possessed a mentality that refused persistently and definitely to accept what she described as my habit of " doing my stuff " with women that I met from time to time.

The wire said:

"*I came round this afternoon they told me you had gone to farm in the country while I was there that Fengel-Nichoelavitch telephoned and asked if you had gone down to farm I asked what was going on and if there were to be women there he said he hoped so definitely if there are women there and you get mixed up with them I shall not marry you ever Green says you have only got one pair of socks shall I send some more I don't trust Fengel-Nichoelavitch or you either and if you get mixed up with some woman I shall not get you out of it as I have before wire about socks Roberta.*"

I borrowed a pencil from the boy and wrote a reply:

"*I am here on sudden holiday against brain fag do not understand what you mean about women what women why did not Green pack more socks dont bother to send any I can buy some at Barrended close to here surprised at your attitude when you know that you are the only woman I have ever really loved unselfishly did Fengel-Nichoelavitch say anything else besides asking if I was down here am probably leaving here to-night to go somewhere else where more peace doctor says must have peace love Pierre.*"

I gave this wire to the boy, who said that he would get

it sent off first thing in the morning and that I was lucky to have got the wire because the post office was really shut for business at seven, but as he was riding home this way he had brought it. I gave him a shilling and he informed me that Barrended—the nearby town—was a rather nice place and only five miles away if one went across the fields, also that there was a very good public-house called the Anchor and Cowslip a mile and a half down the road.

On my way to the Anchor and Cowslip I found myself regretting that I had not worded my reply to Roberta differently. The bit about " probably leaving here to-night " was silly, because Roberta would guess at once that I had put that in merely to stop her wiring again or even coming down. She would know perfectly well that I should not leave here so soon after my arrival. Also it had been foolish of me to ask the question about Alexis. This in any event would constitute an excuse for more wires, and I knew that if Roberta had the idea in her head that some mysterious woman were down at the farm she would expect the worst and might even come down and investigate.

However, after an hour at the Anchor and Cowslip things seemed more cheerful. The inn was an old one with a definite atmosphere, and the people using it were amusing. Also it was far enough off the beaten track to miss the usual crowd of people who dash about in small cars all the summer trying to find inns in out-of-the-way spots.

It must have been about a quarter to eleven when I left the place and I dawdled back smoking my pipe and admiring the weather, which, if you remember, was rather marvellous. I felt at peace with the world and began to hope that perhaps, after all, Alexis would not come down and start something; that possibly circumstances had changed for him since he had written me. Of course, this idea was ridiculous because Alexis never began anything

16

that he did not finish, and I knew perfectly well that he had got me down to this out-of-the-way farm for some definite reason; that, once again, he was using me merely as a pawn in some scheme which was afoot and over which he was certain to collect from somebody or other.

I got back to the farm at eleven-thirty. It was a wonderful night and the moon was full and shedding a radiance over everything, that seemed vaguely hypnotic. As I walked round the end of the farm I looked up and saw that there was a lighted window which would be in the long passage running to my room, and as I continued walking and was nearly underneath it there came to my ears the sound of people quarrelling.

I could distinctly recognise the voice of Pig-face, talking in French in abrupt short sentences—rather like a machine-gun—punctuated occasionally by a reply in a feminine voice—that of the pretty woman, I imagined.

At the same moment I heard the window above opened and something hit me on the head.

I stopped dead with a feeling that the sensation of being struck had not been unpleasant, on the contrary, it was soft, pleasant and reminiscent of something. I stooped down and picked up the object, and was surprised to find that it was a handful of lingerie. The handful consisted of a pair of crêpe-de-chine " steps-ins " in what looked in the moonlight like a rather pleasing shade of pastel green, and two ivory satin and lace nightgowns—and very swell ones they were too. They had obviously been recently unpacked, and from the silken bundle there emanated the impression of a perfume.

Suddenly I remembered what it was. It was a perfume called *Chez Samarkand,* and it was bottled in rather beautiful square bottles with stoppers shaped like crescents. Also it was a perfume which Alexis used to give to women, because I remember him telling me that he had once taken several thousand francs worth of bottles of the stuff in payment for services rendered to an impecunious merchant, and that he found it convenient to give to women at such times as he wanted to give things to them.

As it seemed more than probable that the underwear belonged to the lady who was with Pig-face—I imagined her to be his wife, of course—I wondered if she had ever met Alexis and had the perfume from him. After all, I have known stranger things.

I put the things under my arm and opened the side door to the farm with the key I had been given and went inside. Along the passage running off to the left, which ended at the kitchen—which was immediately under my own room—was a light, and thinking that the farmer's wife might be there, and wanting a cup of tea, I walked along and put my head round the door.

The room was empty, but there was a tea-tray ready on the table, and a brass kettle and tea canister were standing beside it, so it looked as if some one intended to make tea.

On the table was a large bowls of eggs and an egg-poacher stood ready on the kitchen range.

I went in and sat down and filled my pipe. Someone would be along in a minute, I thought, and I might cadge a cup of tea. I was right in this surmise because after a minute or two just as I had got my pipe alight and was seated by the table, the door opened and the woman came in—the one from upstairs.

She was amazingly beautiful. She had on some sort of pale-blue silk wrap and a little lace cap.

We smiled at each other, and I got up and pointed to the step-ins and nightgowns on the table where I had put them.

"Someone threw those out of the window," I said. "For the moment it was raining lingerie. I thought they might be yours."

She nodded. When she spoke it was in a charming,

stilted, carefully pronounced English. I imagined that she was either French or Russian, I couldn't make up my mind which.

"Yes," she said, "they are mine. My husband threw them out of the window. He was unpacking and he is verry hungrry and he always gets quite angrry when he is hungrry."

I grinned.

"Does he always throw your clothes out of the window too?" I asked.

She shrugged and smiled. Then she took an egg from the dish on the table and broke it into the poacher on the range.

"I am going to make poached eggs," she said, "and tea. Do you want tea?"

I said I did. I went on smoking and watching her whilst she made the tea and prepared the eggs. She didn't say anything during this process, but she seemed extremely neat and practical in everything she did. Her movements were quite nice to watch. For some unknown reason I thought of Roberta and wondered what she would say if she had known that I was sitting in the farm kitchen with a charming woman in a pale-blue wrap and a lace cap, making tea.

When the tray was ready she poured out a cup of tea and put it with the milk and sugar on the side of the kitchen table for me. I helped myself and asked if I might carry the tray up for her. She said no thanks, she could do that for herself. We said good-night very pleasantly to each other and she went off with the tray.

After she had gone I sat there smoking and drinking my tea—she made tea very well too—and wondered about her. I wondered whether it was merely coincidence that she used the perfume called *Chez Samarkand,* or whether she knew Alexis, who had, in one of his more expansive moods, presented her with a few bottles. Certainly she seemed an "Alexis" type of woman. She had what he would call allure and a certain *chic* which would appeal to his ever roving eye.

I amused myself with such considerations until nearly half-past twelve by the kitchen clock, at which time I knocked out my pipe, turned off the light and went off to my room and to bed.

I went off to sleep immediately, and the next thing I knew was being awakened by the sound of a long, low feminine yelp. It was the sort of squeal a woman might give if someone stuck a pin into her.

Because I always note the time when anything interesting happens, I looked at my wrist-watch, which has an illuminated dial, and saw that it was three o'clock. At the same moment the door of my bedroom opened and someone switched on the light.

It was the woman. She presented the most extraordinary sight. Her face was almost entirely covered with cold poached eggs, the liquid parts of which had run down and formed an amazing colour scheme on the front of her nightgown, which I noted was one of the ivory satin ones which had fallen on my head earlier.

She leant up against the wall gasping, reminding me of an attractive goldfish. I sat up in bed and tried to look as unconcerned as possible.

"Is anything wrong?" I asked her. "You seem to be in difficulties, and I thought you were going to appease your husband's hunger with those poached eggs."

I got out of bed, walked over to the washstand and handed her a clean towel with which she began to wipe the oleaginous mess from her face.

"My husband is verry verry angry," she said. "He refused to eat the poached eggs when I brought them up and he is also very annoyed with me. Earlier he threw a cup of tea at me but missed me. I have nevaire seen him so angry before and I think I am verry frightened. Also he says that it is possible that he will kill me verry shortly.

which I do not like at all. I think that you ought to protect me if you don't mind."

I sighed. Before long, I thought, I shall find myself up to my neck in a mass of trouble all of which will be caused directly by Alexis and his accursed habit of taking me for granted. I thought I'd find out a little more about this.

"What is all the trouble about?" I asked her. "Are you quarrelling seriously with your husband, or does he often behave like this?"

She shrugged her shoulders.

"Sometimes he does, sometimes he doesn't," she said, "but he is not pleased with me because I will not give him something he wants. So first of all he threw a book at me, then the tea, and now the eggs. Also," she continued plaintively, "I find I am becoming verry cold."

I gave her my dressing-gown.

"Oh, come on," I said after a minute, "let's go and see him."

I walked along the passage to the next room. Behind I could hear the little high heels of her mules tapping on the wooden floor. When I got to the door of their room I opened it and stepped inside. She came in after me.

The room was large with a double window looking out on the south of the farm. On each side of the room was a single bed and sitting on the one on the right, in the process of thinking deeply, was Pig-face. He looked at me belligerently.

I didn't feel at all good. It was a delicate situation, and experience has taught me what usually happens to a man who interferes in domestic quarrels between husband and wife.

"Look here," I said, "I don't know what all this is about, and I don't care, but I am certain about one thing, and that is you can't hit a woman."

He looked at me with a nasty sneer.

"Oh, I can't, can't I?" he said. "Hein?"

He sprang forward suddenly, and picking up an entire

poached egg which lay on the carpet in front of the fire-place, flung it with unerring aim at his wife. It hit her directly on the nose and burst.

I must say I had a great desire to laugh. The situation was sufficiently grotesque to appeal to my somewhat over-developed sense of humour. But I felt that it was incumbent upon me to do something, so I advanced towards him in what I imagined to be a thoroughly antagonistic style. He observed this, put his fists up in a manner which he considered indicative of the prize-ring, and sprang at me. As he came forward, like all inexperienced fighters, he put his head down, so that with the mildest upper-cut I was able to knock him off his balance.

He fell heavily against the wall, but with an agility surprising in such a large man he bounced forward, hit me in the stomach with his head and knocked me flat.

Then I really lost my temper. I got up and went for him in earnest. Two minutes later he was lying on his own bed gasping like a very fat trout. The woman in the meantime had sat down in an arm-chair on the other side of the room and had regarded the whole of this scene with a certain detachment for which I had a great admiration. It reminded me of that detachment which Alexis was always able to summon up after he had got everyone else into trouble and was able to sit on the outside of things looking in.

"Now look here," I said to him. "I don't want to be mixed up in your private affairs, but you definitely can't knock your wife about or throw poached eggs at her whilst I am here. You must understand that. As for you, madam . . ."

But she had gone. I thought that possibly she had gone off to see Mrs. Garrage and arrange about getting another room to sleep in. It seemed hardly likely that she would want to spend the rest of the night in the same room as Pig-face after the scene which had just occurred. Anyhow,

I sincerely hoped that this would be the end of this bother and that I might get some sleep.

I went out into the passage and closed the door behind me. Then I walked along to the head of the stairs and peered over. It seemed that I had been right in my surmise because, hanging over the banister-rail, I could see her talking at the door of the farmer's bedroom with the woman of the house.

I went back to my room, got into bed and went to sleep.

Next morning after breakfast I went out into the garden and smoked my pipe. It was a wonderful day, the sun was shining, and I felt that indefinable gaiety of spirit which comes to me on occasion. I hung about till eleven o'clock and then made up my mind to take a long walk to Barrended and back.

When I got to the farm gate I saw the telegram boy riding along towards the farm and with a sigh I realised that Roberta probably had something more to say.

In this connection I should point out that I have spent much time in trying to break Roberta of the unfortunate habit of sending very long expensive telegrams and telegraphic night-letters. Roberta was a woman who never wrote an ordinary letter because she thought letter-writing was troublesome. She said she preferred the telephone, but she seldom used it. She would spend as much time over the concoction of a £2 telegram as it would take a normal person to write a letter. I went to meet the boy and found as I expected that he had a telegram for me. Roberta said:

" Think your telegram very mysterious I have spoken to Nichoelavitch and like him better than before he has promised to let me know the truth about situation at the farm and why you are there I do not believe that you are going anywhere else rather think that you intend to put

me off the scent please understand that I have breaking-point and shall not stand very much more of this mystery await your wire."

This made me very angry. I have often wondered why it is that women like Roberta who are quite intelligent, charming and good to look upon, should become so fatuous when they suspect that there are other women in the case. Roberta had a definite complex about other women and I am perfectly certain that if she had no one to suspect she would be very unhappy.

But as I have said before I was quite angry about this wire and wrote one to her in which I told her not to talk rubbish and simply signed it. But the receipt of this telegram rather dispelled the feeling of elation I had and walking to Barrended did not appeal to me very much after all.

I wandered back into the farm garden just in time to be caught by the farmer's wife who told me that Mr. "Nickelvitch"—as she called him—was on the telephone. I went inside and spoke to Alexis.

I asked him what the devil he meant by having conversations with Roberta about me and saying he would keep an eye on me. He replied quite glibly that she had telephoned him and seemed rather upset about what I was doing down here, and it had seemed best to him that he should quieten her down and prevent her from coming down by saying that he would let her know exactly what was happening. He also said that it was quite essential that he should meet me at the Anchor and Cowslip at two o'clock, and that he would explain the whole position to me and I would see that the business was not half as mysterious as I thought.

I told him that I would be there.

When I had finished telephoning I went back to the garden, lit another pipe and wandered around. Presently Pig-face approached. He was looking very glum and came

directly to where I was standing and began to apologise
for the night before. He said he was fearfully sorry about
the whole business, but that his wife had annoyed him
and that he had lost his temper with her.

"You understand," he said, "that I am very fond of
Georgette. In fact," he went on, "I am madly in love
with her, but she has a flair for causing me the most
intense annoyance. However, I will see that there are no
more disturbances."

I said it was quite all right, and that I quite understood
how these things happen, and then he clicked his heels,
made a funny little bow and went off.

As the day went on I cheered up considerably and at a
quarter to one I walked round to the Anchor and Cowslip
and had some bread and cheese and half a pint of beer.
At two o'clock precisely Alexis appeared in the bar
parlour.

He was wearing a marvellously cut light-grey suit with
a blue silk shirt and collar, blue silk socks, beautifully
polished brown shoes and a shot-silk tie in which oyster
grey seemed to be the predominating colour.

I thought he looked like a gigolo and told him so. He
shrugged.

"My dear Pierre," he said with superb nerve, "I have
always known that you were jealous of the way I dress,
but let's get down to the business in hand."

"Nothing would please me more," I said. "First of
all I don't know why I ever came down to this place.
Secondly, the couple who are staying in the farm seem
quite mad, and thirdly, I think I'm going to clear out
pretty soon."

I told him of the happenings of the night before, and
he listened attentively. When I had finished he drew up
a chair close to mine and began to talk.

"Now listen, Pierre," he said. "You must understand
that all this is the most delicate business, and that if it
can be successfully accomplished there is a great deal of

25

money in it for me, and as for you, well, you will have had another experience. The situation is this:

" The couple staying at the farm are not all that they seem. The woman Georgette Zuiche has for a long time been an agent for a Central Power. She is very trustworthy and altogether reliable, and unfortunately she cannot be bought.

"Some time ago I discovered that she had in her possession some plans of new fortifications which have been erected in the vicinity of the Meuse, together with a description of the newest thing in artillery—a large-calibred, quick-firing gun. I tell you that she had those plans and I tell you that she still has them.

"Very well," Alexis continued, fingering his tie delicately, " I have been informed by the Government of a country which is held closely by treaty to your own, that it would give me a great deal of money if I could secure those plans. Naturally I want the money, but I had to think of an idea, because ordinary methods are of no avail with Georgette. But knowing her *penchant* for falling quickly in love, I looked around and discovered amongst my somewhat peculiar associates a man called Zuiche.

"Zuiche has been everything from schoolmaster to *agent provocateur*. I came to the conclusion that if he played his cards properly Georgette would marry him. Well, my plan succeeded. I arranged that they should meet, but kept myself carefully in the background so far as Georgette was concerned, and three months afterwards they were married.

" So far, so good, because it seemed to me that Zuiche would be easily able as Georgette's husband to obtain information from her about where the plans were and also what their eventual destination was to be. But not only did Zuiche fail to secure this information, but also he handled the job so clumsily that I am afraid Georgette became suspicious and this hitherto loving pair began to have some serious quarrels, because, as you have seen, Georgette can be very annoying if she wants to be.

"I thought it was time that I did something about it, and so I arranged a meeting with Georgette which appeared quite accidental, and managed, by being very charming and sympathetic, to get from her the story of her unfortunate marriage with Zuiche. She was in great despair about this marriage which she said had been a mistake from the start.

"In the meantime I had discovered something else. Zuiche, it appeared, was a naturalised Englishman and therefore the process of marrying him had automatically turned Georgette into an Englishwoman, a fact which was rather favourable to my plans.

"I told her that the obvious thing for her to do would be to divorce Zuiche, and that I was certain that if I talked to him about it and put the thing to him in its proper light that he would consent. Her reply was that she would be very glad to divorce Zuiche but that as they were both English a divorce in this country would be necessary and that it was not at all an easy thing to get.

"However, I reassured her and said I would talk to Zuiche about it. Then later I told her that whilst Zuiche would not allow her to divorce him because he had religious scruples, he would consent if she would be the offending party. I said that all we needed was a co-respondent and evidence.

"Well, I played my cards very well," continued Alexis with a pleased smile, "and the situation at the farm is the result. The man who is staying there with Georgette as her husband is the co-respondent, who is named Quingare, one of my own people, and he was going to get those plans from Georgette.

"You see," he went on, "when she came down here it was arranged that after they had supplied the evidence necessary for the divorce at the farm, they should leave within the next two or three days for Switzerland, and

27

that Zuiche would then bring his action for divorce. As Georgette was closing down her flat in London I knew that she would have the plans on her and I instructed Quingare—the man who is with her at the farm—that he must get them by hook or by crook.

"I think, therefore, that when she came to you last night and said that Quingare had been knocking her about because she would not give him something that he wanted she was referring to the plans."

I looked at him in amazement.

"But look here, Alexis," I said, "you don't mean to tell me that you got this unfortunate woman in this farm with a co-respondent, whose business is to ill-treat her until she divulges where those plans are? You can't go on like that—you can't hit a woman."

Alexis raised his eyebrows.

"No?" he said, " oh, can't you? You wait a minute, Pierre."

"Apparently," he went on, lighting a cigarette, "Quingare's methods were not acute enough. He should have gagged her first. I have always found it expedient to gag a woman on these occasions."

I grinned.

"If you are using force to try and get information from a woman, and you gag her first, how is she able to give you the information?"

He shrugged his shoulders.

"I take the gag off eventually, Pierre," he said. "Sometimes I pinch them very hard, and then they invariably talk. I once took a photograph of a copy of the secret military treaty between France and Russia merely by tickling the soles of the feet of a Commissar's wife with a hen's feather dipped in sweet oil," he continued reminiscently.

He thought about this for a moment evidently with the greatest pleasure. Then he continued.

"Now, it seems to me that Quingare has failed. Possibly he's not what you call tough enough—I consider the best *agents* invariably have a touch of the sadist about them—but I have got a scheme. To-night I shall come to the farm myself, and you, Pierre, will let me in. Quingare will assist while I deal with the charming but reluctant Georgette, and I promise you that she will talk."

"Oh, really," I protested, "and you think that I'm going to be a party to this business of torturing a woman in order to discover the whereabouts of certain plans so that you may make a lot of money. You must think I'm a fool."

He spread his hands.

"Pierre," he said, "I don't think that you are a fool. On the contrary, I think that occasionally you are quite intelligent. Please consider the situation. All I ask you to do is to let me into the farm by the side door at about half-past twelve to-night. If you do that, I shall, with great pleasure, inform your charming fiancée, Roberta, that she has been quite mistaken about there being any woman business down at this farm, but if you don't, how I should hate to tell her that last night this so beautiful Georgette was in your room, wearing your dressing-gown, and that such unutterable orgies had been going on that the farmer's wife insisted that she sleep in a room by herself at the other end of the farm. Roberta will not like that—will she?"

I looked at him in amazement.

"Alexis," I said, "what an unutterable cad you are."

He shrugged his shoulders once more.

"I know, Pierre," he said, "a lot of people tell me that, but what is one to do. Anyhow what are you going to do?"

I thought for a moment.

"I don't see what I can do," I said eventually, "except let you into the farm at half-past twelve. Otherwise it looks as if you are going to blackmail me to Roberta, and I shall have more trouble."

He got up.

"That is excellent," he said. "Now I must go to Barrended, because I have some business there. Don't worry, Pierre, your responsibility ends when you let me into the farm to-night. After that I look after every thing."

He put on his grey soft hat, gave the brim a tweak, regarded himself in the mirror over the mantelpiece with great satisfaction and went off.

I was almost speechless. I was amazed at the effrontery of Alexis in thinking that I would be a party to his plot, which had all the elements of a fourth-rate drama. However, I did not intend to allow him to concoct some cock-and-bull story for Roberta's benefit, and anyway I had considerable time to think out what I was going to do about it.

I had another half-pint of beer and went for a walk, deciding eventually that I would let Alexis into the farm as arranged at twelve-thirty, tell him exactly what I thought about him and throw him out, after which I would inform the unfortunate Georgette of the plot that was afoot against her.

Having made up my mind on this line of action I became decidedly brighter, in fact I found a certain enjoyment in the situation.

At half-past twelve I was standing at the end of the shrubbery by the back door of the farm. It was a lovely night. I don't think I have ever seen such a wonderful moon, and the hill on which the farm stood seemed bathed in a silver radiance. I had spent the afternoon wandering about the country, making up my mind as to just what I was going to do with Alexis. I had thought of saying something about my conversation with him to Georgette Zuiche, but I had come to the conclusion that this was not the dramatic thing to do.

I must point out that I have always been blessed—or cursed—with a definite sense of the theatre, and I divided the night's entertainment into two parts. First, my big scene with Alexis on his arrival when I proposed to tell him exactly what I thought about him and if necessary to set about him, because it was quite obvious to me that Alexis, although possessed of a certain charm, especially where women are concerned, was really a most unutterable outsider in his heart, who was prepared to stop at nothing in order to achieve success in his very subversive operations.

Secondly, I anticipated the big scene upstairs with Georgette which would take place after I had dealt with Alexis. I saw myself poised rather dramatically in the centre of the bedroom informing her that this Quingare— the co-respondent who she believed loved her and whom she loved—was nothing better than a tool of Alexis, a man simulating passion in order that he might get from her the plans and information which she was so carefully hiding.

This looked a very good scene to me. I saw her turning on Quingare with flashing eyes and telling him just where he got off the tram, after which she would throw her arms about my neck and thank me profusely.

So that I was in an altogether amicable frame of mind when I heard the crunching of Alexis' footsteps on the gravel path and after a few seconds he appeared in the moonlight. He was wearing a dark suit and looked very cheerful.

"Ha! So you're here, Pierre," he said. "I knew that you would be intelligent. Now just where is Georgette's room?"

"Wait a minute, Alexis," I whispered. "Before I open that door I want to have a little talk with you. Don't you think it is pretty low of you to go breaking into that woman's room and, assisted by this rat Quingare, to use foul means in order to get your way? Do you think it is sporting?"

He shrugged his shoulders.

31

"My dear Pierre," he said, "don't be childish."

Before the last word was properly out of his mouth I hit him squarely on the nose and he disappeared into an adjacent rhododendron bush. It took him a few seconds to extricate himself and when he got up it seemed by his attitude that he did not intend to be troublesome. He looked at me rather pathetically and I could see the end of his very flexible nose twitching in the moonlight. His right hand was in his pocket.

"Look here, Pierre," he said, "do you think this is playing the game?"

As he spoke he withdrew his hand from his pocket and threw something in my face.

I don't know what it was but it was awful. I experienced an overwhelming sense of suffocation mixed with a weird smell of aconite. Then I knew nothing else.

When I came to, I found myself underneath a bush where Alexis had dragged me. I looked at my watch and I could see that it was five-past one, so obviously I had been unconscious for about half an hour. My head buzzed and my eyes were watering. I felt like nothing on earth. Also I was quite furious with myself for having been caught napping by Alexis. If I'd had any sense I would have known that he would come prepared for trouble from me, and been ready for it.

I got to my feet and walked up and down the garden until my head had cleared somewhat. Then I entered the farm and began quietly to creep up the stairs. As I ascended I wondered what these two devils were doing with the unfortunate Georgette. I felt quite miserable about it all, and, although I was prepared to set about both of them if necessary, I didn't think I'd have very much of a chance against their combined weights.

My worst fears were realised when as I approached the bedroom door I heard voices talking in low tones punctuated by a sort of sob or moan. This would be Georgette I thought. I stood outside the door for a moment undecided, then caught hold of the door-knob, flung open the door and with a bravado worthy of any crusader sprang into the bedroom, to stop dead on the other side of the threshold with my mouth wide open with amazement.

On the left-hand side of the bedroom, Georgette was doing some needlework on what looked like another pair of eau-de-nil step-ins. Lying at full length on the bed on the right, smoking a very large and foul-smelling cigar, gazing at the ceiling with a placid expression on his face, was Quingare, whilst the unfortunate Alexis was lying on the floor with his head in the fireplace in a most parlous condition. Both his eyes were black. His nose—that sensitive organ for which I had such intense admiration —was bleeding. His shirt and collar were torn open and such had been the ferocity of the attack made on him that the right-hand lapel of his lounge-coat was almost entirely torn off and was hanging to the floor held by a mere thread.

Georgette looked at me with a charming smile whilst Quingare contented himself by turning over on his side and regarding me with a bovine expression.

" Good-evening," said Georgette, " as you see, monsieur, there has been a little trouble again. But nothing very important, and I hope that you were not disturbed greatly."

" Not at all," I said, " but exactly what has happened? Of course," I went on, " it's no business of mine, but I really am rather curious about all this."

She looked inquiringly at Quingare, who nodded his head at her, and then went on puffing his cigar.

" I will tell you," said Georgette, " you see this person here "—she indicated Alexis—" is not at all a nice person. But first of all let me introduce you to my husband, Monsieur André Zuiche "—she gestured towards the man on the bed—the man who I had thought was Quingare. " You see," she went on, " it appears that Alexis originally introduced André to me so that we might get married, and then he thought it would be easy for André to obtain possession of some documents which I had—documents that Alexis wished to sell.

"Well, although André and myself fell very much in love with each other, we quarrelled very much, monsieur, because all true lovers quarrel, and at one time I thought that the marriage was a failure. Then the crafty Alexis suggested to me that having become an Englishwoman through my marriage with André it would be necessary for any divorce to take place in this country. And he arranged that a man by the name of Quingare, whom he presented to me, should come down to this farm with me so that the necessary evidence of misconduct might be assumed. I agreed to do this."

She put down her needlework and helped herself to a cigarette which I lit for her. Then she went on.

"But I changed my mind," she said. "I came to the conclusion that I was really very fond of André, and that I didn't want to be divorced from him. So I went and told him the whole story, and when Quingare appeared yesterday to bring me down here, André, who as you know can be very ferocious, gave him a most terrible hiding. Then we came down here together. We did not bother to tell Alexis about our decision.

"To-night," she went on, "thinking that Quingare was here with me and not my husband, he broke into the farm in order to force me to disclose the information that he wanted and to hand over the documents."

She smiled.

"But he was very unfortunate," she said. "You can see what André has done to him."

I nodded. Not only could I see what André had done to him, but I thoroughly approved the process.

"All right," I said cheerfully. "All this looks very good to me, but tell me, Madame Zuiche, don't you think it is very foolish of you to go about the place with important documents in your possession, documents to valuable that people like Alexis here are prepared to go to any length to obtain possession of them?"

She smiled.

"But I have no documents, monsieur," she said. "I delivered them three months ago to their destination."

"Excellent," I said. "Now all that remains to be done is for us to decide what we are going to do with Alexis."

Zuiche took a hand in the conversation.

"I don't care what's done with him," he said, "so long as he doesn't interfere between Georgette and me. If he does I shall murder him. I desire nothing better than to murder him."

"Hush, little cabbage," murmured Georgette. "You cannot murder people like that."

She turned to me.

"He once killed a man over me in Paris-Plage," she said with a smile, "but that was a long time ago, and I do not wish Alexis to be entirely dead."

"Quite," I said. "I quite understand your feelings, but as Alexis has broken into the house, obviously for some illicit purpose, I think he should be handed over to the police."

I smiled amicably at Alexis, to whom the dawning of consciousness was returning. He looked at me with the bleary eye of a sick fish.

"Yes," I continued brightly, "I think I had better go downstairs, ring through to Barrended Police Station and get an officer sent over to take him away. That seems to me to be the right thing to do."

Georgette looked brightly at André and André nodded ponderously. She smiled at me.

"Thank you very much, monsieur," she said, "we should like that."

At the door I turned and regarded Alexis again. He had managed to raise his head from the ground and was supporting it on one hand. He was gazing at me with an expression of intense hatred.

35

I smiled back at him and went down to the telephone.

Next day at noon I rang up the Barrended County Police Station, who informed me that Alexis, who was incarcerated in a cell beneath the police station, had been allowed to communicate with friends in London, and the necessary arrangements had been made for him to be released on bail later in the day, probably about six o'clock. I then lit my pipe, got my hat and wandered off in the direction of the Anchor and Cowslip.

On my way I met the telegraph boy, and with a sudden sinking feeling I realised that if the police had allowed Alexis to telephone through to friends in London in order to arrange about bail, that they probably would not have prevented him from telephoning Roberta. I imagined the story which he would have poured into her not unwilling ear, and my heart sank.

It was therefore with a feeling of great despondency that I took the telegram from the boy. It was from Roberta, and it said:

" *Of all uncivilised monsters extant I think you are the worst Mr. Nichoelavitch has telephoned me this morning the stories of your orgies with four foreign women you will never dare to come near me again cannot understand how I ever failed to see through the veneer of your weak and superficial character hiding beneath the surface of civilisation nothing but conglomeration of unbridled lusts and passions under cover of artistic temperament never wish to see or speak to you or hear from you again make no attempt to write or telephone me cannot find any words to describe your appalling conduct and moronic sub-normal tendencies shall be at your rooms at eight o'clock to-night and expect a full explanation from you Roberta.*"

I considered this wire for some time, after which I asked the telegraph boy if he would like to take me back into Barrended on the step of his bicycle. He said this was against regulations but a half-crown put that matter right.

When we arrived in Barrended, I walked along the High Street until I found the offices of the Barrended *Courier & Gazette,* which I entered and demanded an interview with the editor, who, I was informed, was at that moment judging a pig contest somewhere in the vicinity, but that I could wait.

I waited. Half an hour later the editor returned. He was a jovial individual and one who moved with the times, inasmuch as he had apparently thrown up uneconomical farming for the more congenial and profitable job of running a local newspaper.

We found we had much in common, and after we had walked to a nearby hostelry where we consumed an enormous quantity of whisky, I had not only supplied him with a very highly flavoured and dramatic version concerning the activities of an international agent—Alexis Fengler Nichoelavitch—in the Barrended vicinity, but I also obtained a promise from him that he would run a special edition providing I would contribute £25 to the cost thereof, and put it on the press right away.

We then went back to the newspaper office and composed a leading story on Alexis which if not entirely truthful was sufficiently factual to avoid a libel action, backed up as it was by an interview with the chief constable.

At five o'clock I was supplied with the first copy off the press, and in the meantime two or three local correspondents for London papers, all of whom had been well primed with the story from the offices of the Barrended *Courier,* had been getting on to the London " Evenings," who were pretty certain to use it, there being a dearth of news at the time.

At five-thirty I replied to Roberta's wire:

" Nothing more hateful than suspicions of a jealous

woman my holiday down here ordered by my doctor owing to the condition of my heart and nerves entirely wrecked by your unjustifiable suspicions fed by the lies of sex-mad Fengler Nichoelavitch who apprehended in woman's bedroom is at present moment frothing in strait-jacket in local gaol here awaiting unprintable criminal charges suggest you read London papers this evening when possibly even you may realise full extent of injustice which you have done to a man who if not exactly noble in character is pretty swell anyway have no wish to continue knowing you after this climax to three years passionate devotion to woman with suspicious mind am leaving here late to-night to seek strength of open country if doctors think I have necessary strength which local eminent physician doubts Pierre."

After which I returned to the newspaper office, collected the editor, who had information concerning another famous hostelry in the vicinity, where the "beer was just like cream," and together, he and I, arm in arm, set out to seek the strength of the open country.

THE DEATH ON PANHANDLE

I

I RECKON that ef you was a deputy sheriff down in Pecos County so long as I bin, you wouldn't get yourself all het up about what these smart guy detectives do way out east in New York.

I reckon that Ma Macallam was just as good a detective as any of these eastern fellers. I'll even say she was better. Ma was a funny 'un. She was tall and thin and scraggy. She had a jaw like a man's and a fringe of carroty hair. She had eyes that was blue and twinkled all the time, and they sorta looked through a guy when she was talking to him.

When she was married to Sparks—who, take it from me, was a bad-tempered stingy old cuss but a durned good sheriff—ten years before, Ma was just the sorta usual Texas school-marm lady gittin' on in years and durned glad to marry anybody, but I'm telling you that as a sheriff's wife she was the cat's pyjamas.

Old Sparks never believed in none of these new-fangled police methods. It was Ma who learned finger-printin' an' ballistics an' photography, and after a couple of years she was as good on all that sort of stuff as any of these new-fangled guys down in that Federal Department in Washington.

I reckon that none of us boys round Pecos County ever knew how hot Ma was until one night Sparks Macallam —her old man that is—got hisself ironed out down at the gas station at the end of Main Street.

It is a nice night and there's a moon. Sparks, Ma and me is sitting in the front room playing three-handed poker when the telephone goes. I answers it and durn me ef it ain't Stevens Mack who is sheriff for Llano County which lays east of Pecos.

Mack sez as how he's got some news for me and he don't mean maybe. He sez as how that Eddie Kelligan, who is servin' a ten to fifty years' sentence for murder in Worth jail, has bust out and is on his way in a car what was waitin' fer him.

He has got some woman with him and Mack reckons that the girl is Lily Melander who was always sweet on Eddie. Mack says too that he's seen Kelligan pull up outside the Llano gas-station, but bein' late—he reckons about eleven-thirty—the place was shut up.

He reckons that Kelligan is needin' gas becos outa the

top window of his frame-house Mack sees Eddie trying to bust open one of the gas pumps, but whiles he is limbering up his gun in order to go an' talk turkey with Eddie they drive off.

Mack reckons that Sparks had better look out for hisself, because he reckons that Eddie is coming this way to fill Sparks fulla lead owing to the fact that Sparks is the guy who sent Eddie up.

Five years before Eddie Kelligan shoots Ma's brother Buck over some difference of opinion—some folks says it's about Lily Melander—an' then he makes for the foothills on the Panhandle. Sparks is away at the time down in Santon or some place buyin' horses an' when he gits back and hears as how Eddie has ironed out his brother-in-law he gets right het up an' he goes off and brings Eddie in.

When the trial comes off Eddie ain't got no real sorta defence—everyone around here knew as he's said he'd get Buck—an' he ain't got no alibi an' in spite of the fact that he says as how Sparks has framed him for sumptin' he never done he gets a ten to fifty year jail sentence which is enough to annoy any guy, huh?

Accordin' to Mack it looks like Eddie might be a-comin' this way.

Well, I hang up and I tell Sparks an' Ma cocks an eye listenin' to what I got to say. But Sparks ain't worried, he gets up and he puts on his belt with his old .45 in it, an' he reckons he is going to drive down to the gas station to wait for Eddie and the girl.

Ma says how come and why don't he hang around there until Eddie shows up and starts something, but Sparks says that maybe Eddie will try to bust the pump at Pecos gas station and then turn off and make for the Texas Panhandle which is where all the bad men go fer.

Sparks reckons he is going to drive down to the gas station and wait around for Eddie and get him one way or another when he shows up.

I says that I think Sparks is right and I'm going to get my gun when Sparks says that it don't take two of us to handle Eddie Kelligan and that he is seeing this business through on his own.

I don't argue any because you can't argue with Sparks anyway, and he goes off. Ma don't say nothin', she just sits there playin' a game of solitaire, and when the old man has gone she says as how she reckons it's durned silly for him to go off on his own after Eddie Kelligan who is anyhow a killer and who is pretty hot on the draw, and who seein' as how he has got this dame with him ain't going to come along quiet like no lamb. I think maybe she's right, but I say, "Oh, hell, I reckon Sparks can look after hisself!"

Well I'm telling you Sparks don't come back. We sit around there until three in the mornin', and I limber up my shootin' iron and I drive down Main Street to the gas station. I guess it's a quiet an' lovely night, the moon shinin' over the hills and the shadows of the frame-houses throwing funny shapes across the street.

When I git down to the gas station there ain't a sign of Sparks, but his car is standin' there on the side of the roadway. I git out and I look round and I find Sparks. He's lying behind the garage in a hole what they use for chucking dirt in and he has been shot clean through the pump.

I reckon this don't look so good to me and I reckon it's going to be pretty tough tellin' Ma that old Sparks has got his, because even if Sparks is a cantankerous and mean cuss, which was just what he was, I reckon she was sorta fond of the old buzzard.

Anyway, it ain't any good goofin' around, so I git back in the car and I drive back and I tell Ma that there ain't no doubt at all but that Eddie Kelligan has ironed out Sparks good and proper, and I reckon we gotta do somethin' about it.

41

She don't say anything, she just sits there looking at the cards in front of her with the light shining on her carroty hair.

Then she says as how she reckons that Sparks was a durned fool to go to meet Eddie solo.

I tell her to take it easy and I git into the Ford and I go round and I git Hick Marshal, Buck Vyners, George Macklin and Jay Pelosi, who is all deputies like me, and we has a meetin' and after the way we do things in Pecos, we unanimously elects Ma Macallam to be a right and proper sheriff of Pecos County for the remainder of Sparks' term which is two years to go.

We then goes back and she is still there playin' solitaire.

We tells her that we reckon as how we have made her sheriff and what are we doing about this Eddie Kelligan. She says:

"Well boys, by cripes I reckon we're going to get this killer and I reckon I ain't going to bed until I get the guy that bumped off Sparks all set for the end of a noose."

We then fix up each of us boys should raise a posse and take the usual routes that the bad men go for. I elect to take the Panhandle road because I've gotta feeling that I reckon that that is the way that Kelligan has gone.

So we git off. I drop Ma at the gas station which is on my way because she reckons she wants to have a look at Sparks. When we get down there she shows me how Sparks was shot in the front of the garage because you can see in the dust where he's been dragged round the back. We also see that none of the petrol pumps has been broke open. So we reckon that Eddie and this dame of his has got some gas some place else before they got here.

I kin see too where their car has turned around, so it looks as if I was right about their making for the Panhandle, so I leave Ma right there and I pick up six boys with everything from old army rifles to a new mauser automatic that Willie Schultz has won in a raffle and we get off after this Kelligan.

42

I reckon we was moving some. Willie, who is driving the car that I'm in, is hitting up seventy-four miles an hour one time an' it's about five o'clock in the morning that ahead we can see a maroon car parked in on the side of the road. It looks to me as if this was the Kelligan outfit, but I can't see anybody movin' and I think at first that the two of 'em have jumped the car and are makin' for the foothills. Anyhow I'm not taking no chances, so we git out of our car an' spread out and creep up—Indian stuff.

An' when I git there I'm more surprised, becos I can see that Eddie Kelligan is asleep in the back of the car with his arm round the dame's neck who is sleepin' on his shoulder.

I see that there's a little trickle of blood that has dried on Eddie's forehead just as if some guy has bounced him on the nut and there they are sleepin' like a pair of babes.

I call up the other guys and I say come and have a look at this and we stands around the car looking at these two guys who are sleepin'.

After a bit we wake 'em up and I tell Eddie that he had better come along back to Pecos because we want to talk considerable to him about ironing out the sheriff at the gas station. The girl starts to say somethin', but I say shut up sister, we don't want no talkin' now.

So Willie Schultz and me and Eddie drives back in their car and Eddie's girl and the rest of the boys go back in the other. I give 'em word that when they get back they are to park the girl in the back cell at the lock-up and I'll stick Eddie in the front one when we get him back because it ain't right for these two to frame up some story between theirselves.

Going back Eddie don't say much. He's looking all dopey and when I say this he says yeah he reckons it's because of the smack on the nut that he got down at the gas station. He also says that it's no necessity for a lot of palooka about this business, becos he bumped off Sparks Macallam down at the gas station. I tell him that this is fine and that there's nothin' like a confession for saving a whole lot of trouble around here but that anyhow this ain't the place to make no confession and that he can do it when he gets back to Pecos where we can write it all down.

He says that is all right by him and that's the way it is.

When we get back to Pecos we are there ahead of the other bunch. I stick Eddie in the lock-up and I go and find Ma who is sitting upstairs playing solitaire, and I tell her that Eddie has confessed to ironin' out the sheriff so she says bring him in and take down his confession.

So they bring Eddie in.

"Hulloa, Ma," he says, "how're you making out? I'm durned sorry I had to iron out Sparks, but you know how it was between him and me."

"Listen, Eddie Kelligan," says Ma. "You know you're a durned no good ornery crittur. Sit down in that chair."

Eddie sits down and she is watching him like a cat. After a bit she tells him to get on with the confession which I am writing down at the side-table as he says it.

Eddie says that he and this dame has come over from Llano County and that they pulled up at the gas station to bust a pump to get some gas. He says that Sparks comes out from the side of the garage and says, "Hulloa, Eddie, what're you doing around here?" and that just as the sheriff is saying this Eddie pulls out his gun and lets him have it. He says that this is all there is to that.

Ma says that's all right. So Eddie shot Sparks through the window of the car which was open, and Eddie says yes that's how it was.

Ma then asks which way Eddie's car was pointing and Eddie says that he had turned the car round towards the Panhandle road. Ma then says well anyway where was the sheriff because if he came round by the side of

44

the garage he would have to be standing on the right of the car. Eddie says that's how it was.

Ma says O.K. an' then she shoves a box of cigarettes over towards Eddie and says wouldn't he like to smoke some. Eddie says Yeah and he takes a cigarette and lights it. After he has a few drags he says now he reckons that this is the end of the business so far as he is concerned, but there ain't no need to hold the girl becos she ain't got nothing to do with this ironing-out of the sheriff at all.

Ma says maybe but the law is the law, and that as she is the right and proper sheriff of Pecos County she is goin' to do this thing the right way and see justice done proper.

After this she tells Willie to take Eddie away an' stick him back in the lock-up.

Eddie gets up and he says that is all right by him but he don't see what the use is of holdin' this girl around here for nothin' when he has made a confession. Willie then takes him away.

I tell Ma that this is good business getting this killer so quick and I tell Ma how we found the car parked on the side of the Panhandle road and both these guys asleep in it like a pair of kids, and that it was funny when you came to think that they had a car full of petrol that they didn't try and give us the go-by at all.

Anyway, I says that I reckon that Eddie has saved us a whole lot of trouble and a trial by comin' clean like this.

Ma don't say anything while I'm talking. She is just sitting looking at the table, but when I've done, she looks up and she says:

"Don't you talk like a durned fool, Bud Swisher. Eddie Kelligan never ironed out the sheriff. I tell you he never done it. I saw burn marks on the front of the sheriff's waistcoat and shirt and whoever shot him had the gun not three inches from his chest.

"I saw where Eddie turned the car round to make for the Panhandle road and I saw where the sheriff was standing—I oughta know his footmarks—*on the left-hand side of the car in front of the bonnet, just the place he would stand*. And that means that if Eddie had shot him from the car there wouldn't be any burn marks round the wound."

I say well I'll be durned, that is a thing that I would never have thought of.

Ma says yeah and she'll tell me something else, that when she asked Eddie to have a cigarette she's seen he's got a scar down his right forefinger, a two to three-day-old scar that wasn't even healed proper, and that when he took a cigarette out of the box he couldn't bend his trigger finger because it was stiff.

"You mark my words, Bud Swisher," she says to me, "Eddie Kelligan never killed the sheriff. There's something screwy going on around here."

And as she is sayin' these very words in busts Buck Vyners.

"Say Ma," says Buck, "you bet you're right, Ma, he never done it, the girl done it. She just confessed an' here's the gun she done it with."

II

Ma sits lookin' across the table at Lily Melander. She is holdin' the gun by the barrel with a silk handkerchief so she don't muss up the fingerprints on the gun. Ma was hot like that an' you bet she had got a lot of these eastern guys beat to track dust on them detective stunts.

Lily Melander stands up lookin' at Ma saucy like. She is a nice bit of a girl, thin maybe, but she has got what the men go for an' I reckon Lily has caused a whole lot of trouble around Pecos since she was big enough to stand lookin' at. But it is a fact that she is stuck to rights

46

on Eddie an' she always said as how if she got a chance she'd help him bust jail.

"Well, Lily," says Ma. "So you done it, huh? I guess you say you ironed out the sheriff?"

Lily don't say nothin', she just nods.

"Well, let's have it," says Ma.

Lily spills it. She tells how she fixed to help Eddie bust out an' that they was a-makin' for the Panhandle. She don't say nothin' about their havin' tried to bust the gas pump at Llano.

She says that just as they stop outside the Pecos gas station the sheriff comes out from the side-wall shadow an' says what about it. Lily says that Eddie is goin' to git out of the car when the sheriff draws his gun an' hits Eddie over the head with it, an' Eddie sorta drops back on his seat right out unconscious like.

She says that she reckons that this burns her up a lot an' that she has got a gun—that Eddie don't know anything about—parked under her coat. She says she pulls it an' lets the sheriff have one right through the heart, an' that he drops down there in the dust an' that she gits out an' drags him around to the back where he won't be seen fer a bit.

When she gits back to the car Eddie is still dreamin', an' so she pushes him outa the drivin' seat an' she drives off.

Then they make for the Panhandle but Eddie is all dopey with the bounce on the nut that old Sparks handed to him an' she is tired to bits, so they reckon that they'll take it easy for a bit becos they don't think that any guy will find Sparks for a bit. Anyway they go on sleepin' an' the next thing she knows is that we are there a-lookin' at her.

Ma says oh yeah and she asks Lily where the sheriff was standin' when she fired at him. She says that she reckons that Lily must have fired outa the window over the front of the car from the front passenger seat becos the sheriff was standin' on the left of the car in front of the bonnet—that she seen that by his footprints—an' Lily says yeah that's how it was.

Ma says Lily where'd you get the gun from an' Lily says that she's had it fer years an' that she found it one day on the Big Spring foothills. Ma says when an' Lily says that she can't remember the day but that it's some years before.

Ma says O.K. Then she is quiet fer a bit an' she don't say nothin', she is just sorta lookin' at Lily. Lily is standin' there with her hands sorta clasped an' I can't help thinkin' that it's a durned shame fer to hang a girl like this girl becos she looks a right smart girl to me. Then Ma says sudden like:

" Say, listen, Lily, you an' Eddie come from Llano, an' you had lots of gas in the car that you got some place else between there an' here. If you was makin' for the Panhandle what did you want to come to Pecos fer when Pecos is right outa your way? You coulda hit straight across to the Panhandle."

Lily don't say nothin' for a bit, and then she says they just wasn't thinkin' much about the way they was goin', that they reckoned they could make the Panhandle easy enough via the Pecos road.

Ma says all right take Lily away an' lock her up, an' then she lights herself a cigarette an' she sits there drawin' down the smoke jest like any man. I reckon she smokes forty of them Mexican weeds a day—an' presently she begins to sorta look funny about the mouth.

After a bit she says to me to go an' get Eddie back some more an' I go down an' gits him.

When he comes in he says what's it all about an' that he has already spilled the beans about the business an' that he done it.

Ma says can that stuff Eddie, becos we know that you never done it—Lily done it.

Eddie gits all het up an' says that it ain't true an' that he done it, an' Ma asks him what is the make of the gun that he ironed out the sheriff with an' I notice that she has thrown a cloth over the two guns—the sheriff's an' Lily's—on the table.

Eddie hums about a bit an' then says that it is a Smith an' Wesson forty-five an' Ma gives a grin an' lifts up the cloth an' shows him that it is a Getsburg Positive forty-five, an' she says that just about fixes up Lily's story becos you never even knew she had a gun with her an' that just about lets you outa this.

Eddie says shucks he knows what he is a-talkin' about an' that he done it, and Ma says listen Eddie you don't know nothin' about what happened at the gas station becos you was unconscious from that bounce on the nut the sheriff give you with his gun an' she lifts up the other end of the cloth an' she picks up the sheriff's gun with the cloth and shows me the butt under a magnifying glass that she has got, an' I can see some black hairs on the butt an' a little dried bloodmark, an' it is easy to see that they are Eddie's hairs.

Eddie don't say nothin' to this an' Ma says to take him away an' lock him up again, so Buck Vyner takes him outa the room an' I ask Ma what is on her mind becos it is stickin' out that the girl has done the job like she said.

Ma says this is all right but that there is one or two things that she don't git about all this. She says that it is durn funny that the pair shoulda come to Pecos at all; that they coulda saved miles an' time by runnin' straight from Llano to the Panhandle an' that she woulda liked to know what they come to Pecos at that time in the mornin' fer.

She says too that it's stickin' out a mile that they would not a' stopped at the gas station at all if it hadn't been fer the sheriff bein' there; that they would a' gone straight

49

on through Pecos becos she could see where the car was turned round, an' she reckons that Eddie turned it after the sheriff called out to them to stop.

Then she picks up the girl's gun, an' she looks at it an' she turns it over an' over in her hands holdin' it by the muzzle with a cloth.

Then I says this is an easy case. I says that there is no shots fired out the sheriff's gun an' that there is one shot fired outa the girl's gun an' that was the bullet that she ironed out the sheriff with. Ma says that's O.K. an' here is the empty cartridge case that she found down at the gas station where it had fell when the shot was fired an' does that mean anything to me?

I say what the hell should it mean to me an' she says Bud Swisher ain't you got no sense at all you durned ornery crittur. Didn't that girl Lily say that she shot the sheriff outa the window of the car? Well, if she shot him outa the window the empty cartridge-case oughta have fell back into the car and not into the dust down at the gas station.

I say that's as maybe but what the hell when the girl has confessed to ironin' out the sheriff is the use of all this workin' out of clues and whatnots when all we has to do is to hand this pair over to Mack so he kin take 'em up to Worth or some place where they have got a real jail.

Ma says that's all right but there's a lotta screwy business in this here shootin' an' she don't like some of it at all. She says that she's got a whole lot of ideas a-rushin' around in her head an' that she believes that Eddie never shot the sheriff an' that the girl is trying to pull the wool over our eyes over somethin'.

Presently she lights another Mexican an' she goes upstairs an' she's up there fer a while an' then she comes down agen an' she is smilin' sorta funny an' she says that she reckons that she is beginnin' to see a spot of daylight.

She says to bring in Lily some more an' so I goes an' gits Lily an' she comes in an' says, say what is all this palooka about when I have already said that it was me who ironed out the sheriff an' why can't you let the thing go at that?

Ma sits there a-lookin' at Lily an' she says: "Say Lily, I guess you an' Eddie was goin' to git married wasn't you?" Lily blushes as red as fire an' Ma says "I thought you was. Why didn't you tell me?" Lily says "What the hell has this got to do with the sheriff gittin' ironed out?" an' Ma says "Maybe nothin' an' maybe somethin'."

Then she says, Say Lily, where was you when Sparks went after Eddie after he had ironed out my brother Buck? An' Lily says that she wasn't around until after Eddie was jailed, that she was down in Laredo with some outfit that had hired her. Ma says "What'd you do when you come back?" an' Lily says as how she went back to Big Spring.

Ma waits a while an' then she says "I guess you went back to Big Spring to see my brother Buck didn't you Lily, I once heard tell that Buck an' you was stuck on each other a bit."

Lily says maybe that's how it was but that she really wasn't stuck on Buck she just sorta thought she was but that anyhow when she got back to Big Spring Buck had been ironed out an' Eddie was in jail.

Ma says huh huh an' then she says, "Say Lily I reckon it took some time fer you to figure out just how you was goin' to get Eddie outa Worth jail didn't it?" An' Lily laughs an' says you betcha it took a helluva lot of figurin' and a lot of dough an' that she never knew it was so hard to grease prison guards so as to stage a getaway. Ma asks where she got the dough from an' Lily says she guesses she worked pretty good an' hard an' saved it up.

Ma says that she is pretty stuck on Eddie ain't she, an'

Lily says she guesses she is but the way things is goin' it don't look as if it's goin' to do either him nor her a helluva lot of good.

Ma says well anyhow life is a durn funny proposition an' she tells me to take Lily away to the lock-up an' that she kin have a packet of cigarettes if she wants one. I say O.K. and do not let on that I have already slipped Lily a packet becos I think that if a girl is goin' to get stretched on a rope for ironin' out a sheriff she is entitled to all the smokes she wants beforehand like.

Well, after I have locked Lily up, I get round to Buck Vyners's place which is nearby an' I drink a couple of glasses of straight whisky with him, an' I ask him why it is that Ma is making such a palooka about this business when it is sticking out a mile that it is the girl who ironed out the sheriff, and while we are talking we hear a lot of shooting going on, and Willie Schultz tells us that Ma is experimenting with the girl's gun, and that what she ain't been doing in the line of taking fingerprints off the guns and such-like is just nobody's business at all.

Buck and Willie and me thinks that Ma is a bit screwy over this business, but we think that maybe she is a bit queasy about sending Lily up becos she knows that this girl will get slung up, and we reckon that maybe she is trying to find some extenuating circumstance or somethin'.

After a couple of hours I feel that I'm gettin' a bit impatient becos it looks to me as if we oughta get these guys over the Worth somehow, which is a long ride, unless we are going to ask Mack of Llano County to take 'em over. The boys reckon that I oughta go and have a word with Ma about this, and I go in and I find her a-sittin' in front of the table, and I see that she has got photographs of the fingerprints on the girl's butt-handle and photographs of bullets which she has been firin' through soft wood.

I tell her that we boys think that we oughta get Eddie

and Lily moved back to Worth as soon as we kin do it, as otherwise the Worth people will be raisin' hell over our not sendin' a jail-breaker back.

Ma lights a cigarette and she looks at me through the smoke. It looks durned like as if she has got a tear in her eye, but maybe it is the tobacco smoke.

"You shut your head, Bud Swisher," she sez, "I ain't sending neither of them back to Worth. I'm probably going to spring 'em out to-morrow."

By this time I think that Ma has gone screwy. "Say, listen Ma, what is this? I says. One of these guys has ironed out the sheriff, it must have been one of 'em, becos there was only the three of them down at the gas station, and here's you talking about springin' 'em."

Ma grins. "Bud," she sez, "you just don't know nothing. It wasn't Eddie that ironed out the sheriff nor yet Lily. Neither of 'em shot him, and if you come round and see me to-morrow morning I guess I'll be able to tell you all about it. Now scram outa here!"

III

NEXT morning Willie Schultz and Buck Vyners and me goes round to Ma's place to see her about this business. I have told the boys what she has told me the night before and we think that Ma is a bit screwy. At the same time we know that she has got a whole lot of brains under that carroty hair of hers and that she's usually right about most things.

We go up and we find Ma sittin' at the table playing solitaire.

"Say, listen boys," she says, "just park yourselves around here and smoke, because I got something to tell you.

"I guess you all is thinkin' that I'm a bit screwy over

this business, but I reckon that I've got this thing worked out proper now."

Buck Vyners grins. "That's all right with us Ma," he says, "only it stands to reason that somebody shot the sheriff, don't it? I guess he wasn't struck down by some invisible guy, huh? Bud here says as how you says that Eddie Kelligan never done it nor yet Lily Melander. Well, who the hell did do it?"

Ma looks at him old-fashioned.

"The sheriff done it hisself" she says. "He shot hisself. Now don't start a lot of talkin', you Bud go and git them two an' bring 'em up here. I guess I sorta want 'em to hear about this."

I gits down to the lock-up an' I brings up Eddie and the girl. I fixes 'em up with chairs an' they sit there lookin' surprised like.

Ma says: "I just told the boys here as how the sheriff shot hisself down at the gas station—which you well know Lily Melander. He was an ornery mean old crittur but I guess that this here suicide was about the meanest bit o' work he ever done."

"Say Ma," says Buck, "what did he want to do it fer?"

"You shut your head Buck Vyners," says Ma. "I reckoned to surprise you boys, but you got to reckon that this here story starts a long way aback.

"Bud, do you remember when my brother Buck was shot dead on the Big Spring foothills five years ago? Now we sorta took it for granted entirely that the feller who shot him would be Eddie, because we knew that Buck was sweet on Lily, and we knew that Eddie was sweet on her too and wasn't the sorta guy to have anyone hanging around his girl—especially my brother Buck.

"The sheriff was away at the time and when he came back he goes out after Eddie, brings him in, takes him over to Worth and gets him tried. Eddie gets a sentence. Now what none of you knew and what the sheriff didn't

54

know was this: That I took the bullet out of my brother Buck's body and I kept it ever since in a box upstairs. I thought maybe it'd come in useful one day. I was right!

"All right! Now let's get to this shooting business. There was a lot of things struck me about this as bein' screwy. The first one was why didn't the sheriff take Bud here along with him when he went to get them guys. Bud was hangin' around and he wasn't doin' nothin'. That looked a bit funny to me.

"The second thing is why did these two want to come to Pecos at all. If they was makin' for the Panhandle why didn't they get straight across from Llano.

"The third things is that when I looked at their car marks on the road I see that they was drivin' past the Pecos gas station comin' this way, and that the car is turned suddenlike in the middle of the road.

"I guess Eddie Kelligan turned the car round after the sheriff hailed him and not before. If that was so then they wasn't makin' for the Panhandle, they was coming down this way. What for? Well, that's an easy one, they was coming down to see the sheriff.

"And he knew they was comin' down to see him and he didn't want nobody to hear what was goin' to be said, which is the reason why he went down to the gas station to meet 'em there.

"I reckon I know what happened down at the gas station. It was something like this.

"The sheriff calls out as they're drivin' past, and Eddie turns the car round. Then he stops it. The sheriff comes up to the car window and says something to Eddie. Eddie probably gives him a wisecrack and the sheriff who has got his gun in his hand bounces Eddie on the nut with it. Eddie goes out unconscious like.

"This gets Lily all het up. She tells the sheriff a few. She tells him what Eddie and she have come over to Pecos for, and she shows him the gun she's got.

"Well, boys, you know what Sparks was like. He

was a hard, mean, ornery crittur. He was a good sheriff but he was a bad man. When Lily Melander told him what she had to say to him, and when she showed him that gun, I reckon that Sparks knew the game was up, but being the old snake that he was, he gets one big idea to even up with Lily.

"He stands there and he tells her that he is a-goin' to shoot hisself, becos nobody will believe that he has shot hisself. They will believe that Eddie done it. After all Eddie has just broke jail and the first thing he was likely to do was to iron out the guy who sent him up.

"So Sparks stands there and tells the girl what's in his mind. He says that she won't ever be happy becos either she or Eddie or both of 'em will swing for shootin' him and he sticks the muzzle of his gun against his chest and he pulls the trigger. Ain't that correct Lily?"

Lily Melander nods. "You said it, Ma," she says. "Eddie was out in the driving seat. He never knew a thing. Sparks stood there an' he turned the gun around in his hand an' he held it pointin' to his heart, just holdin' it loose like with his thumb on the trigger, an' he explains that he is holdin' it like this so that directly he has fired the bullet the gun is goin' to drop outa his hand, so that it ain't goin' to look like suicide, an' he says that if I try to put the gun in his hand afterwards my fingerprints will be on it, an' that would make you know it was me, an' that if I wiped the fingerprints off you would see there wasn't no fingerprints at all and you would still be suspicious like an' know that one of us had wiped 'em off so as to make it look like suicide, an' that you would reckon that we had got the sheriff's gun off him an' shot him with it."

Ma grins: "Correct," she says, "an' that is why I found the empty cartridge-case a-layin' close up to his footprints in the dust.

"Well," she goes on, "Lily has one hell of a time. Eddie is lying back in the car unconscious and Lily knows what the sheriff has said is right. So she gets out of the car and takes his gun and she puts one of the cartridges out of her own gun in the place of the one he's fired so that she can prove that she shot him with her gun, but what the silly girl don't see is that the cartridges in the sheriff's gun was Smith & Weston 45's and the cartridges in her gun was Getzberg 45's. You can see the stamp on the case.

"None of you boys noticed that there was an odd cartridge in the sheriff's gun. Then she drags the old man round to the back of the garage. She pushes Eddie out to the passenger's seat and she drives off.

"Now when you guys come up to 'em Eddie is just sorta comin' to, and she ain't no time to tell him what's happened. Eddie hears that Sparks has been ironed out, and naturally concludes that the girl has done it, so he says *he's* done it, but I knew he never done it, becos he didn't even know what the make of the girl's gun was.

"Then we has the girl up and she tells her story and the story she tells is exactly the story that the old cuss Sparks knew she'd have to tell. But it don't get nowhere with me because I've been noticing a lot of screwy things about this business.

"I knew that if she'd fired that shot at the sheriff out of the car the empty case would have been inside the car and not on the ground.

"Then I got to wondering what it could have been that would make her wait all these years, save money and plot and plan to arrange a jail bust for Eddie just so they could come over here to Pecos to see the sheriff about something.

"Well, use your imagination, boys, people don't break jail just for the purpose of going and visitin' their friends, do they? I reckon they had something on the sheriff. I was right. That's why I asked Lily all them fool questions. I was trying to get at something."

We are all sitting around looking at her with our

mouths open. Willie says, "Well, it sounds all right, Ma, but what did the sheriff want to shoot hisself for?"

Ma looks at him and she grins.

"I'll tell you, Willie," she says. She picks up the girl's gun. "You see this gun, boys," she says. "I've been trying out with this gun and the bullets. I got photographs of the bullet tracks and I got the bullet that I took out of the body of my brother Buck five years ago, and the bullet that killed him was fired out of this here gun."

She hands us the photographs, and it is plain to see that what she says is right.

I whistles. "Cripes, Ma," I says, "then this means that Lily ironed-out your brother Buck! But how could she? She was down to Laredo at that time."

Ma grins again. "Yes, she was," she says. "Don't you boys remember that I asked Lily where she got that gun, and don't you remember that she said that she found it on the Big Spring foothills after she came back from Laredo.

"Well you boys remember that the day Buck was killed was the day that Sparks had gone off down to Santon to buy horses. I remember that day, too, becos it was Sparks' birthday, *and I gave him this gun that morning as a birthday present.* But he never went down to Santon to buy no horses, he went down to Big Springs foothills instead and he shot my brother Buck with the gun I give him—this gun!"

We sits there with our mouths open, staring.

"You see," Ma goes on quiet-like, "when he come home that night he told me a story about how he lost the gun, and I've been wondering for a long time who this girl Lily was that he used to talk about in his sleep. You can put two and two together, can't you, boys?"

Willie whistles.

"You see," says Ma, "when Lily comes back from Laredo she finds the gun. She finds that Eddie Kelligan

58

has got a sentence for shootin' Buck. She goes on quiet-like putting two and two together until she finds out that this gun that she found was Sparks' gun. Then she knows that what Eddie said at his trial that he'd been framed by Sparks, is the truth. So she don't say nothing. She just waits until she can frame a jail-break for Eddie, and they were comin' over to tell Sparks that the game was up. They brought the gun to show him. I reckon Sparks knew that the girl had that gun, and I reckon he knew that I'd identify it as the gun I gave him on his birthday. That's why he went down to the gas station.

"That's why he wouldn't take Bud along, an' that's why he wouldn't let 'em come here. He knew that once they got here that I could identify that gun I give him, he knew that Lily here had got an open an' shut case against him, an' the mean ornery old cuss thought out a plan so that he could still fix 'em."

She gits up an' lights up another Mexican.

"See here, Bud," she says, "you ring through to the warden's office at Worth an' tell them smart-guy fellers that Eddie Kelligan is innocent of that shootin'. Tell 'em that I got an open an' shut case against my husband, Sparks Macallam, late Sheriff of this County, for doin' it, an' that he's proved I'm right by shootin' hisself. Now you all git outa here."

So we all gets out, but after a minute I gits back an' I says, "Ma, I reckon we boys are mighty sorry about all this here business. It ain't so good for you."

She looks at me an' I kin see that there is a tear in her eye.

"Sparks was a mean old cuss," she says. "I knew he was always sweet on Lily in the old days. He was a nasty murderin' old cuss . . . but I loved him, Bud. . . ."

She sorta pulls herself together.

"But," she says, proud-like, "I ain't havin' no miscarriages of justice around here. No, sir, not while I'm Sheriff of Pecos County!"

A SQUARE DEAL

Spike and Callaghan ran a detective business on the fifteenth storey of the Trip Building—corner of Main and Twenty-third. When you got out of the elevator their door was facing you. On it was "Spike and Callaghan. Investigation." The door was kicked about a bit, but Spike couldn't find the money to have it repainted. Anyhow, their clients didn't bother about doors much.

Inside the outer office punching a typewriter was Effie Perm. She wore 4-in. French heels and red hair. She had sex appeal plus. Clients got burned up over Effie, but they never got anywhere much—well, not often. She was wise.

On the other side of her office was Spike's room. Callaghan worked outside most days. Spike was sitting inside with his big feet on the desk smoking cigarettes and thinking. Through the closed door he could hear Effie's typewriter. It annoyed him, because he didn't know what there was to type out anyway.

Spike was tall and loose-jointed and hard. His eyes were big and red—a bit close together under a bunch of curly black hair. He had a long nose and a dog's jowl. He'd done pretty well everything before he started the detective business. He looked like that too.

He was rolling himself a cigarette when Effie came in. "There's a dame to see you," she said. "You'll see her. She's Molly Fakyt—Cario's girl."

Spike whistled through his teeth and shot his legs off the desk. Then he grinned.

"Show her in, Beautiful," he said. "Maybe we've got some business."

Effie showed the woman in and went out. Spike

motioned the woman to a chair opposite the desk with a move of his head.

"Well, honey, what can we sell you?" he asked. He grinned at her and blew out a mouthful of smoke.

She sat down. She was as pretty as a picture—blonde, and with a figure that made you think. She had blue eyes that laughed all the time. She was dressed to kill, and everything fitted. Spike thought she was the sort of girl he'd been looking for for a long time. He blew out a lot more smoke, through his nose this time. She opened her black silk handbag that lay on her lap and took out a cigarette. There was a fat roll of thousand-dollars bills in the bag. Spike saw that too.

She settled herself in her chair and smiled at him. She was as cool as an icebox.

"Say, listen, Mr. Spike," she said. "I've heard a lot about you an' your organisation. They tell me you're a great guy. Well, here's how it is: I'm in a bit of a jam, and there's a little thing you could do for me, maybe."

Spike nodded. "I'm listening," he said.

"Jim Cario's put the finger on me," she went on, still smiling. "He's got an idea that it was me that tipped the cops off about the Lanyard bump-off in Chicago. He's wrong, but it's no good arguing with Jim anyhow. So I thought that Chicago might not be so healthy for me, because he told a girl friend of mine that he'd shoot me on sight. That's why I heard San Francisco calling."

She blew a smoke-ring across the room and watched it fade.

He put his legs back on the desk.

"So what?" he said, looking at her.

She crossed her legs, stubbed the cigarette against the sole of her patent shoe, and neatly flicked the end into the waste-basket.

"I got a long-distance from Chicago this morning," she went on. "Cario's on the run. He knows they'll get him this time, an' he says he's goin' to get me first. He's comin' here to-day on the train—Central depot—seven o'clock."

Spike nodded.

"Well . . . that's easy," he said. "All you do is tip off Colson at police headquarters, an' he meets Cario with the bomb squad an' pinches him. . . ."

She laughed.

"Have a heart," she said softly. "Don't you know Jim Cario? If they did pinch him he'd get out of it for long enough to bump me—or one of his boys would. I'll feel safe when he's dead an' not before."

He rolled another cigarette.

"Yeah . . . an' I suppose I meet him down at the Central depot and bump him off for you, is that it?" He grinned cynically.

She leaned towards the desk.

"That's just it," she said. "You do. But you do it like this"—she wriggled her chair closer, and a whiff of perfume distended his nostrils.

"Listen here," she continued. "Here's the layout, an' it's good. Supposin', at seven o'clock to-night, when Cario's train pulls in, I'm down at the depot—an' you're hanging around with me. All right: what happens? Jim gets out of the train, an' when he gets to this side of the barrier he sees me. What does he do? He reaches inside for his gun, don't he? An' what are you doin'? While he's pulling it you shoot first. You're all ready, see? Then what happens? Why, you're the big private dick who shot one of America's toughest gangsters just as he was goin' to bump off a lady friend. Get me?"

Spike whistled through his teeth.

"I got you," he said quietly. "Gee, it's a swell idea." He began to roll another cigarette. "Say, lady, what's an idea like that worth?" he asked, grinning at her.

She opened her bag for another cigarette.

"Ten thousand dollars and a thousand on account now," she answered coolly. "Do we trade, big boy?"

62

He took his feet off the desk.

"I'm sold," he said, still grinning. "Cash in."

She got up and stretched. Then she took a thousand-dollar bill from her bag and handed it to him. He put it in his waistcoat pocket. "Where're you staying?" he asked.

She was powdering her nose in front of the office mirror. "I'm at the Comindale Apartment on Penworth Street," she said.

He rolled another cigarette.

"O.K.," he said smiling. "I'll pick you up there at six-forty. An' I'll take the other nine thousand at half-past seven," he added.

"That's O.K. by me," she said. "Well . . . I'll be seeing you. . . ."

She walked out.

Spike took out the bill and looked at it. Then the door opened and Effie came into the room. She stood looking at him, her hand on her hip.

"It's one hell of an idea, Spike," she said.

He snarled. "Listenin', hey?"

"You bet," she said. She sat down, crossed her legs and held out her hand for a cigarette.

"Say, Spike," she said, watching him roll it. "You know I'm strong for you . . . well . . . I got an idea that Callaghan's pulling a fast one on you over that last bit of business you did with Steiner."

He threw her the cigarette.

"You're telling me," he said. "He's a lousy partner, but I can't shift him. He knows too much an' so does that wife of his. I don't like that momma."

"Sure," she said. "An' she don't like you. Say, listen, why don't you get Callaghan to do this Cario job at the depot? It's his line all right. He can surely shoot."

He looked at her quickly. "What's the big idea?" he asked suspiciously.

She looked at him smiling.

"It's a hell of an idea, Spike," she said. "But I wouldn't like to suggest anything that'd burn you up. . . ."

"What is it?" he interrupted. "Cut out the nice stuff!"

She inhaled from the cigarette.

"Well . . ." she said slowly. "Supposin' Callaghan goes down to the depot with this dame instead of you; an' supposin' things go as she says. Just imagine: Cario reaches for his rod, but before he can pull it Callaghan fires, but for some screwy reason his gun don't go off . . . well, what happens?"

Spike looked at her through the smoke.

"Cario lays off the dame an' bumps him first," he said shortly.

She nodded.

"Sure he does; an' before he can turn the heat on the dame, supposin' you were standing down by the news-stand and pluged Cario before he could get the dame. See? You'd get the ten thousand an' you'd be rid of a lousy partner," continued Effie, "an' if somebody slipped a few blanks into Callaghan's gun it would be just too easy."

Spike stubbed his cigarette out on the desk. They looked at each other; they were both smiling.

Spike got up.

"Listen, honey," he said. "You got a helluva brain. Just go outside and ring Callaghan. Tell him to pick up this dame at a quarter-to-seven. Tell him the layout—just what he's got to do, an' tell him you'll meet him outside the Colindale, an' give him his gun, so as to save him the trouble of comin' round here for it. Got it?"

"I got it." She got up. "An' how do I break, Spike?"

He slipped his arm round her waist.

"You should worry, kid," he said. "I guess you an' me will take a little vacation to-night. Now go an' get busy."

64

She went out. Spike could hear her outside, phoning Callaghan; telling him what he had to do.

He went to the safe, opened it, and took out two .38 automatics. One he slipped into a shoulder holster under his left arm. From the other—Callaghan's gun—he withdrew the clip, slipped out the first four shells and bit out the bullets. Then he closed down the empty ends of the cases and loaded them back into the clip. When he had finished he saw Effie Perm standing in the doorway. He handed her the gun.

"Give that to Callaghan, kid," he said. "Then go home, pack your kit, and wait for me at your apartment. I'll be there at nine o'clock. So long, baby."

He watched her put on her coat and hat and go. Then he closed his office door, rolled a cigarette, and reached for the telephone. He rang Molly Fakyt at the Colindale Apartment.

"Listen, beautiful," he said. "I got everything fixed. There's just one alteration. My partner Callaghan's goin' to handle the job, but I'll be around. Another thing: I got an idea that you an' me ought to see a bit more of each other, hey?"

She laughed. "Why, sure," she said. "Anything you say if this job breaks right."

Spike grinned.

"Don't you worry. Listen; you pick me up at the office here and bring your bags with you at seven-thirty. Bring the money with you. I got an idea that you an' me ought to take a look at New York. Got it? So long, sweetheart!"

He hung up the receiver.

Spike leaned up against the rear side of the news-stand and watched. He could see Molly Faykt and Callaghan pushing their way through the crowd towards the arrival platform. Callaghan had his hand in his right-hand coat pocket.

Five minutes afterwards Spike saw Cario come through the barrier. Molly Faykt stepped forward and he saw her. She was laughing. Cario stuck his hand inside his coat for his gun, and, at the same moment, Callaghan stepped forward, pulled his gun, levelled it and pulled the trigger. Nothing happened. Cario swung round, fired three shots into Callaghan and, simultaneously, Spike, shooting from the hip, put four shots into Cario's stomach. Molly Faykt faded into the crowd.

Spike dashed forward and knelt at Callaghan's side. He was dead. Looking up, Spike saw Colson of Police Headquarters.

"Well, ain't that tough, Spike," said Colson. "I was here to collect Cario. We were tipped off about him. That was great shootin' of yours. Sorry about Callaghan."

Spike nodded sadly.

"That part ain't so good, Colson," he said. He took Callaghan's gun out of the stiffening fingers and slipped it, with his own, into his pocket. Then he went off. Outside the station he took a cab back to the office. On his way he heard the ambulance bells. He guessed they were collecting the bodies.

Spike was sitting with his feet on the desk, rolling a cigarette, when Molly Faykt arrived. She had changed her clothes, and he thought she looked swell. She sat down opposite Spike.

"Well . . . it worked," she said. "Gee, but I'm sorry about that Callaghan. He was a nice guy."

"Sure he was," said Spike, "but careless about his gun. It must have jammed, I suppose."

She opened her bag.

"Here's the pay-off," she said, smiling.

He looked at her and grinned.

"You hang on to it, Gorgeous," he said. "We'll spend that together."

He got up and stepped towards her. As he moved the telephone jangled. It was Effie Perm.

"Well, Spike," she said. "How're you making out?"

"Pretty good, Effie," he said softly. "Everything went fine, didn't it? Hang around. I'll be along for you at nine o'clock."

He heard her laugh.

"Like hell you will—you double-crossing rat," she said. "Listen, Marvellous, just after I left the office to take Callaghan's gun along to him, I found I'd left my gloves. So I came back for 'em, see? An' I heard you makin' your little arrangements with that dame, Molly Faykt, on the telephone. So you're ditching me, hey?"

Spike snarled. "Well . . . so what?" he snapped.

She laughed.

"So this! Just this little thing. I'm speakin' from the tobacco kiosk next door to the office. I've spilt the whole works to Callaghan's wife. And *is* she burned up! She's on her way up now in the elevator, and boy, she's got a tommy-gun under her fur coat an' it ain't loaded with blanks, neither. So long, Spike!"

Spike dropped the receiver.

He was sweating. He looked at the woman opposite and at the safe where the guns were.

But there was no time.

The door opened and Mrs. Callaghan, with a nasty smile, began to spray the lead.

THE MAN WITH THE RED BEARD

I

THERE are some murderers who are possessed of an almost supreme intelligence. Luckily, they are rare; for it is my confirmed belief that a carefully-planned murder, in which care is taken to obviate such outstanding pointers as *motive, opportunity* and *desire to kill,* will succeed in three cases out of six. In nine cases out of ten carelessness or failure to foresee obvious events are the factors which bring the murderer to the gallows, and not the especial ability of the forces of law and order.

Some years after the War I had occasion to visit my Paris office. At this time the greater part of my business was in France, where, owing to national temperament, and a curious mentality on the part of crooks generally, there are more opportunities for successful private investigation.

I had completed my business and was about to return to England when I received a visit from an old friend and client—a Frenchman—Jules Varnier.

Varnier asked me to see a friend of his—one Gustave Jacquinôt—who was in a very difficult position and wished to consult me.

So I stayed in Paris, and two days afterwards Jacquinôt appeared.

He was a man of some fifty-five years of age; well set-up and attractive in appearance. He was a wine-merchant and owned an extensive business, his headquarters being in Provence. He told me an amazing story which I will recount as briefly as possible.

The facts were these.

68

Some fifteen years before, Jacquinôt had been the head cashier in the offices of a firm of Italian merchants. Their business, situated in Rome, was extensive, but their accounts system was, according to him, obsolete. It was for this reason that he had great difficulty in tracing the source of certain financial defalcations; but eventually, after a preliminary period of single-handed investigation, he was able to bring to book two men employed in his department who were responsible for the thefts. One was a man named Philipe Varouille and the other, his accomplice, a clerk named Atola.

Investigations proved that these two men had not only been swindling the firm for a long period, but their criminal career had embraced other and more nefarious activities. Varouille was sentenced to eleven years' imprisonment. Atola received six years.

Two years after their trial, Jacquinôt, who was a careful and thrifty man, had retired from his firm and, with his savings and the handsome present which his employers made on his resignation, set up for himself as a wine-merchant and had succeeded.

Looking at him as he sat, a rather distinguished figure, on the other side of my desk, I could understand that he was the type of man who would succeed under any circumstances. I said something to this effect. He shook his head and smiled rather sadly.

" There is a proverb," he said, " which says that virtue brings its own reward, but I do not think it applies in this case, because, as a result of my discovery of these robberies fifteen years ago, I am now in danger of my life.

" In point of fact," he continued, " I believe that shortly I shall be a dead man."

I smiled.

"Threatened men live longest, you know," I said. " Tell me who or what are you afraid of?"

" I am afraid of Varouille," he said simply. " After receiving his sentence he behaved very badly in prison.

69

Italian prisons are not nice places. He got no remission for good conduct. In fact, an additional eighteen months' imprisonment was added to his original term. He was released two-and-a-half years ago, and, candidly, I had forgotten all about him until three months ago.

"One day I was sitting in my office in Provence, when I was informed that a gentleman wished to speak to me on the telephone. I answered it. It was Varouille.

"He said that he hoped that I had prospered during the years he had spent in prison. Then he went on to inform me that he was going to kill me, in his own time and place. He suggested that it would be rather disconcerting for me not to know when I was going to be shot.

"Before I could speak he rang off.

"Needless to say, I was terribly perturbed; but nothing happened, and after some time I thought that, possibly, he had changed his mind. Naturally, I wanted to believe that it was some horrible form of joke on his part.

"But soon after I had come to this conclusion my business took me to Madrid. One evening, in that city, he telephoned me again and reminded me that he was still 'looking after me,' as he put it, and that he would strike in his own time.

"Since then I have travelled extensively, as is necessitated by my business, and in no less than five different cities in Europe he has telephoned me to tell me that he is still biding his time.

"This thing," continued Jacquinôt, "began to get on my nerves badly, and when I returned to France three weeks ago I talked the matter over with my friend and your old client—Jules Varnier—and he advised me to come and see you about it. That is why I am here.

"And it seems," he went on with a wry smile, "that I have not come too early, because this morning he telephoned me and informed me that he was going to shoot me within the next fortnight."

I lit a cigarette, mainly so that I might have time to

think. I felt a deep sympathy for the man sitting on the other side of my desk.

"What about the police?" I said. "Don't you think that they could handle this business very much more effectively than I could?"

He shook his head.

"I have discussed that matter with Varnier," he said, "and we agreed that it is useless to go to the police. You look surprised, but have you forgotten the circumstances of the case? I spend the whole of my time travelling between the different agencies of my firm. One week I am here, the next week in Barcelona. After that, perhaps Oporto; then on to Rome. How can I ask for police protection?"

He smiled.

"I should want half the police in Europe looking after me," he added. "It would be all very well if I were permanently in Paris. Then there is another point of view. Supposing that this was Varouille's idea of being revenged—to threaten to shoot me so that I would do all these things, so that I would get police protection in such places as it was possible and make myself look ridiculous, or so that I would stop travelling altogether. In fact, so that I might neglect the business which I have so carefully built up during the last thirteen years."

I nodded.

"I see your point," I said, "but I prefer to think that Varouille is in earnest. After all, it is no good being wise after you are shot, Monsieur Jacquinôt."

He shrugged his shoulders.

"I agree," he said. "And that is why I have come to you. Varnier tells me that you are a man of resource. What can you suggest?"

"It is very simple," I said. "There is not much that I can do. But I can do this. I can have you shadowed night and day by two of my best men. I can employ somebody else to keep a smart look-out for this Varouille.

It will be an expensive process for you, but I see no reason why it should not answer."

He nodded. "And if your men see Varouille," he said, "and if he tries to shoot me?"

I smiled.

"I don't see why one of them should not shoot first," I said. "They would be quite entitled to. If we saw that Varouille was actually in the act of shooting you, we should be entitled to protect you. Let's consider this thing sanely," I went on. "Let's get all the facts. What actually did Varouille say to you this morning?"

"He rang me up at my hotel," he said, "at ten o'clock He said: 'Hallo! Good-morning, Jacquinôt. You see, I'm still here, my friend. I think you have had long enough. I shall shoot you within the next fortnight.' Then I heard the receiver click. I had no time to say anything."

"Well, he sounds determined," I said. "Tell me, is he easily recognised? What sort of man is he?"

"You could recognise him anywhere," he said. "He is of most distinctive appearance. He has red hair, red eyebrows and a little, square, red beard. I saw him four days ago. He was walking along the Grande Boulevard Montmartre with his hands in his pockets, smiling, peering about him. He is very short-sighted and wears horn-rimmed glasses with thick lenses, and his shoulders are bowed."

I laughed.

"Well, we shan't have much difficulty in recognising him," I said. "Now, Monsieur Jacquinôt, listen to me. I propose to take a full statement from you. When I have done this I shall unofficially see a friend of mine who occupies a fairly responsible position at the Sûreté and I shall inform him of the facts. This will cover us in advance in case we have to have a little pistol practice with this Varouille. In a moment I am going to ring through for two of my best operatives. They are both crack shots and I propose that these two men shall keep an eye on you. They will not worry you, but they will be on duty outside your hotel or near you wherever you go. That, at least, will give you more confidence."

"I feel better already," he said.

"All right," I said. "Let's get to work."

I took a full statement from him and sent for two operatives—Valatz and Olly Stevens. Valatz was a Frenchman and Stevens an Australian. They were two very sound men and good pistol-shots.

Jacquinôt described Varouille to them and I gave them their instructions. It was also arranged that he should telephone me immediately he intended to leave Paris. Then I would get in touch with connections of mine in any city which he proposed to visit, so that they would have representatives to meet him on his arrival there.

It seemed to me that the only way we could make certain of getting Varouille was either to seize him in the act of endeavouring to shoot Jacquinôt, or, if the worst came to the worst, to shoot him before he could carry out his threat. Jacquinôt realised, as I did, that it was quite impossible to get Varouille arrested merely because he had telephoned a threat. He would deny that he had ever telephoned and it would be impossible to prove that he had done so. Had he made the threat personally, it would have been a different matter.

After Jacquinôt had gone, I thought over the whole business carefully. I imagined Varouille spending his thirteen years in Italian prisons, feeding his mind on thoughts of vengeance. Probably he was a little insane. In any event, it was more than probable that he would, at some time, endeavour to carry out his threat.

Next morning, I had Jacquinôt's statement carefully typed out. Then I rang up my friend at the Sûreté and went round and informed him unofficially of the position. He agreed that I had done the right thing and that the only possible way to deal with the situation was to keep

Jacquinôt under observation and to try and get Varouille red-handed.

Three days afterwards, at eleven o'clock in the morning, my private telephone rang. I answered the call. It was Jacquinôt.

His voice was tense and I could hear that he was controlling himself with difficulty.

"Varouille has telephoned again," he said. "He rang up five minutes ago. He said that he hoped that I was happy here, in Paris, and that I had better make the most of my time. Then he laughed—a devilish sort of laugh—*and told me that he would be with me at four o'clock this afternoon*. What am I to do?"

His voice trailed off nervously.

"Don't do anything," I said. "Just stay where you are. I think that Varouille is bluffing. After all, if the man intends to murder you this afternoon he isn't likely to advertise it by telephoning you first. Why, for all he knows, you might have a room full of policemen waiting for him!"

"Are you going to do anything about it?" he asked.

"Most decidedly," I replied. "That's what I'm being paid for, isn't it? I'm going to do this. Valatz and Olly Stevens will be on duty at the reception office at your hotel as usual. They will check up on anyone who asks to see you. If they are at all suspicious, they will search any visitor. I will put a man on duty outside the front hotel entrance and another one on the back door, and I will come over myself and see you at half-past three. In the meantime, don't worry. Nobody is going to get past Valatz and Stevens—at least, nobody with a gun or a red beard. You'll find that you and I will have tea together quite happily at four-thirty this afternoon!"

I hung up the receiver and, after telephoning to Olly Stephens and giving him the most stringent instructions, I arranged for another three men to go on duty—one outside the front hotel entrance, one at the back, and a third

74

to hang around generally and to act as a telephone link with me in case anything happened. Then I did a little quiet thinking.

I was trying to make up my mind about Varouille. I was uncertain whether he was merely a bluffer who was trying to frighten Jacquinôt, whether he was insane, or whether this telephoned warning was part of some definite scheme. It was an interesting case.

At a quarter-past three, accompanied by my chief assistant, Grenelle, I walked over to the Hôtel du Parc, where Jacquinôt was staying. In the hall, by the reception office, we found Valatz and Olly Stevens. No one had asked to see Jacquinôt, and there had been no sign of anyone answering to the description of Varouille. Dupont, the man on the back entrance—a very keen and observant operative, said the same thing.

It was just half-past three when Grenelle and I got in the lift and went up to the second floor where Jacquinôt's bedroom was situated.

We got out of the lift and turned to the right and walked down the corridor. My client's bedroom was in a short passage on the left of the main corridor. Just as we were about to turn the corner a man dashed past us and shot down the stairs. My heart gave a bound for he was wearing a black soft hat pulled down over his face, and his red beard and horn-rimmed spectacles were quite obvious. It was Varouille!

Both of us, actuated by the same thought, dashed round the corner and through the open door of Jacquinôt's bedroom. He was lying on the floor, with a thin stream of blood running down his face from a scratch on his forehead; but, apart from this and his obvious exhaustion, he was unhurt.

I sent Grenelle off after Varouille and questioned Jacquinôt.

Five minutes before, he said, there had been a knock on the door. He had thought that it was me and had

75

called out. The door opened and Varouille stepped into the room. He had his hand in his right-hand coat pocket and he just stood grinning at Jacquinôt. Then he said: "Well . . . you're going to get it now, my friend," and withdrew his hand from his pocket. It held an automatic pistol.

Jacquinôt sprang at him, but he was no match for Varouille, who was very strong. Varouille held him off easily with one hand, pushing his head against Jacquinôt's mouth so that he could not shout for help. Then suddenly he threw him off, and as Jacquinôt fell to the ground Varouille must have heard the sound of the lift stopping outside.

He put the pistol back in his pocket, grinned, and said: "I'll see you again, Jacquinôt," and ran out of the room.

By this time Grenelle had returned. Varouille had disappeared. We had seen him running down the stairs to the floor beneath, but he had not left the hotel by the front entrance—in which case he would have had to pass Valatz and Stevens—and Dupont reported that no one had departed by the back way. His escape was a complete mystery. How had he got out of the hotel, or—what was still more important—*was he still in it?*

By this time Jacquinôt was more or less himself again, and was sitting on the settee smiling ruefully.

"A pretty close thing, that . . ." he said.

"Too close for my liking," I replied.

I realised that we had to take good care of Jacquinôt. Varouille meant murder.

"You'll have to leave here at once," I said. "You had better take a room at the Petit Grand—it's not a bad little hotel, and I know the proprietor. It's only half a dozen doors away from my office, and we shall be able to keep our eye on you all right."

"Do you think he'll try again?" queried Jacquinôt.

"Of course he will," I said. "Varouille is stark, staring

mad; you can depend on that. Whether it was his twelve
and a half years of solitude in prison, or his desire for
revenge, I don't know, but you can take it from me that
he's a lunatic, and up to the moment he's had the luck of
one."

I went over to Jacquinôt and examined his throat.
There were fingermarks on it where Varouille had gripped
it. On the lapel of his coat were two or three red hairs. I
removed them carefully.

Jacquinôt smiled.

"I pulled those from his beard," he said. "I hope it
hurt him!"

Two hours later we had him settled in at the Petit
Grand. Valatz and Olly Stevens were to sleep in a room
three doors from his own. During the day they were to
guard the narrow entrance leading to the lift and stairs.
There was no back entrance.

I also arranged that the telephone in Jacquinôt's room
should be connected permanently on to the private-wire
telephone in my own bedroom, which was above my
offices.

Then we had a little meeting. Myself, Jacquinôt,
Grenelle, Valatz and Stevens.

"Now we can't take any chances," I said. "No one
but a lunatic would have tried to do what Varouille
attempted this afternoon. He'll try it again. Maybe he'll
have the effrontery to telephone you and tell you when
he's coming. He wouldn't telephone from anywhere
round here, because he will know that we shall be watching this district. I think he'll act pretty quickly, because,
for all he knows, we have already informed the police of
what took place this afternoon.

"Immediately he telephones you, Jacquinôt—if he does
—get through to me at the office and I'll be here in two
minutes. But don't send for Stevens or Valatz. They
must remain downstairs. Remember he's got to pass them
to get at you.

"Another thing—I'm going to send you round a loaded pistol. *If you see Varouille anywhere near you,* shoot him —and shoot first. I don't think you'll have to, but I'm taking no chances."

Jacquinôt seemed satisfied with these precautions, and I returned to my office. Seated at my desk, I switched on the desk-lamp, and taking the two red hairs from my pocket-book, I took a magnifying-glass and examined them. I was, at this time, very interested in Dr. Hans Schaeffer's theories on the effect of character and insanity on human hair, and I hoped to glean something about this Varouille by a close examination of the strength and colour-gland developments of the two hairs which Jacqui-nôt had plucked from his beard. I got Schaeffer's book from the shelf and studied it, and then subjected the hairs to a close examination.

Then I thought for a long time. I was feeling easier in my mind. I felt that I knew what Varouille would do.

I sent for Grenelle and we discussed the matter at length, after which I sent him off to Jacquinôt with a fully-loaded Mauser automatic pistol with an easy pull on the trigger. Then I telephoned to my friend at the Sûreté —Inspector Garreau—asking him to meet me at the Hôtel du Parc in five minutes' time. He promised to be there.

11

Two days passed uneventfully. On the third night, ten minutes after midnight, my telephone jangled. It was Jacquinôt. His voice was shaking.

"He's just telephoned," he stammered. "He's coming round . . . he's coming round *now*!"

"Don't worry, Jacquinôt," I said. "I'll be with you in three or four minutes. *Don't worry!* He'll never get past Valatz and Stevens!"

I raced down the stairs and up the street. Just inside

the hotel entrance were the people I expected to meet—my chief-assistant, Grenelle, Inspector Garreau, and *the Man with the Red Beard!*

Valatz and Olly Stevens were missing. I knew they would be.

"Do you understand?" I asked the Man with the Red Beard. "Has Garreau explained?"

He nodded.

"Come on, then!" I said.

We ran up the stairs and along the corridor to Jacquinôt's bedroom. We made no noise. Outside the room we stopped, and the Man with the Red Beard knocked on the door.

"Come in!" called Jacquinôt.

The Man with the Red Beard stepped into the room. I paused for a split second and then we went after him. Facing us stood Jacquinôt, the pistol in his hand. It clicked twice as he pulled the trigger.

Then he saw us.

Garreau stepped forward and took the pistol from my client's hand.

"*Philipe Varouille,*" he said, "*I arrest you in the name of the Republic for the attempted murder of this man*" —he pointed to the Man with the Red Beard—"*Gustave Jacquinôt!*"

The man I had known as Jacquinôt, *the man who was Varouille,* dropped into a chair with a sickly grin. Then he picked up a still-burning cigarette from the ashtray on the table and looked at me wryly.

He blew a cloud of smoke into the air.

"Well, how did you find out?" he muttered.

"The two hairs I took off your coat-lapel, Varouille," I answered: "*they were dyed horse-hair*. The red beard was false. Varouille, those two hairs are going to send you to Devil's Island!"

An hour later Grenelle, the real Jacquinôt, and Garreau and myself drank a well-earned cup of coffee in my office.

Jacquinôt handed me a cigar.

"Now, m'sieu, will you please satisfy my curiosity, for when Inspector Garreau met me at the railway station to-night he was able to give me the merest outline—just enough to enable me to play my part in this drama," he said with a smile.

I nodded.

"I believe that this is the cleverest murder plot ever evolved by a human brain," I said. "Here is the story:

"I will start from the time when I examined the two hairs under my microscope in this office.

"A close examination showed me that they were horsehair. And I knew why we had been unable to discover the man who had struggled with the supposed Jacquinôt that afternoon in the Hôtel du Parc.

"He had been made up with a false red beard and eyebrows, had worn horn-rimmed spectacles, and, as he had run down the stairs between the two floors, he had torn off his disguise. He had then turned quickly into a room on the first floor. He must have done this, for no one had passed Valatz and Stevens on the front entrance, or Dupont on the back entrance.

"There was a chance that he might still be at the Hôtel du Parc. He would feel quite safe there, because we had moved the supposed Jacquinôt to the Petit Grand.

"I telephoned Garreau and we met at the Hôtel du Parc. Quietly and systematically we examined every guest who was staying on the first floor. There was not one of them who even resembled—in stature or general appearance—the man who had dashed past us on the second floor.

"But one guest who was out and who would be returning shortly had instructed the hotel office that he was leaving that night. His bill was to be prepared.

"We searched his room. Stuck up the chimney of the fireplace was a red beard, false eyelashes, a balck soft hat and a pair of horn-rimmed spectacles!

"We had found our man!

"We waited for him. When he returned we searched him.

"In his pocket was his passport. *His name was Enrico Atola!*

"He realised that the game was up, and in order to save his own skin as much as possible he gave Varouille away.

"Varouille had thought out the whole plot in prison. On his release he had come to France and started a reputable wine business. He gave himself a whole year to make friends with my old client, Jules Varnier. Then he told him the fake story. *He knew Varnier would send him to me.*

"Naturally, I believed his story, and the fake attack on him by his accomplice, Atola, confirmed everything he said.

"Just before Garreau and I arrived at the Hôtel du Parc, Atola, according to instructions, had telephoned Varouille in his room at the Petit Grand. Over the telephone Varouille informed him that two weeks before he had written our friend here—the real Jacquinôt, in Rome, telling him that he wished to make restitution of the money he had stolen twelve and a half years before, that he was lying ill, and asking Jacquinôt to come and see him in Paris when he was wired for. Jacquinôt had answered, agreeing.

"Varouille now instructed Atola to wire Jacquinôt requesting him to come to the Petit Grand where he, Varouille, lay dying and asking for a reply.

"This reply was to be sent to Atola at the address to which he was moving that night.

"We took him round to this address and awaited the reply, which said that Jacquinôt would arrive at the Gare du Nord at eleven-forty-five at night, on the day after the next. Garreau arranged to have Jacquinôt met by one of his men and the situation explained to him.

"I then sent round the automatic pistol to Varouille, but first I had the firing-pin extracted so that although the pistol was loaded it was harmless.

"Then I realised that somehow or other Varouille would have to get Valatz and Olly Stevens out of the way. I told them to fall in with any suggestion that he might make to them.

"Sure enough, immediately Atola, on our instructions, had telephoned Varouille telling him of the time of Jacquinôt's arrival, Varouille came down to them and asked them up to have a drink.

"They went into Stevens's room and Varouille uncorked a bottle of brandy. He drank none himself, saying that it disagreed with him. Needless to say, it was doped. That disposed of Valatz and Stevens.

"Next he hung out of the window and waited until he saw Jacquinôt stop his cab outside the hotel and pay off the driver. Then he dashed to his telephone and phoned me that 'Varouille is coming round.'

"Jacquinôt would have gone straight up to Varouille's room, and Varouille would have shot him dead. Immediately he had done this he would fire a shot from another pistol which he had, put the weapon in Jacquinôt's hand, and the story would have been complete. He had shot the supposed 'Varouille' in self-defence, and I would have been able to corroborate his story in every detail.

"The police—and remember that I had unofficially informed Garreau here of the situation as told me in the first place—would have been absolutely satisfied, and it would have been weeks before the real Jacquinôt's friends would have noted his disappearance. Varouille and Atola had lots of time to make their getaway. With luck, they would never have been suspected.

"Had it not been for the two false hairs, or if Varouille had had sense enough to have had a beard manufactured out of *real* hair, the plot would have succeeded, and Jacquinôt here would be reposing in the Morgue at the present moment under the name of Philipe Varouille, a would-be murderer, whilst Varouille, the criminal, would have been at liberty under the name of Jacquinôt.

"How Varouille must be cursing those two hairs!"

ABIE ALWAYS PAYS

LISTEN youse guys, maybe you read some place about how the woman always pays. Well, I am tellin' you this is a lotta boloney because the guy who always pays is me, Abie Hymie Finkelstein, an' I don't mean maybe.

Maybe youse mugs believe that there is some justice for a swell citizen with sex appeal like I am in this man's country. Well, all I gotta say is that if there is some justice around this dump then I am the King of China playin' baseball with Mae West on Christmas Eve.

Every guy knows that I am a kind-hearted guy who wouldn't hurt some mice, but all I gotta say is that if some thugs will throw Police Captain Dooley O'Hagan down some pit with tigers an' man-eatin' rattlesnakes then I will believe some more in the Superb Court of Judication an' that this here New Deal is New an' not just raw.

I'm telling you that all these plots an' consperions against me is just because I have gotta lotta sex appeal an' dames go for me in a big way because I have got that little somethin' which other guys have not got, an' because like this guy W. Shakespeare, who is signed up with Metro-Goldwyn-Mayer says, Hell is all furry like a woman scorned.

But is this some reasons why that big cheese Police Captain Dooley O'Hagan should make some plots against me all the time, even when I am not doin' anything that is not barred at the Superb Court of Jurisdiction an' the local Elks Lodge.

I am walkin' around to see my goil Lilly Scapalensi, who, even if she is not so hot to look at an' weighs one hundred an' eighty-four pounds, has got some fine prospecks, because she lends me some money that she gets out of her old man's till when he is out with a key I give her for a present on my birthday.

But when I get around there I see there is some plots goin' on because through the glass door at the back of the store I see Lilly cryin' like she was paid for it an' becase Police Captain Dooley O'Hagan is standin' in the shop eatin' cold Schnitzels an' when he sees me he looks like he is havin' lock jaw through rages.

When I go to make some dignified exits he hollers that old man Scapalensi is makin' a lotta charges against me about his goil takin' dough outa the till for me. He hollers at me that if he hears some more about me around here he will pinch me on a charge of blowin' up a sewer in St. Louis last year an' when I say that I was in New Orleans last year he says much he cares an' that he will get some guy who looks like me to blow up a sewer in New Orleans an' charge me with that an' how do I like that. I then say that I do not like that an' he throws a lotta soup at me which would not have been so bad if this guy had been like a gentleman an' taken the can off it first.

Am I burned up? I then go around to work at Rudy Scraut's delicatessen, but when I arrive at the dump Rudy says that Police Captain Dooley O'Hagan has been around there sayin' that I am Public Enemy No. 14, an' that I am not fit to be in the same country with a cash register unless they have got the U.S. navy an' a marine corps to watch same. He then gives me the air.

I am then so full of desperation, but I remember that I have still got a lotta sex appeal, so I go around and I meet up with Rachael Moshinsky, an' I sing to her, "I Cover the Waterfront," so that she starts cryin' with some emotions an' I then tell her that Police Captain Dooley O'Hagan has lost me my job an' that he is a big air balloon, an' she says, "You should worry, Abie, because if you will give Lilly Scapalensi the air I will show you a way you can make plenty dough if you will fall for me in a big way."

I then say so what, an' she tells me that there is some guy has gotta room around at her pa's tenement, an' that she knows that this guy is Killer Bolgutz, who is wanted for murder an' stick-ups all around an' that there is a reward of 2000 dollars for turnin' him in.

I say that if this news is O.K. then Lilly is out, an' that I will be just like Romero an' Juliet to her, although as I hope to tell this Rachael Moshinsky is not even so hot to look at as Lilly, an' is so fat that she cannot even get into a cinema seat.

But this business looks like a big prospeck so I go around to the tenement an' I see this ferocious guy an' I ask him if he is Killer Bolgutz an' he says sure an' what can he do for me. I tell him that he cannot do anything for me an' I rush round to the 13th Precinct an' I see Police Captain Dooley O'Hagan who says what do I want anyway because I am a menace to the public safeguards.

I draw myself up like Clark Gable an' I tell him that he is a big cheese an' that I would not talk with him even if he was a blind man dyin' of cold feet but that I am a good citizen an' that I know where this Killer Bolgutz is hidin' out an' that if he wants to be in on this business he had better speak polite to Abie Hymie Finkelstein otherwise I am goin' to the Superb Court about all this an' also I want 2000 dollars for the reward.

He then shakes me warmly by the hand an' says that there has been a big misunderstandin' between us an' that he is just like a father to me an' that if I will show him where this Killer Bolgutz is he will probably get Mr. Roosevelt to start some new State Departments for me some time.

I say O.K., but when do I get the dough an' he says

that have I considered that dough is a terrible thing. He says that he has known guys to get 2000 dollars an' go to the bad because they have this dough. He also says that if I will tell him where the Killer is he will give me one hundred bucks an' will keep the rest of the reward for me when he gets it, an' will be like he was my own father only better.

I then say O.K. an' he gives me one hundred bucks an' I take him around to the tenement an' he pulls a gun on this Killer Bolgutz an' says are you Killer Bolgutz an' the Killer says sure I am an' then Police Captain Dooley O'Hagan pinches him an' takes him around to the Precinct.

Now I am feelin' pretty good because I am now Public Hero No. 1 with a lotta sex appeal, an' I am just about to buy a new pair of pants from Isaacs store when I see Rachael Moshinski an' she says that she has heard that they have got Killer Bolgutz an' that now I have got some dough I should marry her before I forget about this arrangement.

I tell her that she is all wrong an' that the real romantic guys do not get married an' that if she will see some pictures she will see that this Romero and Juliet do not get married at all, but they are such lovers that they poison each other all the time.

She then says that I am a big punk an' that she knows that this Romero and Juliet stuff is all boloney becase they are not lovers anyhow, but cigar manufacturers becase she has seen the boxes in the store. She also tells me that she will give me a big surprise becase this guy who says that he is Killer Bolgutz is not Killer Bolgutz at all an' that when Police Captain Dooley O'Hagan finds same out he will bring some charges against me that I will get sentences so long that it would have been cheaper for me not to have been born at all. She then kicks me on the shinbones and sweeps off.

I am now in a terrific jam because I know what Police Captain Dooley O'Hagan will do to me, an' I think that in this case I should come clean about all this, so I ring up Police Captain Dooley O'Hagan from the booth on the corner an' I tell him that I have made a big mistake about this Killer Bolgutz, an' that he is not Killer Bolgutz at all, an' then Police Captain Dooley O'Hagan says some things to me on the telephone which I would not say to anybody at all even if they was strapped down with chains so they could not get at me.

He also says that he is goin' to release this guy an' that unless I give him the hundred bucks back again, with another hundred for his damages he has suffered over this business, that he will charge me with a lot of murders and arsons so that I will practically never see daylight again.

I then go home becase I am feelin' not so good, an' while I am there Lilly Scapalensi rings up an' she says that she has been talkin' to Rachael Moshinski, who says that she has pulled a fast one on Abie becase this Killer Bolgutz is the real guy all the time and that this can be proved by some bullet holes he has got in his arms. I then tell Lilly that she is the goil for me an' that I will be just like Romero and Juliet with her, only better, an' that if she can get one hundred bucks out her old man's till to stop Police Captain Dooley O'Hagan starting something with me then I think that we can make a lotta dough.

Lilly then does a big act with the till an' she brings me round the hundred bucks, an' a few minutes after she has gone Police Captain Dooley O'Hagan comes around an' says that he has released this fake Killer Bolgutz who is threatenin' to bring some actions for malicious persecutions against me, an' that if I do not slip over the hundred bucks an' another hundred for damages that he will encourage and assist this Killer to fix me good an' proper.

I then give him the two hundred bucks an' he goes off, an' when he has gone about half an hour around comes this Killer Bolgutz an' says that he is not so pleased at bein' flung outa the can becase he is only safe from some friends of his if he is in prison. I then tell him to keep quiet an' I will fix him, an' I then ring up Police Lieutenant O'Leary at the 12th Precinct an' tell him that I have got Killer Bolgutz—the real guy—up in my room an' that he should come around an' get him, and also that I would like the reward good an' quick.

Police Lieutenant O'Leary says that I am the berries an' that he will see that I get some straight shootin' from him even if the 13th Precinct cops do say that I taught the forty thieves their business, an' he dashes around with a patrol wagon with tommy-guns and takes away Killer Bolgutz in the wagon, an' he says that I should go straight around to the District Attorney's office an' get the reward.

So I dress myself up a bit so that I am looking full of sex appeal and that little something that the other guy has not got an' I get around to the District Attorney's office an' when I get there I see that there is one helluva argument goin' on outside between O'Leary and the 12th Precinct cops and Police Captain Dooley O'Hagan an' the 13th Precinct guys who have now heard that this Bolgutz is the real feller, an' all these guys is arguin' an' fightin' amongst themselves like you never saw.

So I slip into the District Attorney's office an' after a lot of palooks an' signin' papers they give me two thousand bucks an' am I feelin' good or am I, because if I can now get out of this burg before Lilly Scapalensi can get all passionate about me I can see some nice prospecks with this dough.

But outside Police Captain Dooley O'Hagan is waitin' for me, an' he looks at me like I was a rattlesnake with stings an' he says do I think that I am goin' to get away with all this stuff around here an' what do I think that I am that I should pull one on him like I have. He also says that old man Scapalensi has missed another hundred bucks from the till an' that he is goin' to charge me with takin' the dough from Lilly an' that the old man has marked the bills so it is a cinch that I am for a long sentence that is unless I like to give him the two thousand bucks reward in which case he will probably get me off an' will be like a father to me.

I then tell him that he is nothin' but a big cheese an' that I have just told the District Attorney that the bills taken from old man Scapalensi's till has been given to Police Captain Dooley O'Hagan an' that if they are all marked it don't look so good for him. I then leave him lookin' like he was going to have a whole lotta paralytic strokes all at once.

I am now feelin' very good an' I go around to my room an' I realise that it is my sex appeal that makes all these dames so passionate about me an' just as I get around there I see a newsboy shoutin' an' I buy a paper an' it says that owin' to the argument between the 12th and 13th Precinct cops as to who was to have Killer Bolgutz the news about him bein' pinched has got all around town an' that while they was takin' him back to the 12th Precinct a lotta friends of his have stuck up Police Lieutenant O'Leary an' the 12th Precinct cops an' that Killer Bolgutz is escaped again.

But much I care because I have handed this guy over two times an' I have also got the reward.

But when I get up to my room I find that there is Killer Bolgutz an' some thugs all sittin' round an' Killer Bolgutz says that unless I hand over the two thousand bucks then they are goin' to give him an' me the works.

Now all these thugs havin' got pistols an' guns there is nothin' to do about anything except to give them the dough, after which they go off takin' Killer with them an' also a new overcoat that I got outa some cloakroom last week whilst the attendant was asleep.

So now I am even robbed of my clothes because of this sex appeal I have got which is a terrible thing, an' I think that after all Lilly Scapalensi is not such a bad goil an' she has got some prospecks an' so I ring her up an' I say that even though I have not got any dough I will be like Romero and Juliet to her some more, an' she says oh yeah well she will tell me something an' she tells me that Police Captain Dooley O'Hagan says that he has heard that Killer Bolgutz was seen comin' outa my place with a lotta thugs an' that he is goin' to arrest me for harbourin' criminals.

So it looks like there is nothin' left for me but to get outa this burg good an' quick before Police Captain Dooley O'Hagan starts bringing a lotta false charges against me at any moment.

But I hope that some guy in the Superb Court of Judication will read this becase then he will know that really I am a straight guy but that I have gotta lot of sex appeal which gets me in bad with dames an' that it is not becase I am not honest but only becase I have got that little somethin' which other guys have not got that these plots are goin' on against me all the time.

A DOUBLE DOUBLE-CROSS

I

IN an attractive villa between Nimes and Avignon lives Roanne—to be precise, Roanne Lucrezia Loranoff. It was believed by the assortment of individuals who still meet, occasionally, in the little room upstairs at Père Benoit's, in Ostend, that Loranoff was not her actual surname but that it was a much more important name. John Varnak of the yellow beard and loud laugh—that same Varnak who was stabbed last August in a mean alley in Leningrad—said that she was a princess. It was, however, agreed that the point was immaterial. She was Roanne—which was sufficient.

In the years which followed the ending of the war, when open diplomacy was so fashionable that the secret service and intelligence departments of every country were worked to death, Roanne functioned very adequately. She was one of the few aristocratic young women who had escaped from the Soviets with no harm, except a twisted little finger—caused by some ruffian tearing off a too-well-fitting ring—and a desire to annoy anybody who was a man.

She did none of the things which *émigrées* did. She left the stage, the Parisian cabarets and New York society severely alone. She called herself Loranoff, and spied—most excellently. In a year she had made a reputation on counter-espionage work which made old hands jealous. Half a dozen countries employed Roanne at different times. But she served only one master at once. She was dependable. Male secret service people, carefully warned against her wiles, went down like ninepins. In 1920 she rifled John Varnak's despatch-case while he, driven desperate by the pain of her supposed toothache, wandered about Milan at three o'clock in the morning in search of a dentist. He said afterwards that he knew it would happen, but that he " couldn't *not* believe her," when she said she was hurt.

From her feet upwards she was the woman that most men dream of. She was supple and slim, but not too slim; her taste in clothes and her method of wearing them were exquisite. Her skin was like milk, and when she pulled off her hat, you expected, for some reason, to see black hair. You did not. She was an ash blonde. Even women gazed after her when she walked. This was Roanne, who, at this moment, lives at the Villa Lucretia between Nimes and Avignon.

II

WHEN Duplessis stepped off the boat at Dieppe, Roanne, standing on the railway side of the *octroi,* spotted him immediately.

Maltazzi (she was working for Italy at this time) was with her, and she spoke quickly to him.

"Listen, Maltazzi," she said. "That must be Duplessis. Somehow I shall get into conversation with him in the train. But do not let him see you."

Maltazzi nodded, and went off to the train. Roanne watched Duplessis get into a first-class carriage which was unoccupied. Then she pulled up the big chinchilla collar of her cloak round her face, gave a little tug at her cloche hat, darted one quick look at her stockings (like all well-groomed women, she hated the wrinkle which sometimes appears under the knee, even in the best silk stocking) and ordered her porter to put her suitcase in the carriage where Duplessis sat. The porter, somewhat clumsily, knocked the suitcase against the doorway, slightly tearing the leather cover and attracting for a moment the attention of Duplessis, who was reading. He looked up and saw both the tear in the suitcase cover and Roanne, who was just about to enter the carriage. Duplessis looked at Roanne's face and forgot all about everything else.

That look was sufficient for Roanne. The momentary gleam which had appeared in the grey eyes of Duplessis, and her quick glance at his humorous and sensitive mouth, convinced her that he would be easy prey; providing always that he had not been warned and had not recognised her from one of the innumerable dossiers which every Intelligence record possessed.

As a matter of fact, Duplessis had not the remotest notion, at that moment, that she was Roanne. He realised simply that she was a remarkably beautiful woman with a wicked little gleam in her eyes; that she had a twisted little finger—he was observant, was Duplessis—and that the idiot porter had torn the patent-leather corner of her suitcase. The first realisation nearly ruined Duplessis; the last saved him.

Probably every man who has done Secret Service work has a complex about beautiful women. His mind, so continuously occupied with the fact that " the other side " may be employing some international beauty to trap him, becomes more than cautious about them and, paradoxically, that makes them more attractive.

The train moved off on its way towards Paris. Duplessis sat in his corner, reading a magazine and stealing covert glances over the top at Roanne. She, in the diagonally opposite corner—her plan of campaign definitely settled—composed her features into an expression of heartbroken sadness, and twiddled nervously with her lace handkerchief. Beneath the long lashes her eyes watched Duplessis, who was obviously interested.

For half an hour Roanne did nothing. She sat and looked sad. Then, after some decided twitching of her long fingers and with a spasmodic movement which betokened intense effort of self-control, a sob broke from her. She put her hands to her face, her body relaxed, and she sobbed, bitterly and openly. Roanne was an excellent actress.

It worked. Within three minutes Duplessis was sitting by her side, offering condolence, sympathy, asking if he could do something—would she like some tea? Tea was so refreshing; such a stimulant to the nerves. Roanne, still sobbing, admitted that she would like tea, and Duplessis, rather pleased with himself, went off to get it. While he was gone Roanne arranged her face against his return, and Maltazzi, observing from his distant part of the train the peregrinations of Duplessis in search of tea, grinned a little cynically. He knew Roanne.

It was very natural that, after Duplessis had procured the tea and after Roanne had drunk it, Duplessis should endeavour to find out what the trouble was, and if he could be of any assistance.

You have heard already that Duplessis was not an amazingly clever man. His business in the Secret Service was mainly confined to opening reluctant safes for the more clever people, who afterwards dealt with the contents. Being entirely innocent at the moment as to what his mission to Paris might be, he did not suspect Roanne in the remotest degree.

Punctuated by the most charming sobs and with an occasional sidelong glance at Duplessis which was not without its effect, Roanne haltingly told her story. Her name was Marie d'Enverde. Her mother had died, leaving her certain bonds, payable at sight, in the charge of her young brother Etienne. Etienne, it appeared, was a bad young man; he drank, he doped; in fact, he did everything that he should not do. Also, he refused to hand over Roanne's legacy.

"Why not take proceedings against him?" Duplessis asked, naturally enough.

To this Roanne replied that she could not bear the publicity. In any event, too much had been heard in Paris of the doings of the aforesaid Etienne. After another little outburst of tears, during which Duplessis sat by Roanne's side and patted her hand in a manner which grew less fatherly every moment, Roanne went on to say that in a fit of desperation she had even hired a burglar to break into Etienne's flat, open the safe and steal the bonds. But alas! the cracksman could not open the safe. It was a marvellous safe, an entirely new invention, a Duplex safe. Duplessis smiled at himself at hearing this, for in all probability he was the only man in Europe who could open a Duplex safe.

So that, continued Roanne, life was entirely impossible. She was almost penniless. Yet, in this safe of her brother's reposed a small fortune of a million francs, which was rightfully hers, though she could not obtain it. She indulged in another spasm of tears, this time on her comforter's shoulder.

Then the idea came to Duplessis. A wonderful idea! Of course, it was the idea that the clever and beautiful Roanne had intended should come to him—the idea that *he* should open the safe! He pointed out to Roanne that he was an engineer occupied in the manufacture of safes, that he knew all about them and that the whole thing would be easy. Roanne was very diffident. She took a great deal of persuading, but eventually she allowed herself to be persuaded.

"It will be quite, quite simple, my dear, my very dear friend," she murmured eventually, "because, you see, my brother will not be at his flat to-night. It is the first-floor flat, Thirty-seven, *Rue Clichy*. The concierge is a friend of mine. I will telephone him that you will be there at nine o'clock to-night. I can give you a key of the flat. Luckily, I have one in my handbag."

She opened her handbag and gave Duplessis the key.

"Oh!" She gave a little exclamation. "Here is something else too. Here is an exact replica of the leather case in which the bonds are. I had it made for my unsuccessful burglar to leave in place of the other one, so that my brother should not miss it too quickly. Will you take this and leave it in the place of the one which you take out of the safe? And then if you do open the safe, do you think you can bring my bonds to me at the Hotel Continental? I shall be there at ten o'clock. And perhaps," continued Roanne, with a positively devastating glance, " you might care to have supper with me."

Duplessis agreed to everything. By this time, like many much cleverer men, he was head-over-heels in love with the exquisite Roanne. And when the train arrived at the Gare du Nord he was congratulating himself on being lucky enough to be able to do her a service.

On the station she bade him an affectionate farewell and got into a large car which awaited her. Duplessis watched the car until it disappeared in the dusk.

Two hundred yards from the station Roanne's car pulled up. Maltazzi jumped from a following taxicab. He hurried to Roanne's car, opened the door and smiled at her. She sat back in the corner, wrapped in her cloak. Her eyes were shining.

" Well?" asked Maltazzi.

" My friend," said Roanne, " it worked. This Duplessis was easy. At nine o'clock he will go to the flat and open the safe. Therefore the occupant of the flat, Bayarde, who would guard those papers with his life, must somehow be removed. You must find a way to do that."

" Easy," said Maltazzi. " It has been arranged that I call on Bayarde to-night with reference to some business in which he is interested in Paris. I am supposed to be one Gauteuil, a commercial traveller."

Roanne laughed. " Maltazzi," she said, " you don't look very much like a commercial traveller, but if you put on your hat a little straight, and get your shoes dusty, and— yes!—take my suitcase, you will probably look the part

96

much more; but please return my suitcase carefully—my evening gowns are in it."

Maltazzi nodded and picked up the case from the floor of the car. "Easy," he said again. "When I get into the flat I shall ask Bayarde to examine some papers. As he does so I shall press a wad, soaked in chloroform, over his nose. There is no one else in the flat and I shall drag him into the next flat, which belongs to one of my men. He will see that Bayarde remains there sleeping quietly until our friend Duplessis has done his work."

"Excellent," said Roanne.

Maltazzi nodded and lit a cigarette.

"It is all very well, mademoiselle," he continued. "I can arrange all that easily enough, but supposing this innocent Duplessis takes it into his head, after he has opened the safe, to examine the papers. He will quickly discover that, far from being bonds, they are copies of two important secret treaties. What will he do then? Why, obviously, he will take them to his own chief in Paris and all our trouble will have been for nothing. What a curse it is that I could not get that safe open myself!"

"I've thought of all that," replied Roanne. "It's quite possible our charming Duplessis will examine the papers, in which event he would, as you say, take them straight off to his chief. It is even possible that he will report to his chief this evening. If so, he would be told that he has been sent for by his own service to open the identical safe in the *Rue Clichy* in order that Britain may have these papers, and then the affair will become a little difficult; but I'm hoping he will be so inspired by my distress over my wicked brother"—here Roanne laughed softly—"that he will put off reporting to his chief until to-morrow. With regard to the second point, that he examines the papers when he *has* opened the safe, that, my friend, must be dealt with by you."

"How?" asked Maltazzi.

"Easily enough," said Roanne. "When Duplessis

leaves the flat in the *Rue Clichy* to-night it will be quite dark. He must be set on by three or four *apaches*. They will take everything on him, papers, watch, chain, money, everything. It will look like an ordinary robbery. We shall in any event get the papers, and all that remains for my poor Duplessis to do is to come to me at ten o'clock, with tears in his nice eyes, and to inform me that, after actually getting my bonds from my wicked brother's safe, they have been stolen from him in the street. Quite simple, isn't it?"

Maltazzi laughed. "You're a clever woman, Roanne," he said, looking at her with sincere admiration. "I can arrange that. It will be dark when he comes out, and as there have been one or two robberies in the neighbourhood of the *Rue Clichy* during the last week, no one will think anything of it."

"Excellent!" said Roanne. "But one thing, Maltazzi. My nice Duplessis must not be hurt. I shouldn't like that. He was so kind to me. He got tea for me, and patted my hand, and was so sympathetic."

Maltazzi smiled again. "Rest assured, mademoiselle," he said, "we shall not hurt him. I will promise you that."

He raised his hat and, quite pleased with himself, disappeared into the crowd. He would not have been so pleased had he realised that in the business of chloroforming the unfortunate Bayarde he, Maltazzi, would forget Roanne's suitcase and leave it on the floor in the corner of Bayarde's sitting-room. All of which goes to prove that the cleverest international agent, like the most foolish criminal, can make a mistake.

Duplessis, having watched Roanne's car out of sight, took a cab and went straight to the rooms where he stayed when in Paris, near the *Grand Boulevard Montmartre*.

Roanne had made one mistake in assessing Duplessis's character. He was not the type of man to disregard his duty, and his first business, after dumping his attaché-case in the corner, was to ring up Slavin—who was at that time Chief of the British Service in Paris—and to ask him whether he was wanted immediately.

"Oh, no, Duplessis," said Slavin cheerily on the telephone. "I want you to do a job for me, but it can easily wait until to-morrow. Still, I'd like to talk it over with you, so perhaps you will come round to my place about ten to-night."

Duplessis said he would. He thought that he could have the little business in the *Rue Clichy* finished at nine-thirty, dash round to Slavin, hear what he had to say, and then make straight for the Hotel Continental and Roanne.

The very thought of Roanne stirred Duplessis. Dimly, in some remote place at the back of his mind, a vague idea of marrying Roanne was germinating. How he was going to do this he had not the remotest notion, but the idea was there. He realised also that the first step towards making this vague idea a little more practical was to carry through successfully the business of returning to Roanne her bonds.

He bathed, put on a dinner-suit, ate an excellent dinner, and at ten minutes to nine, having put his little kitbag of tools, most of which were his own inventions, into the pocket of his overcoat, he took a taxi to the *Rue Clichy*.

He paid off the cab on this side of Zelie's and walked slowly towards his destination, examining the houses carefully. Soon he realised that a postcard-seller, whom he had noticed when he got out of his cab, was sidling behind him. The man whispered hoarsely in his ear. *" M'sieu,* everything is arranged. Mademoiselle's brother is out and the concierge has been amenable to reason. It is the first-floor flat; your way is clear before you. *Bonne chance, M'sieu!"*

Duplessis nodded, and walked on. He turned casually into the entrance to Number Thirty-seven, acknowledged the greeting of the concierge and ran quickly up the stairs. The front door of the flat yielded easily to his key. He looked quickly through the rooms until he found the safe. Then he switched on the light and set to work.

Opening that safe was one of the toughest jobs which Duplessis had ever experienced. It took twenty-five minutes' hard work and it was nearly half-past nine as he swung the ponderous door open. Before him, on the steel shelf of the safe, lay the leathern wallet, the exact duplicate of the dummy in his pocket. He had put out his hand for it when his observant eye fell on something in the corner—something which made him start. In the corner of the room was a very ordinary suitcase; *but* the corner of this suitcase was torn. Duplessis immediately recognised it as Roanne's case, which the clumsy porter had torn when putting it into the railway carriage at Dieppe.

I have said that Duplessis was not an extraordinary clever man, but, very naturally, he asked himself why this case should be in the flat. Why, for some unknown reason, should this case, part of Roanne's luggage—which should have gone with her straight to her hotel—be in this flat in the *Rue Clichy?* Either Roanne had been there herself or someone else had brought it there. Was it likely that Roanne, who was such bad friends with her brother, would come round to the flat, and, if she did, leave her attaché-case there?

Duplessis's eye fell on the clock on the mantelpiece. It was twenty to ten. He remembered his appointment with Slavin. The very thought of Slavin suggested something to Duplessis. The idea came to him, for the first time, that Roanne was not all that she seemed and that, possibly, he had walked into a trap.

He tiptoed out of the flat and looked down the stairs. The concierge was deep in conversation with two rough-looking individuals, one of whom was the man who had told Duplessis that the way was clear in the *Rue Clichy*. Then Duplessis realised that when he got outside he would probably be set upon and the wallet stolen.

There was a telephone in the corner of the room, but he knew that it was no use telephoning the police. It isn't usual for employees of the Secret Service to get mixed up in foreign police courts. Suddenly the whole thing became clear to Duplessis. Slavin wanted those documents in the safe! And Duplessis had been sent over to Paris because he was the only man who could open it. These other people, whoever they were, wanted them too. And he, like a fool, had walked straight into the trap that had been laid for him.

For some minutes Duplessis stood in the middle of the room, thinking deeply. Then he walked over to the attaché-case and opened it. In it were three evening gowns. Their flimsiness and the suggestion of perfume which greeted Duplessis's nostrils reminded him vividly of Roanne.

An idea came to him and he laughed quietly to himself. Then he went to the telephone, found the number of the Hotel Continental, rang up the hotel and asked for Mademoiselle d'Enverde. A few minutes later the sound of Roanne's soft voice came to him over the telephone.

" Mademoiselle," said Duplessis, " I am delighted to tell you that I have just opened the safe and that the leather wallet containing your bonds, which, of course, I have not opened, is in my hands."

" Excellent!" said Roanne softly. "I am so indebted to you, Monsieur Duplessis—my dear Monsieur Duplessis —how can I ever repay you?"

"Quite easily, mademoiselle," replied Duplessis. "I have been thinking. You remember you said that I might come to you for supper. Would it be asking too great a reward for my services if I asked you to have supper with me at ten-thirty at the Café de la Paix? If that is agreeable I will call for you at ten-fifteen."

"But how I should love that, my friend," said Roanne. "But, alas! I have no evening gowns. . . ." Duplessis's heart leapt when he heard this. "Do you mind if I come in a day gown?"

"Mademoiselle," said Duplessis, "I am terribly disappointed. You see, I think that I am very fond of you, and all the while I was working on this safe I had a little picture in my mind, a picture of us supping together, with you wearing the most wonderful evening gown. I thought," said Duplessis, "that it would probably be a black one. I am certain you would look so nice in black . . ." he remembered the black gown in the attaché-case.

Roanne laughed. "Very well, my friend," she said, "you have deserved well. I will wear a black evening gown. It is a little inconvenient because my evening gowns are not here, but I will send for them. Nothing is too much trouble for you, my good friend."

Duplessis murmured suitable thanks, said "*Au revoir*," and hung up the receiver. Five minutes later, having shut the safe door, he noisily descended the stairs, said "Good-night" to the concierge, and turned into the *Rue Clichy*. Seven minutes later a very burly individual, coming suddenly out of a side street, neatly tripped Mr. Duplessis. With great promptitude four other individuals who appeared out of the shadows which abound in the *Rue Clichy* held him down and very systematically relieved him of everything in his possession, including his tiepin. They then disappeared as quickly as they came.

Duplessis got up, brushed himself, and, with a beatific smile, got the first cab which appeared. In it he drove straight round to Slavin who, when he had heard Duplessis's story, laughed long and loudly; and that, if you know anything about Mr. Slavin, was a very strange thing.

IV

At ten minutes past ten Duplessis called at the Hotel Continental.

Roanne received him smilingly, but, as he shook hands with her, Duplessis's face was a picture of abject misery.

"Mademoiselle," he said, "I do not know how to tell you the terrible news. I hope you will understand. When I left the apartment in the *Rue Clichy* to-night I was set upon by *apaches*. They took everything that I had, including the wallet with your bonds in it. I would have rung you up sooner, but I could not bear the thought of your disappointment."

Roanne smiled. She was looking utterly delicious in a black evening gown—the top one in the attaché-case, Duplessis noted with satisfaction.

"My poor friend," she said, "do not be concerned on my account. Naturally, I am sorry that the bonds are lost, but since I last saw you certain business has taken place which will mean that I am to receive a large sum of money. Therefore do not let us think any more about these bonds which have been the cause of so much trouble. Let us go and sup and talk about more pleasant things. For you must know," said Roanne admiringly, "I am beginning to feel quite an affection for you."

And this was true. In spite of her varied acquaintance amongst some of the cleverest men in Europe, Roanne really felt herself attracted to this rather quiet and straightforward Englishman, this specialist in opening reluctant safes of whom she had made such good use.

At this moment the telephone rang loudly. Roanne, with a murmured excuse, went to it. After a moment's conversation she called through the door leading from the sitting-room, in which they were, to her bedroom. "Marie, there is somebody downstairs, a Monsieur Leblanc, who insists on speaking to me personally on an urgent matter. I don't know him, and I don't want him up here. Go down and see what he wants."

The maid went off, and Duplessis smiled to himself.

Two minutes afterwards the maid returned and informed Roanne that Monsieur Leblanc was sorry, but that he must see her personally. It was a matter of the utmost urgency, and Roanne, with apologies to Duplessis, went downstairs.

Immediately she had gone Duplessis turned to the maid. "How silly of me," he said. "I have just remembered. The Monsieur Leblanc downstairs wishes to see me, and, knowing that I should be with mademoiselle, he has probably asked for her by mistake. Run after her and explain. And tell him he must come and see me to-morrow morning."

The maid, looking rather surprised, went off. As the door closed behind her, Duplessis dashed across the room and into Roanne's bedroom, from which he emerged in time to seat himself in his original chair as Roanne and her maid returned.

As they sat over their coffee, Roanne watched Duplessis covertly. She felt that he would make a nervous confession of love at any moment, a process to which she was quite accustomed, for most men proposed to Roanne at some time or other.

But she found herself rather interested in the forthcoming avowal from Duplessis. She felt that it would be different. He looked troubled and his hand, holding the coffee-spoon, trembled a little.

Eventually he spoke, and she, with a little inward and gratified sigh—in which women indulge on these occasions

—braced herself to listen with much pleasure. Her surprise grew as Duplessis continued speaking.

"Mademoiselle Loranoff," said Duplessis—she sat back a little at that. So he knew her name!—"I am very unhappy because I am very fond of you and I feel that the news I have to break to you will make you hate me. However, I will tell you at once that the wallet, which your friends took from me on the *Rue Clichy* this evening, is the dummy one which you yourself gave me. . . ."

Roanne smiled a little. She was a good loser.

"So . . ." she murmured, "and the real one?"

"By this time safe at the British Embassy," said Duplessis. "You see, mademoiselle, I am not at all a clever man. When I received instructions to report here, I could not guess that it was to open that safe of Bayarde's in order that my own people might get hold of those plans. I believed your story and was keen to help you, because I had already become interested in you. . . ."

Roanne's eyes were glistening.

"How did you get the papers away from the flat in the *Rue Clichy*?" she asked.

Duplessis grinned. "That was quite easy," he said. "You see, the first thing that aroused my suspicions was your suitcase in Bayarde's flat. When you left me at the Gare du Nord it was put into your car. I noticed this. Directly I saw it at the flat I recognised it because I had seen porter tear the corner slightly getting it into the carriage at Dieppe. Then I began to suspect you and when I saw the concierge whispering with the man who had spoken to me in the *Rue Clichy* I thought that I should probably be set on directly I got out of the flat.

"Therefore, having discovered that your evening gowns were in the suitcase and that the top one was black, I telephoned you, and asked you to wear an evening gown, knowing that you would probably send round for the case. I then hid the real wallet in the empty pocket in the lid of the suitcase, and put the dummy in my pocket. As I thought, you sent round for the suitcase. You remember the mysterious Monsieur Leblanc who called to see you while I was with you at the Continental? Well, this was a young gentleman in the employ of our service here, and I used him to get both you and your maid out of your suite while I went into your room and took the wallet from the suitcase which lay open on your bed.

"The Embassy messenger was awaiting me here in the cloakroom when I arrived with you, and I handed him the wallet."

Duplessis looked at her. He looked thoroughly miserable. Roanne, looking into his eyes, came to the conclusion that Duplessis was a thoroughly sound Englishman and that he was not half such a fool as he liked to pretend.

"I am sorry, mademoiselle," said Duplessis, "that you have lost this little game. I am a loser too."

Roanne smiled and her eyes were very soft. Remember that she was very much of a woman and that Duplessis was the first man to outwit her.

"M'sieu Duplessis," she said, "you are the only man who has ever beaten me at my own game. I think that I like being outwitted—the experience is new. But you must be punished. I shall, therefore, marry you! Well——?"

It took Duplessis five minutes to recover his breath and another twenty to be persuaded that Roanne was speaking the truth. When he told Slavin the next morning that worthy refused, point blank, to believe him.

But the fact remained that "Roanne Lucrezia Loranoff," sometime Princess Roanne Lucrezi Demiroff, and now Mrs. John Duplessis, lives in an attractive villa between Nimes and Avignon, and awaits the periodic return of her spouse, who, in the intervals of feeding chickens, occasionally points out how clever she is and what an awful fool she must think him.

When they ask Duplessis—in the little room upstairs at

Père Benoit's, in Ostend—how he got Roanne to marry him, he says he doesn't know.

And, strangely enough, although no one believes him, he doesn't!

THE BUMP-OFF

SOME guys has been ruined by janes an' some by wood alcohol; but I am a guy what has been ruined by some stuff called ethics and because some wise palooka called W. Shakespeare tips off the Big Shot some boloney about ridicule bein' worse than death.

Do I get all burned up when I see guys pointin' at me in the street an' sayin' that I am the feller who used to be Red (Two-Gun) Maloney, the best bump-off man in town?

This business is all because of a buddy of mine who I thought was a regular guy an' who played me for a sucker an' who is the cause of me havin' to drive this liquor truck like an ordinary sap—me, who bumped off Frenchy Harris, Little Ike Schnitzler an' Machine-Gun Caselli in one night—all separate jobs an' nice work.

You gotta take life like it comes, an' when it don't come so good what is a guy to do?

You heard of McGonegal? Yeah. Well this McGonegal was a buddy of mine. That guy an' me used to play around Capardo's wharf on East River when we was kids. Now will you listen to what that guy did to me?

Him an' me was workin' for the Big Shot in a big way. McGonegal an' me was muscle men. He got the orders an' looked after the liquor delivery an' I was doin' any bumpin' off that came along an' blastin' shop-fronts when they got tired of payin' for protection.

One night something breaks. Issy Marcovitch who is

the Big Shot's contact man comes to me when I am sittin' in Schmidt's speak-easy an' tells me that he has got a piece of news what ain't so good—in fact, it's bad, an' he don't mean maybe.

He buys me a shot of rye and he proceeds to inform me that McGonegal has been shootin' his mouth around town an' has got in bad with the Big Shot owin' to his havin' talked too much to some newspaper guy what works on a tabloid.

So the Big Shot says that McGonegal should be bumped off pronto as a lesson to other guys whose mouths is too big. Issy also says that the big feller is very appreciative of my nice work the week before when I blew the front wall out of some brewery, an' that I am the guy who is to bump McGonegal off.

Now I take it very bad that the Big Shot should elect me to bump McGonegal owin' to said McGonegal bein' a pal of mine and a regular fellow when sober, but in any event business is business so I tell Issy that I will pay special attention to this job an' that I will bump my old pal McGonegal so nice that he will be playin' harps before he knows what has hit him.

Issy Marcovitch says this is O.K. by him but that this piece of business must be done pronto in order that other guys workin' for the racket shall not go about drinkin' cut liquor an' talkin' to newspaper men; said newspaper men bein' a menace to any honest-to-God racketeer. This is Tuesday night an' I tell Issy that by Friday morning we shall all be buyin' wreaths for McGonegal an' that I will personally buy him a very big lily wreath because he is a buddy of mine and we was kids together.

Issy then scrams out of it and I am sittin' there talkin' about a baseball game with some guy who is buyin' me rye with some money I took out of his pocket when Schmidt comes an' tells me that McGonegal is on the wire.

I go into the phone-box an' McGonegal who is cussin'

like a rattlesnake informs me that some guy has wised him up that the Big Shot is goin' to have him bumped off an' that I am elected for the job. He also says that this is a lousy business for reasons which he says after the jane at the telephone exchange has told him that she will disconnect him if he don't pipe down on the cussin' as he is usin' words that even she ain't ever heard before.

McGonegal then says that he don't mind bein' bumped off providin' same is done in a legitimate an' proper manner. He says that he knew the spot was comin' to him owin' to him havin' talked too much to this newspaper guy; but that I am a so-and-so and a so-and-so because he knows that I have got myself elected to bump him off simply because I owe him eighty-two dollars and ten cents, an' because I have not returned to him the blue suit with two pair of pants that he lent me in order to look ritzy with at the Ironworkers' Frolic last week.

I tell him that he is talkin' out of his elbow an' after a lot of pressin' he comes round to the speak-easy where I proceed to inform him that I have not elected myself to bump him, but that I have been tipped off to effect same by Issy Marcovitch.

I also say that I am a fair-minded an' legitimate guy an' that he certainly has a grouse comin' to him over the eighty-two dollars and ten cents, an' the suit of clothes, an' I also say that any guy who would get himself elected to bump a buddy of his when he is owin' same money is no sort of a guy but a two-faced four-flushin' twicer.

We then have some more rye an' it is arranged that I shall not bump off McGonegal until I have paid him the eighty-two dollars an' ten cents and returned the suit an' two pairs of pants after havin' same pressed up.

McGonegal then says that this is all okey doke, but that what the hell is the good of dough to him if he is goin' to be bumped off; also he has got no use for his suit when he is in a casket with flowers all around it. But he says that he does not want to make things tough for me so he will accept this thing provided that I send the eighty-two dollars an' ten cents to his girl who is workin' for some feller who runs a snide poker game in Oklahoma, an' that when she tips him off on the phone that she has got the dough then I can bump him any time I like an' that he will give me the suit an' two pairs of pants as a mascot.

Havin' fixed this up we beat up some guy in the corner because he looks like some other guy who McGonegal says he does not like very much an' we part the best of friends which we have been ever since we was seven years old.

Next mornin' I discover that I am in a bad spot because it is very easy to send eighty-two dollars an' ten cents to some jane in Oklahoma supposin' you have got same, which I have not got. The result is that on Thursday mornin' I have only got sixty-two dollars towards this money, which is all the money there was in the safe at Ye Olde Englyshhe Bunne Shoppe on Firty-First an' Cleveland, after I have opened same with a pineapple.

Also Issy Marcovitch is ringin' me up and pressin' me to get on with the business of bumpin' McGonegal off as per instructions, an' refuses to advance me any dough until same is performed as per schedule.

So on Thursday night I take a chance an' send the sixty-two dollars to McGonegal's girl in Oklahoma, hopin' that she will not report the shortage to McGonegal, because I am not to know am I that said girl is a proper vinegar cat. Also I am very keen to get action in this matter as I know that unless I bump McGonegal pronto the Big Shot will be askin' questions which is not such a hot business if you know the Big Shot.

But am I wrong? On Friday mornin' McGonegal rings me up and when I say so what he proceeds to inform me that I am seventeen degrees lower than a pink rattlesnake; that I am a low mobsman without hope of resumption, an' that I would stick up an old lady for her imitation horn-rims any day.

By which I come to the conclusion that the vinegar cat in Oklahoma has given McGonegal the low-down on being twenty dollars and ten cents short in the kitty, an' I know I am right when he informs me that he is not goin' to be bumped off by any guy that would do a thing like that to him.

He also says that he has been sittin' up all night drinkin' rye an' thinkin' out ways that he can make me look like a nickel's worth of Limburger cheese after a Mickey Mouse convention, an' that he has got the big idea.

He says that he is goin' to bump himself off by jumpin' off Capardo's Wharf on East River an' that he is goin' to leave a note for the coroner sayin' that he is takin' this step because he is sick of hangin' around waitin' to get bumped off by me!

I am now in a proper hot spot an' when I ring up Issy Marcovitch an' tell him about this bezusuz, he says that my only chance is to get down to Capardo's Wharf an' bump off McGonegal before he can perform the high divin' act, otherwise the Big Shot will most certainly iron me out good an' proper, an' that if any more stuff gets into the newspapers I can go book myself a nice table down at the morgue.

Issy also adds that for a gunman I am behavin' like a big cissy an' that he could have bumped off a couple of thousand guys while I have been flirtin' round with this proposition.

I now see that I must get myself some very quick action otherwise I am goin' to lose a whole lot of my reputation for my nice work in the past. So I get myself a Yellow Cab an' I rush down to Capardo's Wharf where I see a lot of guys standin' about the place, an' when I ask some guy what is all this palooka about he tells me that McGonegal has jumped off the wharf with a bottle of rye in each pocket an' a picture of the vinegar cat in Oklahoma in his mitt, and that some newspaper guy who has

III

been trailin' around after McGonegal has jumped in after him an' pulled him out, after which both these guys drunk all the rye and McGonegal then proceeds to tell the newspaper guy—who is the guy at the tabloid—the whole works.

I am now feelin' very full of grief because I sense that there is a whole lot of trouble comin' to me an' I know this idea is right because when I go back to Schmidt's there is Issy Marcovitch waitin' for me with a couple of gorillas.

Issy Marcovitch then hands me a special edition of the tabloid an' there smacked across the front page is the story about McGonegal havin' been put on the spot an' how the gangsters was foiled by this newspaper guy.

Issy then goes on to inform me that I am nothin' but a big raspberry. He says that I have got no ethics an' that the Big Shot is burned up like a rattlesnake, because everybody is laughin' at him an' some guy has told him that a guy called W. Shakespeare has said that ridicule is worse than death.

I then offer to bump off this guy W. Shakespeare for nothin' as a guarantee of good faith, but Issy says that the guy is already dead so I figure that some other guy must have bumped him off already.

Issy Marcovitch and the gorillas then put me on the train an' I am sent off to this one-eyed town an' I am forced to drive this liquor truck at twenty per week, on the understandin' that if I show my eyelids in Chicago any more that I will be ironed out pronto an' will not be given any funeral either—which is an insult to a guy like me.

An' I cannot bust myself into any racket because my reputation as a bump-off man is absolutely ruined over this business, an' all this is because of my bein' a good feller to McGonegal who is drinkin' rye whisky an' talkin' to newspaper guys all the time an' nobody can bump him off because the newspapers are so hot about this business.

All this should show any guy that he should never be kind-hearted but should bump off everybody pronto and not go hangin' around with ethics which is what Issy Marcovitch said I had not got.

The only good thing is that some guy bumped off this W. Shakespeare which is a thing I wish I had done personally.

An' although I am a guy who does not wish any harm to any other guy I would like to feed poison to that vinegar cat in Oklahoma who has put me in this spot and who has broke up the friendship between me an' my old buddy McGonegal who was mean about twenty dollars an' who I hope will fall off the top of the Flatiron building.

THE HUMOUR OF HUANG CHEN

IN the early part of the 18th century, in the north-east of the Province Shan-Si—almost within sight of the spot where the Great Wall sweeps towards Yenan, there dwelt Huang Chen, who called himself Lord of The Thousand Stars.

He weighed nineteen stones, and his rat-tail moustaches hung but eighteen inches from the ground. Also he claimed descent from Chin Shing Huang Ti, who built the Great Wall in 246 B.C.

With seven thousand spears he raided, robbed and extracted protection-toll, a process in which he found much food for laughter.

Below, on the other side of the Valley of Flowers, below Fien-Sing, there lived Li-Tok, the rival of Huang Chen. He was thin, sardonic, and without humour.

These two feared nothing save each other; and, during forty years of successful banditry, terminated on the one side by the death of Li-Tok—the circumstances of which are about to be related—they lost no opportunity for vengeance of the most diabolical kind, carried out with that urbane courtesy expected from Chinese gentlemen.

The evening sun was shining below the foot-hills behind the Valley of Six Great Stones, when Huang Chen, gasping a little for breath as he sat beneath a canopy of purple silk supported on camphor tree poles, saw in the distance a horseman galloping madly towards him.

Huang, who was suffering from a period of inactivity and an attack of indigestion following a heavy meal of dog's fat and rice mixed with hot spice, glanced with apparent nonchalance towards the rider, and his expression was still urbane when the man, a broken arrow sticking out from his breast, dismounted some twenty yards from the canopy and staggered towards the War Lord.

"Oh Father of the Moon!" he cried. "Hear me! May yellow dogs defile the graves of my ancestors, but this morning, the dew still being on the grass, Li-Tok, with a thousand spears, raided across the Valley of Flowers and hath burned to the ground the Gold Pavilian which you built but last year!"

Huang Chen folded his hands across his portly belly, which, swathed in blue silk worked with golden dragons awed all beholders.

"Ohe, Wo-Sang," he said softly. "Let this thing trouble you less than the arrow which sticks in thy middle. Go . . . die in peace."

The man staggered away and Huang Chen considered deeply. None of those about him spoke, for they were aware of the condition of his mind.

Soon after there came Chen-Hun, one of Huang's lieutenants, and the six men who had escaped after a vain attempt at defence of the Gold Pavilion. They had with them an old man who was blind and whose tongue had been cut out.

"Illustrious one," said Chen-Hun, grovelling on the ground, at the same time keeping his hand over a spear wound on his left side. "I live only that I may one day strike a blow at the accursed Li-Tok. But though the Gold Pavilion is but ashes, still I bring something. Behold"—he indicated the old man who stood apart—"This man, Shadow of the Moon," he continued, "is the most famed physician in all China. The great Ho Tong himself cut out his tongue so that he should never speak of his wondrous cures. This one, Great Master, we found, with six slaves, travelling towards the palace of Li-Tok."

Huang Chen smiled.

"Hath Li-Tok need of a physician, Chen-Hun?"

"Great Lord, he is afraid," the man answered. "The plague is rife in the lower valley, and this physician is the only one in all China who can cure it."

Huang Chen nodded. Then he looked at the physician, who in his red silk robe, his hands folded in his sleeves, stood staring sightlessly before him. The scrutiny of Huang Chen was long, and his keen little eyes concentrated themselves on the parchment-like face of the doctor. Suddenly he began to smile and called to him Wang, his chief lieutenant, and whispered to him for a while.

"Take him away," he said eventually, indicating the doctor, "and put him in a bamboo cage. Let no man approach him, for I say that this doctor is too great to be defiled by the touch of lesser men."

Then with extreme difficulty he got to his feet and waddled uncertainly down the path towards the pavilion. He was very deep in thought.

In the evening when the lanterns swung from the branches of the catalpa trees outside the pavilion, Huang Chen, swathed in a robe of cat-bear fur, sent for his daughter, Rosy Pearl.

"Consider, my daughter," he said, as she stood before him, "the beauty of filial obedience and devotion. It is as the stars that shine from the celestial carpet above, and as the lily which pushes itself through the still surface of the turgid stream. Listen, then, my daughter, with care, for I would not lose you."

Rosy Pearl bowed. " My father," she said softly, " I am as water in your hand."

Huang Chen nodded.

" To-morrow, my child," he said, " accompanied by six spearmen only, your litter will be carried down to the Valley of Flowers. There you will walk and ponder in the sunshine. Upon the other side of the valley, in the foothills, lurk the spies of Li-Tok.

" Sweet child, they will observe you, and seeing the weak escort that accompanies you, they will seize upon you and carry you off to Li-Tok.

" You will go quietly with them, my child, without protest, trusting always in the wisdom of thy father. And when you have been but two days with Li-Tok, then you shall tell him, or his wife, or any one in his house, that a sickness has come upon you.

" Go in peace, sweet Rosy Pearl."

She bowed three times.

" I am much honoured to be the daughter of my father," she said. " Celestial parent, I shall do thy bidding to the utmost."

Two hours after noon on the following day a band of Li-Tok's spears, riding swiftly on the shaggy Manchurian ponies, swept down upon the litter of Rosy Pearl in the Valley of Flowers. They killed the bearers and the six spearmen and went off, the litter swinging between two horses, pleased with their prize yet not knowing how great that prize was.

And at sunset on the evening after a rider, sweating after a rapid journey, arrived at the pavilion of Huang Chen bearing a message from Li-Tok.

Huang Chen received the messenger with grave courtesy and ordered refreshment, then with much nodding of the head and glances at those around him listened to the screed of Li-Tok as it was read to him.

"To Huang Chen, Lord of the Heavens, Beloved of the Gods.

"O, Huang Chen, I, the unworthy Li-Tok, who am not worthy to kiss the soles of thy honourable feet even though they be muddy, send greetings and news.

"Yesterday, spearmen of mine found in the Valley of Flowers a lady so beautiful that they became blinded. They brought her to me and, shading my unworthy eyes, I saw that it was thy daughter, the exquisite Rosy Pearl.

"Oh, Huang Chen, hear me! To keep the white ox secure, then must the chain be strong, and six spearmen are but a poor escort for the daughter of one such as you. But I will return her to thee; with all ceremony shall she return to you when the three boxes of beaten gold which thy serfs stole from my house at Ho-Ping before the last moon shall be returned to me, filled with golden taels and precious stones. For three days shall I await the coming of thy messengers. During that time shall thy daughter live in my yamen with my wives and daughters, and she shall walk with me in my jasmin garden.

"And if, after the three days thy messenger shall not arrive, then, knowing that Rosy Pearl has found disfavour in thine eyes, then shall she be boiled in hot oil. Greetings, Huang Chen.—Li-Tok."

Huang Chen, his hands folded across his purple belly, sighed deeply; then he addressed the messenger.

"Go to your honourable master, Li-Tok, as quickly as the horses which I give you shall carry you," he said. "Bear greeting to him from the unworthy and despicable Huang Chen, who is less than the mud adhering to the wheels of his ancestral coffin-cart.

"Tell Li-Tok that here in the hills we beat our breasts with pity for him.

"Tell him that I sent my daughter Rosy Pearl into the distance of the Valley of Flowers with but six spearmen, because, may the Great Confucius succour her, she hath the plague!

"What miserable fate is this that ordained that only yesterday whilst the men of Li-Tok were busy in the destruction of my Gold Pavilion, my spearmen captured the one physician in China who can cure this foul disease; whilst at this time Li-Tok, his wives and his daughters, must be in sore need of his ministrations.

"Tell the Celestial Li-Tok, whose eyes are as rubies on velvet, that I will make this bargain with him. To-morrow evening let my daughter return across the Valley of Flowers at the northern end where the little stream flows. Let two slaves only accompany her bearing two helmet-casques filled with rubies and pearls and gold taels. And in exchange, at the other end of the Valley, I shall send over this great physician of whom Li-Tok knoweth, to be with him in his hour of need.

"Get you gone in peace, and go quickly!"

The scared messenger needed no second bidding.

On the following night as the stars twinkled from a glowing sky above the pavilion of Huang Chen, the War Lord, sat beneath a catalpa tree, wrapped in a robe of golden tissue. Beside him a slave played upon a reed-pipe softly.

Presently there came Wang.

"Illustrious one," said he, "my heart is as a nightingale. The will of my master whose breath is as the wind sighing amongst the flowers has been done. But three hours since the lady Rosy Pearl, with four slaves bearing two helmets filled with golden taels and rubies and pearls, passed into our hands. At the other end of the valley the physician was delivered by two slaves, according to your word, into Li-Tok's keeping."

Huang Chen cocked an eyebrow.

"It is good," he said. "Send my daughter to me."

Rosy Pearl came to him between the avenue of tea-trees.

"Oh, my daughter," he said, "the strict obedience of the child is as the sound of the waterfall and as the pure note of the laughing thrush. For you there shall be a head-dress of pearls from Li-Tok, and an ankle girdle of double rubies."

Two days passed, and on the third, Huang Chen sent for Ho-Sin, who was a great swimmer and who could creep like a shadow through the darkness. "Go you, Ho-Sin," said Huang Chen with a little smile, "and creep through the darkness on this night, into the Valley of Flowers. Swim the river on this side of the yamen of Li-Tok, and throw the screed which I shall give you into his house. Then escape quickly, for it will not be well with thee if his hand falls upon thee."

Ho-Sin bowed.

"It is done, Lord of the Earth," he said. "Within six hours shall Li-Tok read the screed of my master."

Huang Chen nodded and gave Ho-Sin the screed, taking it from the sleeve of his robe.

It was written in golden paint and red ochre after the fashion of a funeral cover, and these were the words upon it:

"Ohe, Li-Tok, I, Huang Chen, send Greeting. Take with thee to the Shadows the last farewell of Huang Chen. My daughter wandered in the Valley of Flowers in obedience to the word of her father. For I knew that thy men would take her and that you would demand ransom. She had not the plague, O Li-Tok. This lie I sent to thee so that thou should'st exchange her for the physician.

"For—and my heart goeth out to thee, O Father of the Shadows, it was the physician who had the plague. This I saw when first my eyes fell upon him.

119

"Go peacefully to thine ancestors, O Li-Tok.—Huang Chen."

Huang Chen gazed thoughtfully after the retreating figure of Ho-Sin; then, his hands folded in the sleeves of his gown, he waddled away, listening dreamily to the music of the reed-pipe and the glass bells which swung in the camphor trees.

ABIE AND THE GANGSTERS

LISTEN fellers; I am Abie Hymie Finkelstein an' I woik for Rudy Scraut who is the guy with the delicatessen on Forty-fifth and Myrtle.

Maybe you know guys who have been the victims of these gangsters and maybe you know guys who was also the victim of the police department; but I am a guy who has been welted like you never saw by the gangsters and the police department an' everybody else round here.

An' if you say why I say it is for the reason that I am a smart guy with poisonality an' becase other guys is jealous of me becase the dames fall for me in a big way. If this ain't the case then I an an Indian princess with a coupla wooden legs.

One of these days if some gangsters will take hold of Police Captain Dooley O'Hagan an' will put him in a sack and go throw him in the lake then I will start believin' that there is some justice around this burg. Also if some gorilla like Dillinger will proceed to shoot up that blonde dame what took advantage of my sex-attraction then I will believe some more in Father Christmas which is a thing that I do not believe in anyhow.

If I was not a big guy like I am I would be altogether broke up about this business; but you do not have to

120

worry about Abie Finkelstein thank you very much becase I have already got back my noive and am at this time makin' a big play for Lilly Scapalensi who is not so easy to look at but who has some nice prospecks even if her father does say that he would rather see her buried alive with snakes rather than his girl should be married to me. Even this pa is jealous of my sex-attraction.

Well, it is a lovely night like you never saw an' I am goin' home feelin' like a million dollars. I am wearing a hot pertater suit—twenty dollars with two pairs of pants —an' a plaid four-in-hand with a white homberg an' a walkin' stick with a tomato in ivory on the top.

I know I am lookin' good which makes me indifferent to the giant raspberry which the newsboy on the corner hands out to me becase I know that this guy is also jealous of my appeal.

Suddenly I see the blonde who comes into the delicatessen for caviare on Saturday nights. This blonde is the berries an' when she sees me she stops dead like she was suddenly paralysed.

This girl is just like a film star except that she ain't had her face lifted an' I have often thought that she is a classy dame only I do not know if she has got prospecks an' a goil without prospecks is no goil for Abe.

So she comes up to me an' she says Abie I am in a very bad jam an' you must help me out becase you are the sort of a guy like I could fall for some more if I got to know you good, an' if you will do sumptin' for me I will see that you get a hundred dollars an' I will never be able to refuse you nothin' even if I don't like you.

So I says what an' she says that if I will take this big black violin case down to Giekel's speak-easy and give it to some guy called Gatty then this guy will give me a hundred bucks.

I say O.K. sister an' I start off for Giekel's. But on the way I begin to think what is in this case because it is heavy like some dead guy was in it, so I drop in at my room on Myrtle an' I open it up an' inside there is a Thompson machine-gun and six pistols all loaded up like you never saw.

Now it looks as if this dame is tryin' to slip some business over on me, but I remember that I am a smart guy with ideas so I rush around to Krimp's shootin' gallery an' I do some business an' I rush back an' do some more business with these guns an' then I go down to Giekel's an' wait for this guy Gatty.

Presently he comes along an' he is some tough egg an' I hand him the case an' I say what about the hundred bucks an' he sticks one of these guns in my ribs an' informs me that if I do not get in the car that is parked outside he is goin' to blow the top of my head into Queen's County.

So I do not argue with this guy but I do what he says an' we go off to some basement dump where there is a lot of thugs sittin' around drinkin' rye like you never saw an' they tear open the case an' take out the guns. Then the head gorilla says what shall we do with this mug boys becase he might start shootin' his mouth to the cops an' they all say bump him off Joe, but before they have finished sayin' it I am out of a door I seen at the back an' am scrammin' down the street like some mad racehorses.

When I have got myself away I think that this is a bum trick for the blonde to play on me an' I start to use my brains once again so I get into a taxi-cab after I have got the money from Rachael Moshinski who happens to be passin' an' I go to the 13th Precinct an' I see Police Captain Dooley O'Hagan an' I tell him the whole works an' he is very excited an' says that this is the Stripey Gang an' that my information is so hot that maybe he will make me a detective or a police commissioner or something for this.

I say wait a minute an' I ask him if he would like to be the big guy who took the Stripey Gang single-handed an'

I tell him how I have took all the ball ammunition out of them guns an' loaded them up with blanks what I got from Krimp's shootin' gallery.

He then informs me that I am a credit to the United States an' that by the time he is through with me I will probably be chief of the G men, an' that he is also goin' to give me one hundred dollars reward, a free pass for Shombergs waxworks an' a lot of other things. He then says that I should go home an' await further doings.

So I go back home an' one hour later there is a special edition which says that Police Captain Dooley O'Hagan has arrested seven members of the Stripey Gang single-handed, an' that they was all armed with machine-guns an' cannons like you never saw, an' that he is about the bravest guy since Christopher Columbine.

This looks plenty good to me so I get myself around to the precinct an' I see Police Captain Dooley O'Hagan an' I ask him about the hundred dollars an' all the other things an' he says go jump in the lake an' if he has any more of this stuff outa me he will have me arrested under the Mann Act, the Baumes Act, the Vagrants Act and for tryin' to blackmail a police captain.

I am now feelin' not so hot an' I tell him that he is a big cheese an' that he would not have arrested these guys if I had not tipped him off that their guns was only loaded up with blanks, an' I also say that I will take a walk around to the newspaper office an' slip them the works about this business.

He says oh yeah he will show me something an' he telephones through to the newspaper office an' says that if some lunatic named Abie Finkelstein ever shows up he should be held for the police. He then calls in some other guys an' has them throw me into the can on a charge of throwin' a hamburger at an old lady on Forty-second Street last Tuesday. By which you will see that this Police Captain Dooley O'Hagan is a four-flushin' twicer an' that he is framin' me like I was a big ninny.

So next morning when they let me out of the can I start to use my brains some more an' I ask some guy in the precinct if the gangsters who have been taken by O'Hagan have got themselves a lawyer an' he says yes.

So I get around to this lawyer an' I tell him that if he will give me a hundred dollars I will splutter a bibful that will astound the world. He says O.K. an' so I tell him the story about the blanks an' that these gorillas was not really armed with lethal weapons after which this lawyer laughs his head off an' says that he will make O'Hagan withdraw the charge or look like a monkey to the whole world.

He then says I should go home an' that if I will get around to this office the next morning he will hand me a hundred bucks, an' about two hours afterwards there is another special edition that says that Captain Dooley O'Hagan has made one big mistake an' that the gang is not the Stripey Gang at all but a meetin' of a commercial travellers' shootin' club, an' they have all been released, by which it looks like this lawyer has given Captain Dooley O'Hagan the works.

Now I am feelin' very good becase I have taught Police Captain Dooley O'Hagan that he cannot make a sucker out of Abie Finkelstein an' next morning I get around to the lawyer's an' I ask for the hundred bucks an' he gives a merry laugh an' tells me to go jump in the lake, an' that if I try any of that blackmailin' stuff around there he will have me pinched for firin' hayricks. He then calls in some other guy who throws me out on the sidewalk.

I am now feelin' that I am goin' to be very sick any time now becase of the deal I am gettin' around here from one an' all. Becase all the time it looks like I am going to get some money an' all I get is a lot of right royal raspberries from the whole woild. But even at this time my brains begins to work some more an' I get myself a tram an' I go to the basement where the gangsters are operatin'.

And they are all there an' I say howdy boys an' I tell them that I was the big guy who got them out of a helluva jam becase I knew that Police Captain Dooley O'Hagan was after them an' that was why I loaded up them guns with blanks.

The big gorilla then says this mug ain't so bad an' they whip around an' they give me a hundred dollars an' a highball.

I now begin to feel good some more becase I have now got one hundred smackers an' I have also got the low-down on Police Captain Dooley O'Hagan who I reckon is feelin' like a boiled pork chop in a snow-storm, an' I get myself around to my place on Myrtle Street an' as I am goin' up the stairs I hear that there is some goil in my room an' she is singin' "I Can't Give You Anything But Love, Baby," so I guess that this is probably some dame who has fallen for me in a big way.

However I am wrong some more becase it is the blonde gangster goil who asked me to carry the guns an' before I can do anything she pulls out a rod and she tells me that she has got word from the gangsters that they have handed me out a hundred smackers an' do I think that I am goin' to get away with that stuff when I am nothin' but a copper's nose who has been givin' information all around town. With this an' some more wisecracks she grabs the hundred dollars off from me and she tells me that for two pins she will also smack me down. I say that I have not got any pins so she smacks me down anyway an' goes off singing' "Life Is Just A Bowl Of Cherries," which is maybe right so far as this dame is concerned.

It now looks to me as if all my brains was getting wasted around this burg an' that I will not try to get any more money becase there is a lot of plots goin' on any time I get some money. I think also as well that I had better be gettin' along to the delicatessen otherwise Scraut will also be handin' me some raspberries.

So I smarten up some an' I go off an' I am beginnin'

to feel not so bad becase anyhow this business has not cost me anything at all an' I am also thinkin' about Lilly Scapalensi who thinks I am the cat's lingerie when suddenly Police Captain Dooley O'Hagan springs out of some doorway an' says that he is pinchin' me an' that I better not try to avoid arrest. I say that I am not tryin' to avoid arrest but he calls the patrol wagon an' handcuffs me an' takes me to the precinct.

So I ask what these guys are chargin' me with an' Police Captain Dooley O'Hagan says that he has found a whole load of pistol an' machine-gun ammunition in my room on Myrtle an' he is chargin' me with bein' in possession of ammunition.

I say have a heart I told you all about that an' he says oh yeah smart guy I don't know what you are talking about an' that if I think I can get away with all this stuff around the thirteenth precinct I had better think some more. He also says that if he has some more trouble with me he will also charge me with some murders that the police have not solved yet an' that he would charge me with a murder that happened the night before in Illinois only it is too far for me to have got in the time.

So then they throw me in the can some more an' I am there for four days an' they then bring me up before some judge who says that I am a disgrace to the city an' that he will make an example of me like hell an' that if Police Captain Dooley O'Hagan who is a great an' good guy had not pleaded for me he would probably have given me a ten to fifty years' sentence but as it is he will fine me a hundred dollars or three months in the can.

So that will show you guys that it is not easy to make some honest dough around here, an' all these plots to stop me gettin' any money are not doin' me any good as in order to pay this fine I have to borrow the hundred smackers from Lilly Scapalensi who gets it from her old man's till whilst he is comin' out of a jag.

It is not right that old Scapalensi should lose a hundred smackers because of some police captain who is nothing but a big cheese an' a lot of gangsters who are a disgrace to this civilisation like you never saw.

Now all this has happened to me becase I am a smart guy an' a swell dresser, becase if I had not been a smart guy then the blonde goil would not have picked me out which shows you that it is not always so good to have a lot of sex-appeal like I have got as it is liable to get you into troubles with swell dames except in the case of goils like Lilly Scapalensi who is not such a hot looker but who has got a whole lot of prospecks an' the key to Pa Scapalensi's till.

THREE MEN ON TAMPA

SOMEWHERE east of Kei in the South Borneo Sea is an island which is so small that few maps bother to show it. It is called Tampa, and often there comes to my mind a mental picture of this island, baked in the tropical sun, with a white beach running up to a line of low foothills, and, behind, hills covered with dry scrub.

Somewhere on these hills is a broken-down shack, and somewhere behind the shack is a rough grave marked with a boulder.

When I feel most prosaic I am inclined to remember this grave and smile, realising that romance with a capital R still lives, even in the life of a detective!

About four and a half years after I began my career as a private detective I received a letter from a gentleman for whom I had acted on one or two occasions. He was in business in the North of England, and was a man of undoubted position and integrity. In his letter he informed me that a friend of his—a Mrs. Haasen—would be calling on me shortly and seeking my professional assistance. He recommended her, and hoped that I would be able to help her.

In due course Mrs. Haasen came to see me. She was a woman of about forty-five years of age, and she had once been very beautiful. In point of fact, she was still an extraordinarily fascinating person.

She told her story with a certain hesitancy, which my instinct told me was assumed. I am quite used to meeting people; I am also very used to hearing all sorts of confidences. The cupboards containing many family skeletons have been opened in my private office and, as a result, I have acquired an ability to assess people at their true worth. Very naturally, I sometimes make mistakes, but I do not think that I am often mistaken.

This was her story.

Some eight years previously she had found herself stranded in South Borneo. Her father—her only known relative—who was manager of a tobacco plantation in that country, died suddenly, leaving her penniless. She had no friends, for her father was a quarrelsome drunkard, and they had lived a lonely life.

During the month preceding her father's death she had made the acquaintance of three individuals who had arrived in that part of the world five or six weeks previously. They were rather a mysterious trio. One was an Italian named Guelva; the second a tall, good-looking Swede named Haasen; and the third an Englishman named Scutters.

Guelva was attracted to her, and proposed marriage. She accepted him, and married him immediately. She told me quite candidly that she did not love Guelva, but that she had to "do something." She knew nothing of him, but, after marriage, learned quite a lot.

Guelva drank, and in his cups was inclined to become confidential. He told her that he had information that, on one of the small uncharted islands south of Kei, he had reason to believe there existed buried treasure. His idea was to find it.

Haasen, the rich Swede, was putting up the money, and Scutters, who seemed to be a well-educated Englishman who had come down in the world—a man of the remittance type—had also been engaged to take part in the expedition.

Guelva suggested that she should accompany them. Mrs. Guelva, as she then was, agreed.

She told me quite frankly that she was sorry afterwards that she had gone with them, as she believed that there was some quarrel between Haasen and Guelva, of which she was the subject.

A few days afterwards the expedition set off, and they sailed for Tampa via Ceram and Kei.

Tampa, apparently, was an unattractive place, but they were all in good spirits.

A tent was pitched not far from the beach for the use of Mrs. Guelva, while the three men installed themselves in a broken-down shack which stood on the slopes of a line of scrub-covered foothills a mile from the beach. This shack, according to Guelva, had been erected by some people who had made a previous and unsuccessful attempt to find the treasure.

During the day the three men went off on their exploration which was based on a chart possessed by Guelva. They would return in the evening to the shack, where Mrs. Guelva would prepare the evening meal.

There was no doubt, she informed me, that her husband was, by this time, thoroughly jealous of the attentions paid her by Haasen, the Swede, who was inclined to treat the other two male members of the expedition with an ill-concealed jovial contempt.

At night, after she had returned to her tent, the men gambled, and Guelva almost invariably won, which, apparently, did not improve matters between him and Haasen.

It was on their eighth day on Tampa Island that the tragedy occurred.

At three o'clock in the afternoon Scutters came running down the beach, white-faced and excited. After a lot of beating about the bush he informed the woman that there had been an accident. Guelva, her husband, had been standing on the edge of a deep gully; Haasen had taken a pot shot at a bird, had missed, and had shot Guelva through the head. Guelva had rolled down the gully— dead.

Scutters pointed out that he had buried Guelva. He had not waited for Mrs. Guelva to see the body of her husband because, as he told her, the face was terribly disfigured, and the legs broken by the fall.

Haasen, said Scutters, on observing the result of his fatal shot, had dashed off into the scrub, overcome with grief.

The next day the three of them had a meeting and decided to give up the expedition. The chart, which Guelva had possessed, was a rough affair, and, without his personal knowledge, was of little use to them. They returned to Borneo, and from there to Singapore.

Here Haasen, who appeared to be quite overcome at the results of his unlucky shot, had proposed marriage to Mrs. Guelva. He informed her that he had wanted to marry her immediately he met her, but that Guelva, " as usual, had got in first."

She agreed; for, if anything, the Swede was a much more desirable husband than Guelva. He had money, and, beyond the fact that he had a sudden and fierce temper, he was a good-natured, easy-going fellow. He paid off Scutters, who left them.

After their marriage they had settled down in England, in the country, near a provincial town, where they had lived ever since; and, at the moment, they were occupying a furnished flat in London.

I listened to Mrs. Haasen in silence. Her story was certainly interesting, and I was impatient to come to the crux of it, to know just why she was seeking my assistance.

"I expect that you are wondering why I have come to consult you," she continued in her low and attractive voice. "But, after all these years of peace, this tragedy has reawakened.

"A week ago I received a letter from the man Scutters, who is in England. He informed me that he had been very unlucky during the last few years, and was now stranded in Liverpool—penniless. He suggested that I should ask my husband to remit to him immediately a large sum of money, and that, in the event of his not receiving it within ten days from the date on the letter, he would make it his business to inform the authorities that my husband had deliberately shot Guelva on Tampa Island; that the shot had not been accidental, but was the result of a definite quarrel concerning myself; that my husband was, in fact, a murderer, and that, unless the money was forthcoming, Scutters would divulge his knowledge.

"You will realise the situation," Mrs. Haasen went on. "The only witness to the shooting was Scutters, and, though he knows perfectly well that the shot was accidental, there is no doubt that he could cause a very disagreeable situation."

"What does your husband say about it, Mrs. Haasen?" I inquired.

"At first he was furious," she replied, "and it was with great difficulty that I dissuaded him from going off immediately and thrashing Scutters.

"I was afraid of this. My husband is a man of hot temper, and I thought it possible that he might do Scutters some definite harm, and that this situation might be made worse. I took the advice of the gentleman who has written you about me. He is an old friend of mine, and he advised me to get in touch with you and to take your advice on this unfortunate business. What do you think?"

I thought for a moment. Mrs. Haasen's story was certainly a strange one. Looking at her, I could easily imagine that ten years before, she had been a person about whom two men might easily quarrel, especially on a small uninhabited East Indian island where temperature and tempers run hot.

Scutters's story, even if absolutely untrue, might easily cause a serious situation.

At the same time, I was not certain that I wanted to handle the case. The story was an amazing one. It intrigued me, and it was a departure from the rather prosaic cases which I was then handling.

"It isn't easy for me to advise you, Mrs. Haasen," I said. "There are only two courses open to you. If you propose to deal in the obvious way with this man Scutters, then it is a case for the police. If, on the other hand, you would think it more advisable to agree to his demands, or partly to agree to them, then perhaps it would be a good thing for me to see him on your behalf.

"By the way, have you the letter which he wrote to you?"

She handed it to me.

I adopted my usual course of action in cases in which I am not quite satisfied with the original information laid before me.

"Let us leave the matter for a day or two, Mrs. Haasen," I suggested. "Let me think it over. Give me the address of this man Scutters, and a description of him, and I will look through my files and see if, by any chance, we have any information about him. He may have tried blackmailing before. Then, when I have

hought this matter over, I will write to you and make a
suggestion."

She agreed, and gave me a description of the man, and
his address in Liverpool, which I wrote down. Then,
after giving me her London address, she left the office.

Left to myself, I considered the matter deeply. From a
professional point of view the case did not interest me.
The story I had heard was interesting, but, as to its entire
truth, I was doubtful. In any event, I came to the conclusion that, pending my decision as to whether I would
officially handle the case or not, there would be no harm
in my making some inquiries about the man Scutters,
and, with this end in view, I sent for an expert assistant
named Baskin.

Baskin, who had been in my employ for some years,
was rather a character. He was an ex-public schoolboy,
and possessed great charm He was a wonderful " mixer,"
and could ingratiate himself very quickly with almost any
class of person.

I gave Baskin Scutters's address and sent him off to
Liverpool with instructions to find out all he possibly
could about Scutters, his antecedents, financial position
and recent movements, and to report to me as soon as
possible—in any event, within three days—so that I might
have his report before writing Mrs. Haasen.

Two days afterwards I received a report from Baskin
in which he informed me that Scutters was " an easy
contact," but that he had little information for me at the
moment, and did not think that he could report further
for some days.

This placed me in a quandary, as, while I was reading
his letter, Mrs. Haasen rang up to inform me that she
and her husband were in the neighbourhood and were
coming in to see me.

Twenty minutes afterwards they arrived. Haasen was
a splendid specimen of manhood, standing well over six

feet. His character was obvious in his face. He was a jovial, good-natured man until he mentioned Scutters. Then his face became diffused with rage, and I could easily understand Mrs. Haasen's unwillingness to allow the two to meet.

Following a long discussion, Haasen suggested, after Mrs. Haasen and I had dissuaded him from the idea of dealing with the matter personally—which process I told him would probably result in more trouble—that I should make it my business to see Scutters as soon as possible, and that if I could obtain from him a statement that his story about the murder on Tampa was absolutely false, I might pay to him the sum of one thousand pounds, provided he agreed to leave England, never to return.

This seemed to me a sensible course to pursue. I told Haasen that I should, if possible, get the statement from Scutters on payment of as little of the money as possible, and that, having secured the statement, there would be small chance of further danger from Scutters, as he would then, of course, be a self-confessed blackmailer, and no one would give credit to his story.

Haasen nodded.

"I tell you," he said in gruff, broken English, "what I speak—it is the truth. Guelva was standing on the edge of a little ravine. A bird flew past. I fired at it. Guelva gave a shriek, put his hand to his head, and fell down the ravine. I lost my head. I, who was in love with his wife, had shot him. I threw down my rifle and ran away. I did not know what to do. When I come back I find the pig Scutters, who tells me that Guelva is dead, and that, besides this, his legs were broken by the fall; that he has buried him because he was not a pretty sight, and his wife must not see him. That is the truth. It was an accident. I would not kill any man like that!"

We discussed details, and then the pair went off, Mrs. Haasen seemingly relieved at the suggested solution to the trouble.

I should like to state that I had not the remotest intention of paying to the man Scutters anything like the sum of one thousand pounds, but I had proved to my satisfaction that Haasen was prepared to pay that sum in order to have the matter cleared up. He appeared to me in a very favourable light, and I had no doubt in my mind that his version of the accidental shooting, which confirmed his wife's original story, was quite true.

The cheque which he left with me was specially cleared and was duly paid.

Next day I went to Liverpool and, during the journey, concentrated my thoughts on every possible angle of the forthcoming interview with Scutters.

I realised that it would be of little use beating about the bush with this gentleman. He had a good case, and circumstances were in his favour. If he were openly to accuse Haasen of murder, the Swede would find himself in a position which would be difficult, to say the least of it. Haasen's marriage to the dead man's wife, following almost immediately on the heels of the accident—a circumstance quite innocent in itself—would actually support Scutters's story that the woman was the cause of the quarrel which had ended so fatally.

But I was optimistic. I visualized Scutters as a weak-kneed drunkard who would do anything for a hundred pounds, and I was quite prepared to pay him something like that sum if he would sign a statement as to the actual facts of the death. Once in possession of this statement, Haasen would have nothing more to fear from the black-mailing Scutters.

When I arrived at Liverpool I found Baskin awaiting me on the platform, his whimsical face smiling, as usual. He handed my bag to a porter and, taking my arm, led me towards the station tea-room.

"I've got some news for you, Chief," he said. "Some extraordinary news. We'll talk about it over a cup of tea. I think you'll have to do some quick work!"

And his news was certainly extraordinary. It was, in fact, sensational.

At eight o'clock that night I saw Scutters. An hour later, after I had finished with him, he signed a statement which was written down in his presence by Baskin.

I did not give him a hundred pounds. I gave him a ten-pound note and advised him to put as much distance between England and himself as was possible, for his own sake.

After which we left him and made for a mean street in the slum area. In a tumbledown house we had another and somewhat more dramatic interview, and next morning I caught an early train to London, perfectly satisfied with my visit.

Immediately I arrived at my office I sent a man out to make some hurried inquiries about Mr. and Mrs. Haasen. As I had imagined, they proposed leaving the country within a few days, and their flat was already in the hands of half a dozen agents.

In the early afternoon I telephoned Mrs. Haasen and asked her to come round and see me, and to bring her husband with her. In reply to her question, I informed her that I had succeeded in getting the statement from Scutters, and she said that she would come round to my office and get it, but that her husband was busy and had asked her to deal with the matter. She said that she would be with me in twenty minutes.

I gave her ample time to leave her flat, and then dispatched a man to go round and bring Haasen himself.

When Mrs. Haasen arrived I informed her that, since telephoning her, I had come to the conclusion that her husband's presence was necessary, and had sent for him, and that we would await his arrival. She appeared surprised, but maintained a perfect composure.

Fifteen minutes afterwards Haasen arrived; and at the same time my staff office—which is situated in another part of the building—telephoned through to me that "Baskin and his friend" had arrived from Liverpool.

Mr. and Mrs. Haasen sat together on the settee opposite my desk. I opened my dispatch-case and took out the statement made by Scutters. Then I gave them both cigarettes.

"I want you both to keep very cool and not to interrupt, however much you may feel inclined," I said. "Especially you, Mr. Haasen. It is necessary that you should listen to this statement carefully."

Haasen nodded.

I then read the statement:

"I, Charles Glanbole Scutters, declare that this is a true statement as to what happened on Tampa Island during the eight days that Enrico Guelva, his wife, Paula Guelva, Rolf Eric Haasen and myself spent on the island, and that the facts hereafter set out, leading up to the accident which happened to Enrico Guelva, are true.

"I met Enrico Guelva at Singapore. I do not know what his business had been, but at that time he was a professional gambler. After a few weeks he told me that he was meeting a Swede named Haasen near Banjermasin in South Borneo, that this Swede was a wealthy man, and that he was going to finance an expedition for the purpose of discovering some treasure which Guelva knew existed on Tampa Island, a small, uninhabited island south of Kei Island in the Banda Sea.

"He informed me that I could join this expedition and would be well paid for my services. I agreed to go with them.

"We crossed from Singapore to Banjermasin and met Haasen, who was rather a simple individual, a great gambler, and very good-natured, but with a sudden temper. We stayed at Banjermasin for about six weeks, during which time Guelva made the acquaintance of a young woman named Paula Gervis, whose father, a tobacco plantation manager, had just died.

137

"Haasen was very attracted to this young woman, who was a most fascinating person. Both Guelva and myself came to the conclusion that he would marry her and would possibly throw up the treasure expedition. This expedition I now knew to be a fake, and that it had been arranged by Guelva simply for the purpose of getting money out of Haasen.

"One day both Haasen and myself were surprised by the news that Guelva had married Paula Gervis. Haasen was furious, but was talked over by Guelva. A few days later we crossed to Macassar, and from thence to Ceram Island. Departing from Ceram in a tug, we landed on Kei Island, but left there next day for Tampa in a sailing-boat, Mrs. Guelva accompanying us.

"Mrs. Guelva had a tent above the beach, and we three men occupied an old wooden shack on the foothills. During the day we would explore the island, guided by a fake map possessed by Guelva, and at night we would return to the shack. After Mrs. Guelva had retired to her tent, we would gamble, and Guelva, who was an expert with cards, almost invariably won.

"There was bad feeling between Guelva and Haasen, and after the third day they began to quarrel, Haasen saying that Guelva had deliberately married the woman just because he knew that he, Haasen, was in love with her, and because he also knew that she was stranded and penniless, and would accept any proposal.

"We all knew that Guelva had fallen out with his wife, for she had discovered that, had she not been in such a hurry, she could have married Haasen.

"On the eighth day, early in the afternoon, Guelva was standing at the top of a deep gully. Haasen had his rifle in the crook of his arm, and suddenly took a pot shot at a bird. Guelva screamed, and I could see that Haasen had shot him in the head. Guelva then toppled over the gully and fell to the bottom. I looked over and shouted to Haasen, 'My God! You've killed him!' Haasen threw down his rifle and ran into the scrub, shouting out something which was unintelligible.

"I climbed down to the bottom of the gully. When I arrived I found Guelva sitting up. He was not badly wounded, for the bullet had merely scored the left side of his face. He asked where Haasen was, and I said that he had run away.

"I bandaged Guelva at once. While I was doing this he told me to dig a rough grave and fill it up, and to tell Haasen that he was dead, that he looked such an awful sight that I had buried him at once. Guelva told me to tell his wife the truth, but that she was to pretend to believe the story, for Haasen would certainly marry her. Guelva was to hide in the scrub until the rest of us had left Tampa, and I was to take him food supplies as soon as possible, and when we had left Tampa I was to get a boat from Kei Island and come over and pick him up.

"I agreed to carry out these instructions, and afterwards ran down to the beach and told Mrs. Guelva the story. She agreed with the plan, and when Haasen reappeared that night she acted up to the situation perfectly.

"The next day Mrs. Guelva, Haasen and myself left Tampa. We went back to Singapore, where Haasen married Mrs. Guelva. He paid me handsomely and I left them there.

"They lived there for some time, and Mrs. Haasen secretly kept Guelva—whom I had picked up off Tampa Island—and myself supplied with money which she got from Haasen, who was clay in her hands.

"When they left Singapore and went to England, Guelva and I followed them. They were living in London and we stayed in the Midlands.

"But the money received from Mrs. Haasen—as she now called herself—got less and less, and Guelva sent me up to London to complain.

"I met her in London, and she explained to me that Haasen had lost a lot of money and had become very tight-fisted, but that she had a scheme by which we could get some more money.

"I was to reappear and send a letter threatening to accuse Haasen of the murder of Guelva unless he paid over a large sum of money. In return I would write a letter absolving him from all blame. The Haasens were proposing to leave London to go back to Singapore, and Mrs. Haasen said that she would manage to destroy my letter, and that when they were in Singapore I could reappear and start to blackmail Haasen again. . . ."

I looked across at Haasen.

"I don't think it is necessary for me to read any more, Mr. Haasen," I said.

He gazed straight in front of him. He seemed numb. But the woman spoke.

"It's a lie!" she said hoarsely. "A dastardly lie!"

"It's the truth, Mrs. Haasen," I said, "and very easily proved." I took up my office telephone. "Send Baskin and Guelva down here," I ordered.

Haasen looked up in amazement.

"Guelva!" he exclaimed.

"Precisely," I said. "We picked him up in Liverpool last night, and I gave him the choice of coming down here or taking what was coming to him. He preferred to accept my offer."

The door opened and Baskin appeared. With him was the man Guelva. I had my foot on the "alarm button" which is fixed to the floor under my desk, for I thought that Haasen would probably spring at Guelva, but he did not move. He just looked at him, smiling quietly.

Guelva stood quite still, a rather foolish smile on his face.

"Tell me," said Haasen. "How did you find this out?"

"Pure chance," I replied. "Candidly, I did not be-lieve this woman's story in the first place, and sent a man

140

down to Liverpool at once to make contact with Scutters. This was easily done, for Scutters is a drunkard who would make firends with anyone who would buy him liquor.

"One night my man—Baskin—took Scutters out for the evening, and they met a Frenchman named Garoulle. Later in the evening they went to a billiard-hall, where Scutters and Garoulle began to play matches for a sovereign a hundred. Scutters lost several times, and eventually agreed to play Garoulle 'double or quits.' By this time he was quite drunk.

"However, he managed to win the game by one point, and, in his excitement, shouted, 'I've won, Guelva! I've won!'

"Neither of them noticed that he had called Garoulle by the name of Guelva, but Baskin here noticed it and reported it to me when I went down.

"It was easy to put two and two together. It was obvious that Guelva was alive.

"When I saw Scutters I told him that the game was up; that we knew Guelva was alive. The bluff worked and he confessed the whole business Then we went round to Guelva and dealt with him. The next step rests with you!"

Haasen got up. He still wore the cynical smile.

"So," he said, "I am not married! I am a free man!"

He looked from Guelva to the woman. She had crumpled up. Her nerve was gone, and she sat with her face buried in her hands.

"My congratulations," said Haasen to me. "I will come and see you to-morrow." He turned cynically to the woman. "Good-bye, Mrs. Guelva," he said, and, with a bow to me, walked out of the office.

When he had gone I spoke to Guelva.

"If I were you I should take your wife and get out as quickly as you both can," I advised. "Mr. Haasen might change his mind, you know!"

He shrugged his shoulders and turned to the door. The woman got up wearily and followed him.

Four years later Guelva died in a foreign prison. I do not know what became of the woman.

A SET-UP FOR PSYCHOLOGY

DAMES don't have any gratitude—which you will see if you take one look at Sadie Perrosino who used to work the frankfurter stand in Schmid's speak-easy on Grape Street an' who ditched me for some travellin' salesman with wavy hair an' no sense of the proper thing.

Sadie is a blonde with an appeal that will knock your eye out. Also, she has a great business sense and is educated so that she can hand you a frankfurter, a wise-crack an' some good advice whilst you are trying to find the ten-cent bit that is stuck in the lining of your pocket.

I am stuck on Sadie for years, and my intentions towards her are absolutely on the up an' up, because she gets me all poetic and I desire nothin' so much than to marry this girl and go off to Arizona with her. That bein' the only State in that part of America where the District Attorneys are not always tryin' to find out where I am for the purpose of pulling me in for something they allege I must have done at some old time around their particular dump.

So I get very hurt when she tells me that she ain't got no use for any guy without capital—which is the sort of guy I am. She also says that I should go get myself a lot of personality an' brains like her friend Willie Tobolsky, the travellin' salesman, who is a smart guy.

This Willie Tobolsky runs a racket selling gas refrigerators on one instalment down to dames who, according to his friend in the supply office, are about to have the gas cut off, after which he collects the refrigerator an' lets 'em off with the rest of the payments.

Sadie says that this Willie Tobolsky was as big a sap as me until he read a book called *Psychology and Power*. She said I ought to read this book an' get wise, an' that if I had a thousand dollars capital she would marry me in spite of my face an' the fact that the District Attorneys of seven different States have got a decided interest in where I am at any given moment.

So I get this book an' I read it, and it seems that this psychology stuff is a business what tells you what another guy is thinkin' about—that is, supposin' he does think.

I then get a big idea and go round and tell Sadie all about it, and she says it is good an' that the book is beginning to work already.

I then go round to see Billy-the-Goat, an' in case you don't know who he is, he is the guy who runs prize-fights at Spitzler's Stadium.

Now most of these fights that Billy runs is set-ups. They're in the bag an' everybody knows who is goin' to win about two days before the fight comes off. The result is that business is very bad for Billy.

I then proceeded to tell Billy that I have got a big idea to fix up a fight between Willy McGuiz, commonly known as the East Side Terror, an' Ike Delarez, who is a tough guy lately resigned from the beer racket over an argument with a cop, which the cop won by usin' an unfair advantage an' a piece of lead pipe.

"The point is," says Billy, "that these two guys have gotta fight and they have gotta fight good."

He says he don't want any of this lying down in the ring an' sleepin', because, three weeks ago, his patrons have almost torn the place to pieces over some guy gettin' knocked out almost before the fight started.

143

I tell Billy that this is all right; that I got a big idea; an' he asks where did I get it from, to which I reply that I got it out of this psychology book.

That evenin', about six o'clock, I go an' I find McGuiz in a beer cellar on Twenty-second Street. He is drinking rye whisky with his manager and is looking very depressed. We get down to business an' I tell these boys that I'm out to fix up a fight between McGuiz an' Delarez and that McGuiz need not bother his head about trainin' because I have already arranged that Delarez shall lay down in the third round after a right hook from McGuiz.

I say that there's not very much to it from the money angle, as the purse is only goin' to be two hundred dollars a side, the winner to take the lot, but it's easy money for them, because all they have to do is to back McGuiz to win.

They think this is a big idea, but I tell them they must be very careful about gettin' the bets on, because, so far as Billy-the-Goat is concerned, this is goin' to be a straight out-an'-out fight to a finish, an' I've practically guaranteed that one of the guys is goin' to be killed in the ring.

The upshot of it is that they ask me will I do the backin' for them quietly, an', after a lot of pressin', I consent to back McGuiz with some friends of mine for seven hundred dollars, which they go an' borrow off some guy who has had a lot of rye whisky an' is not very interested in anythin'.

I then take a walk an' I find Delarez, an' I tell him the same story, only the arrangement I make with him is that McGuiz is goin' to be beat in the third round. I also tell Delarez that he must be very careful how he backs himself, as this idea of mine must be kept very quiet.

In due course Delarez, after goin' home an' rifling the family savings, hands me 600 dollars to back him with, an' everything is O.K.

I then go round to Billy-the-Goat an' inform him that

I've fixed up a fight that will be so ferocious that there's never been anythin' like it, but I'm very concerned about one thing, an' that is, who the referee is goin' to be. Billy considers this matter very deeply an', at last, he says that I've taken such a great interest in this fight that I should appoint the referee, but that it must be a guy who'll be O.K. with both McGuiz an' Delarez.

So I go round an' I see One-Eye-Smith, who is an intelligent an' a broadminded guy, an' I outline the situation to him an' I pay him 300 dollars which I tell him I owe him, because he's a delicate guy an' would not like anybody to suggest that he would take a graft from any man, woman or child to give a wrong decision; after which I go home an' I read some more out of this book which they gave me down at the lecture-hall. It begins to look to me as if this book was good in spite of the long words.

The fight is fixed for ten days ahead an' in the meantime Billy-the-Goat proceeds to work up some excitement in the neighbourhood. He tells a story about how McGuiz an' Delarez have hated each other all their lives; that they was both in love with the same woman an' that they quarrelled so terrible about this dame that she, eventually, went off with a drug-store clerk from Oshkosh, which has embittered them somethin' terrible; an' that this fight between these two guys is goin' to be nothin' less but legalised murder, so much so that they have already got the beds ready down at the hospital.

The result of all this is that the fans in the neighbourhood get a definite idea into their heads that there is really goin' to be a real fight at last at Spitzler's Stadium an' on the night you can hardly get into the building.

First of all, there's a couple of exhibition bouts, an' then the big fight comes on. McGuiz steps into the ring, wearing a happy smile an' a pair of sky-blue pants, whilst Delarez is in red shorts and a black eye from the night before.

One-Eye-Smith gets into the ring an' does his stuff, an' the fight starts. The first round is jus' nothin' at all. Both of these guys jumps about the ring as if they was a pair of kittens, giving each other a playful pat now an' then.

Billy-the-Goat comes up to me, where I'm standin' by the ringside, an' says that it don't look so good to him, because the fans are already shouting their heads off that this is no fight at all. I tell him to wait a minute; that the real business will start very soon.

The second round is very much the same, an' by this time the house is in an uproar, because everybody is yellin' that the fight is a frame-up an', secondly, owin' to the fact that some guy in the gallery has pushed an ice-cream cone down another guy's neck jus' because he's wearin' a stiff collar, which offends the first guy.

By the time the bell goes for the third round the place is in a pandemonium an' I tell One-Eye-Smith that this is where we start to take an interest in the fight.

They spar around for a couple of seconds an' then McGuiz gives Delarez a punch on the nose an' Delarez socks back at McGuiz. From my place in the corner I can hear McGuiz tellin' Delarez that it's about time that he got knocked out, an' I hear Delarez telling McGuiz jus' what he is an' tellin' him that this is where he is supposed to lay down.

The upshot of it is that these two guys get so annoyed with each other not lyin' down that they really start doin' somethin'. The fourth round is terrific. McGuiz is callin' Delarez everythin' that he can think of, includin' some words that even I have never heard before, an' what Delarez is sayin' is awful, but neither of these guys will lie down, as arranged, an' the other guy, thinkin' he's had a phoney deal, starts to do some honest fighting for the first time in his history.

The fight goes on for twelve rounds, when it's stopped by the referee, who says that he's jus' got a tip-off that the police are comin' to raid the place an' that, anyway, the fight is a draw.

However, it proceeds for some time owin' to the fact that they can't drag McGuiz away from Delarez an' that Delarez can't get out of the ring owin' to the fact that he can't see, McGuiz havin' poked his finger in his eye, but, by the time they get these guys sorted out, I have already left the building with a double ticket for myself an' Sadie for Arizona, which is one State where the District Attorney is not interested in me, and one thousand dollars, which is the balance of the money I got from the boys and which I did not back anybody with.

I am feeling very good an' I go straight round to Schmid's speak-easy and there I find Willie Tobolsky, the travellin' salesman, an' he tells me that Sadie has told him all about my little idea an' that he thinks it is great, but that she is very worried in case McGuiz or Delarez should collect me before I have time to get away, an' that, in any case, I should be careful to change the notes they gave me for other notes in case some smart guy remembered some of the numbers, in which case they would know I had not backed anybody.

This is a good idea, so Willie Tobolsky gives me a thousand-dollar bill for the notes and tells me to rush down to Sadie's apartment, where she is waitin', an' pick her up, as she wishes to get out of Chicago with me as quickly as possible.

So I rush round there, an' when I get there I get a note, which Sadie has left, sayin' that she is goin' off with Willie Tobolsky and that I had better not try to spend any of the thousand-dollar bill which he gave me, as same was made by a friend of his and likely to get me into some more trouble with District Attorneys.

The note also goes on to say that I should have read a bit more of the psychology book, which says that you should not put your trust in princes or any other sort of guys, which is a wisecrack that also goes for Willie Tobolsky, who has got my money and also Sadie Perrosino.

All of which will show any guy that it is no good tryin' to make money by honest ways, because some crook like Willie Tobolsky will always get it off you.

So I am now in a very hot spot because the District Attorney for Chicago City is now also looking for me over a matter of Willie Tobolsky's thousand-dollar bill, which, owing to the depression, I have handed to some guy whose eyesight is not so good.

And I also have some news that Willy McGuiz is lookin' for me too with a piece of iron bar to which he is partial when he is not so pleased with any guy, and that Ike Delarez an' friends are aimin' to blow up Spitzler's Stadium any night from now on.

I also have a telephone message from Billy-the-Goat informin' me that if same occurs he will lay informations against me that will get me about 3000 years in the State Penitentiary on about forty-seven different counts.

So now there is practically no place in this man's country where the District Attorney is not lookin' for me, except Arizona, which is too far to walk, and where that dishonest guy, Willie Tobolsky, has gone off with Sadie Perrosino, who is a dame with no sense of gratitude at all and who does not know a good guy when she sees one.

THE DE LANIER TECHNIQUE

I

WILL you consider, if you please, that Mr. de Lanier had reason for discontent, even though his inevitable and charming smile indicated that all was well?

Of course he realised that this was merely an interlude. Something *must* eventually turn up, he thought—mainly because it was necessary that something *should* turn up.

You must know that at the moment Mr. de Lanier possessed fourteen shillings and ninepence—enough for lunch—an attractive smile, a figure that made fat men squirm uncomfortably and register vows about physical jerks, and an eyeglass. These things, together with his wardrobe, constituted, at the moment, his sole possessions.

And he knew that he could expect no help from the fraternity of high-class crooks on the outskirts of which he conducted his operations. The fraternity did not appreciate his aptitude for playing his game just within the border-line of the law. Life, ruminated Mr. de Lanier, was a trifle hard.

He walked slowly up Berkeley Street. Glancing down, he caught a glimpse of his left shoe. Slightly too well worn, the sole was about to part company with the upper. At the same moment it decided to rain. Such things happen at crucial instants. Without any hesitation he turned into the Hotel Reina and made for the restaurant.

He saw her from the top of the stairs. She radiated breeding, and her face showed a poised vivacity which appeared to be charming her middle-aged companion, who, de Lanier's international eye told him, was of the wealthy American class. Her clothes were perfect. She was exquisite.

She looked up and saw de Lanier. Then, with a smile, deliberately beckoned him to their table.

He walked across slowly. Obviously she had mistaken him for somebody, but even as he stood before her the smile persisted. She beckoned him to sit down. He did so.

"I think . . ." began Mr. de Lanier, but exactly what he thought remained unsaid, for at this moment a small foot was pressed softly against his, and an eyelid quivered, almost imperceptibly. It seemed safer for Mr. de Lanier to smile. He did so.

"I'm so glad you've arrived," she said.

Then she turned to her companion and indicated de Lanier with a small suede-gloved hand.

"This," she continued, "is Mr. Shelton, your mining expert."

She smiled again at de Lanier, and once more her eyelid quivered.

"Mr. Shelton," she said, "this is Mr. van Straat, who is buying the El Caras gold-mine from us."

De Lanier bowed. By this time you will know that he was of the type that would try anything once. He was an expert at opportune situations, and this, it appeared, was one of them. This charming woman desired that he should be Mr. Shelton. Her little wink and the soft pressure of her foot had indicated that, at some time or other, there would be an explanation; therefore, for the moment, de Lanier was quite happy to be Mr. Shelton, and as the Americans put it, to "play along."

Van Straat held out his hand.

"Glad to meet you, Mr. Shelton," he said briskly. "I want to hear all about that mine. Come and see me at the Alcazar to-night and tell me what you think about it. Just an informal talk. Your firm's reputation is good enough for me."

The small foot pressed de Lanier's once more. He rather liked it.

"Thanks, Mr. van Straat," he said, and tried to look modest. "We are, justifiably, I hope, proud of our reputation."

He looked, his eyes laughing, straight into the violet eyes opposite. They laughed back.

Mr. de Lanier lunched—with Mr. van Straat. Also he talked about everything else in the world except gold-mines. At two-thirty the American discovered that he had an appointment, but requested de Lanier not to hurry over his coffee.

"I'll get along," he said. "Meet me to-night at the Alcazar—first-floor suite. We'll dine at eight and talk about the mine. In the meantime you can tell Countess d'Iriet all about it."

He signed the bill, made his adieux and departed.

Through his cigarette smoke Mr. de Lanier regarded the still laughing eyes of his companion. Eventually he spoke:

"I am enchanted to meet you, Countess. May I ask questions, or does my responsibility end with lunch?"

He smiled quizzically, and she noted the attractive lines about his mouth.

"Ask on, Mr. de Lanier," she said mischievously.

De Lanier's smile deepened. So he was known!

He rested his elbows on the table and leaned towards her. A subtle suggestion of perfume came to him.

"Question number one. Are you Countess d'Iriet? It's a good Russian name—I know it. Two: Why am I Mr. Shelton? Three: How do you know I am de Lanier? Four: Exactly what is the game?"

She looked at him over the match flame as he lit her cigarette.

"I am Countess d'Iriet. My husband died in Russia three years ago. He left me his good wishes and a string of pearls. I sold the last one two months ago. Two: You are Mr. Shelton because it is most necessary that our

good Mr. van Straat should receive a personal report o
the El Caras mine to-night in order that he may buy a
the shares to-morrow. Three: I know who you ar
because Siriet, Deputy Chief of the Paris Sûreté, pointe
you out to me two years ago as the one internationa
'operator' that the police could not lay hands on—yo
always kept inside the law; and four: the game, as yo
call it, is simply this, there being nothing dishonest abou
it.

"Nine months ago I was in South America and met
charming man—Jean d'Alvarez. He owned the El Cara
mine and wanted to sell it. Then Mr. van Straat, whom
met casually in New York, came along, and I introduce
him as a possible purchaser. Mr. van Straat sent for
mining expert, a Mr. Gerald Stevens. This gentlema
reported on the mine five days ago and told of the di
covery of a pocket of gold. A month ago Mr. van Stra
wrote here from New York instructing Mr. Shelton, th
English mining expert, to go out and confirm Steven
report.

"D'Alvarez arrives in London to-night, and to-morrow
all being well, the purchase will be completed. But th
morning I got a hectic marconigram from him th
Shelton had taken ill and was left behind, and that as Mr. va
Straat's confidence might be shaken by the non-appearanc
of Shelton, who was personally confirming Steven's repor
I must find a substitute. This was possible as van Stra
has never seen Shelton. When I saw you I thought yo
might like to be Shelton—for a consideration."

"Ah," said de Lanier. "And what is Mr. d'Alvare
like?"

"Oh, he's amusing, tall, dark, and very handsome in
Latin sort of way. . . ."

"And you are in love with him?"

"Heavens, no! Why?"

"If you are not, why are you taking all this trouble?"
queried Mr. de Lanier.

152

She regarded him quizzically.

"For five thousand pounds which I receive from Mr. d'Alvarez when the purchase is completed," she said, "and that purchase must be completed. I've got twenty pounds in the world left . . . you see?"

Mr. de Lanier nodded. He saw.

He leaned back in his chair and thought. He couldn't understand it. D'Alvarez . . . one of the cutest fake share-pushers on the Continent. . . . So d'Alvarez was behind this. De Lanier had crossed swords metaphorically with d'Alvarez more than once in his interesting career—and d'Alvarez had always come off worst in the process. But for d'Alvarez to be selling gold-mines! De Lanier sensed that there was dirty work somewhere.

And the woman. Was she telling the truth? Did she believe the deal to be straight and the production of a false Mr. Shelton simply a business move? Another suspicion of perfume floated across to his nostrils and he felt himself becoming a little sympathetic. After all, she was a very beautiful woman, and de Lanier was nothing if not romantic.

"And what," he murmured, "do I get out of this?"

"I'll split my five thousand commission with you," she said. "We'll go halves. And, if you'll let me, I'll give you one of my two remaining tenners on account."

She smiled delightfully.

"I've noticed your left shoe needs dry-docking," she said.

"Thanks," said de Lanier. "You may."

He slipped the bank note into his pocket.

"Incidentally, I'm wondering why I'm doing this . . . but perhaps I know."

She looked astonished.

"I thought you always did things like this," she said. "Things most people wouldn't do."

He smiled.

"I don't," he said.

153

"Then why did you agree?" she asked with raised eyebrows.

"I agreed to do it," said Mr. de Lanier with a little grin, "firstly, because I'm having an interlude—a pretty bad one—but secondly, and more importantly, because I think I like you rather a lot. I like your mouth and the way you talk. I like the way you wear your clothes and your perfume. So I'll take a chance."

He got up.

"Excuse me going, won't you," he said. "I've got to 'mug' up my story for van Straat—all about El Caras. I suppose we shall meet to-morrow when the big finance comes off. *Au revoir!*"

He moved away towards the cloak-room. She watched his slim figure disappear with eyes that were a little astonished.

II

As Mr. de Lanier walked up the rather ornate staircase at the Alcazar to keep his appointment with van Straat, he wondered with a half smile whether his wisdom was departing with the years. Then an incident attracted his attention.

A small page-boy ascending the stairs in front of him dropped from a bundle of letters a pink cablegram. De Lanier picked it up, was about to call to the boy, when he noticed that the missive was addressed to van Straat.

Curiosity being a strong feature in de Lanier's character, he stepped into a convenient telephone-box, and, taking a leather case from his pocket, extracted what appeared to be a small darning-needle. This he inserted in the tiny space left unstuck at the top of the envelope. In a moment the cablegram was in his hands. Mr. de Lanier read it with appreciation, then returned it to its envelope by the same process, stopped the page-boy on his return downstairs and handed it to him with a mild reproof for carelessness. The boy turned back to deliver the cablegram, and de Lanier followed him along the corridor to van Straat's suite.

The dinner was excellent and de Lanier was in good form when he left the hotel at nine-thirty. Van Straat accompanied him to the entrance.

"D'Alvarez arrives to-night," said the American, "and after your excellent report I shall complete the deal here to-morrow as arranged, at twelve o'clock."

He smacked de Lanier on the back with jovial good humour.

"You'd better come along at that time and witness the transfer," he said, "then you can drink a glass of champagne to the new owner of El Caras!"

"I most certainly will," said de Lanier.

He bade his host good night, and made quickly for Piccadilly. Here, outside the Monico, he stood deep in thought, his brain searching for the name he wanted.

Eventually it came—Tony Largasso, who knew every crook in the world, who specialised—for dubious considerations—in their life histories. De Lanier hurried inside and looked up the gentleman in the telephone-book. Then he hailed a taxi and drove off. Midnight found him in another taxi on his way to a dingy flat in Long Acre, and two hours afterward, smiling happily, he meandered back to his flat in Knightsbridge.

It was a beautiful night, and the air was soft and refreshing. Mr. de Lanier found himself thinking of a pair of violet eyes.

"I wonder . . ." he asked himself. "I wonder . . . my little Countess, what you will do? Will you essay to save me, or will you let me sink with the ship?"

No answer being possible, Mr. de Lanier let himself into his flat and slept the sleep of complete innocence.

The Countess heaved a little sigh. The formalities had been completed. On the table in front of the smiling d'Alvarez lay sixty thousand pounds in English bank notes. That worthy, who had noted de Lanier's appearance as "Mr. Shelton" with commendable *sang froid,* was about to pick them up, when without warning the door opened and a burly and quietly dressed individual appeared.

"Sorry to interrupt you, Mr. van Straat," he said shortly. "I'm Chief-Inspector Durrant of Scotland Yard. You've been rather badly had, I think, sir!"

He turned from the astonished van Straat to d'Alvarez, whose smile had frozen.

"Jean d'Alvarez, I have a warrant for your arrest for conspiracy to defraud. Stephanie, Countess d'Iriet, I have a warrant for your arrest as an accessory. I've no warrant for you, de Lanier," he continued. "We only had information as to your part in this business this morning, but I'm going to hold you on suspicion."

"Look here, officer, what does this mean?" said the amazed van Straat.

"Simply this, sir," answered the police officer. "We know this d'Alvarez. He's an international crook. The South American Police have had their eyes on him for some months. Share-planting is his game. Oh, there's no doubt that he's the legal owner of El Caras, but it's worthless. The man Stevens that you took out to report on the mine originally was bribed by d'Alvarez to 'salt' it. They put the gold there that Stevens found. . . ."

"But Shelton . . ." spluttered van Straat, "Mr. Shelton here . . ."

"He's not," replied the Scotland Yard man. "He's
156

harles de Lanier, a very clever person indeed, who has
ways managed to keep within the law till now. The
elton that you had sent to El Caras was knocked over
e head by d'Alvarez and held out there to prevent him
ving you a true report. You had never seen him and it
as easy for them to plant this chap on you with a fake
port."

Van Straat gasped. D'Alvarez shrugged his shoulders
d smiled—he was always a philosopher. The woman
t, very white, her hands clasped.

"I knew nothing of all this," she said. "No one will
lieve me, but I knew nothing. Also, this gentleman,
r. de Lanier, is quite innocent. I persuaded him only
sterday to impersonate Mr. Shelton. Please believe
e. . . ."

She gazed at de Lanier dumbly.

"You sweet thing," said that worthy, most cheerfully.
I wanted to hear you say that. Lock the door, Chief-
spector, will you?"

He picked up the bank notes from the table and put
em into his breast pocket. They gazed at him in aston-
ment.

"The 'Chief-Inspector' here is a friend of mine," he
id smilingly, "and the only time he ever went to
otland Yard he had handcuffs on!

"Now let me explain!"

He turned to d'Alvarez.

"Jean, for once in your life you've been double-
ossed." He indicated van Straat. "Allow me to present
rus Friemer, the cutest crook in the United States. Sit
wn, Friemer, it's no good getting excited! Now I'll
l you what really happened.

"Friemer heard that there was gold in El Caras. He
so heard that you were trying to sell the mine through
untess d'Iriet, although you didn't tell her of your
rky past. He sent a crooked mining engineer, Gerald

Stevens, to vet the mine. Stevens discovers a big vein o
gold, reports to Friemer and then allows d'Alvarez t
bribe him to salt the mine and send a second report t
Friemer. The Shelton sent out by Friemer was anothe
accomplice, sent out for the purpose of belittling Stevens
fake report in order that Friemer might buy the min
even more cheaply.

"D'Alvarez, who believes the mine to be worthless, an
that Shelton's adverse report will prevent the sale, ha
him held in Paris en route and wires the unsuspectin
Countess that she must find a fake Shelton, who wil
report that the El Caras mine is teeming with gold—a fac
which our scheming pseudo 'van Straat' knew very wel
I happened along, and the Countess selected me for th
job, which was lucky for her!

"Last night when I came here to see van Straat, I ha
no idea that he was a crook, but luck was with me. A
page-boy dropped a cablegram addressed to van Straat o
the stairs here. I extracted and read the message. It wa
from Stevens informing van Straat that there was gold al
over the place at El Caras, that d'Alvarez had no idea o
this, and that at sixty thousand the deal was a snip.

"That was good enough for me. I got in touch wit
Tony Largasso, who identified van Straat as Friemer
Then I staged this little comedy with the 'Chief-Inspec
tor,' and here we are!

"Now I'll settle the matter.

"D'Alvarez, I'm tearing up your transfer to van Straa
The mine is still yours. For my services I'm going to stic
to the sixty thousand pounds less what is due to th
Countess and a bit for the 'Chief-Inspector's' troubl
Take my tip and get back to South America. You ca
sell your mine easily. As for Mr. van Straat, this litt
failure costs him sixty thousand, but he can go to th
police if he wants to, although I rather think he'll kee
as far away from them as possible. They want him o

bout fifteen different counts. Inspector, open the door
or Mr. Friemer, I think he is going to be ill!"

One hour later Mr. de Lanier lunched sumptuously at
he Hotel Reina. He appeared to be deep in thought.

"Of what are you thinking, Mr. de Lanier?" asked his
ompanion.

"I was wishing that I had a little more courage," said
Mr. de Lanier—who was inclined to be artistic. "I should
very much like to talk to you of love and kindred topics,
but I do not know whether or not they might interest
you. I need encouragement," concluded Mr. de Lanier.
He looked adequately pathetic.

She appeared concerned, but her eyes were mischievous.
Under the table a small foot pressed his, very gently.

"I am encouraged." murmured Mr. de Lanier, "I shall
proceed!"

And he did.

ABIE IN HOLLYWOOD

LISTEN, youse guys: I am Abie Hymie Finkelstein, the
big song-writer, an' I been framed like you never saw.

Maybe you got histry; maybe you heard of these Dark
Middle Ages when there is this Spanish Imposition?

Here's the way it goes: This Spanish Imposition sticks
guys on some pants-pressin' arrangement they call the
ack. They stretch this guy out an' then the Spanish
mposition says an' how do you like that? If the guy says
do not like that then they stretch him some more for
bein' fresh, an' if he don't say nothing at all then they
make him drink some boilin' oil just to get this mug
civilised properly.

Well, if some guy would give me the address of this Spanish Imposition I would give them a lotta recommendations to get after Police Captain Dooley O'Hagan an' if the Spanish Imposition wants some guy to hold th funnel whiles they pour hot boilin' lead down Police Captain Dooley O'Hagan's neck, then I will do this work for nothin' at all.

So one afternoon my landlord is bein' very insultin' to me about the rent, an' so I get around to Lilly Scapalens an' I am singin' a hotcha number to her what I have comprised myself called "You Got It an' I Got It—So What!" while she is tryin' to get her old man—who is out—to lend me some dough outa the till, only we cannot find the can-opener.

Lilly says that if I would only get down an' use my brains an' write some swell songs I would probably make a lotta fortunes.

Now this is a swell idea so I go home an' I do a lotta thinkin' an' I write a smash hit entitled "You Didn' Know What Love Was Til I Come from Cuba With My Tuba."

When I have comprised this big song success I go out an' I am in a quick lunch when some guy lamps over my shoulder an' says, "Excuse me, but I have been readin' that song, an' did you write it?" An' when I tell him yes, he says that he reckons that I am about one of the biggest smash-hit writers of this degeneration an' that some guys he knows in the song business are lookin' for a big song-writer to go out to Hollywood an' make a lotta dough, an' that I should go along an' see these guys right away an' that he will put a call through that I am comin.

Now does this sound swell to me because I am sick of stickin' around here with Police Captain Dooley O'Hagan chasin' me around sayin' that I am a Public Enemy, an also because I do not think that Lilly is such a swell dame since her old man has got himself a patent lock on the till; an' so I go around to this office where this guy tells me.

When I get around to this dump I see these guys, an' when I have finished tellin' them that I am not the boy from the dry-cleaners I show them my big smash-hit number.

They read this smash-hit that I have comprised, an' they look at me an' they say that I am a sensation an' I should go a very long way. These guys also say that I am a lotta geniuses an' that if I will come back in half an hour they will have a contract all signed up for me to go out to Hollywood to write smash numbers for the Collosus Film Company, that they will have my first-class ticket an' they will give me an advance of 250 bucks.

So I nearly have a fit when they say this, an' then they give me one hundred bucks on account an' tell me to come back in half an hour.

When I go outa this buildin' I am walkin' on nares because now I am a famous geniuses, but I lay off Lilly Scapalensi because I think that if I should tell this dame about this she may get a lotta shocks an' she may also want to marry me because of my sex-appeal an' because I am now a big sensation with dough.

Pretty soon I get back to these guys an' I find I am not dreamin' because there is the travelling tickets an' the contract an' the rest of the dough, an' they say I am to go to Hollywood right away, that I am going to get 2000 bucks a week.

They also tell me that Abie Hymie Finkelstein is not such a hot name for a song-writer, so they have got for me a new monniker, an' that I am from now on Abie Valparaiso, the Swing King from Cuba.

An' when I am in the train goin' to this Hollywood dump I read a book that I have bought at the depot which says *How to Treat Film Stars*. It tells me that film stars are so temperental that most of the time they don't even know what they are doin', an' that any time they get wise to themselves they are no good because they cannot act. An' it says that the right way to treat a film star is to tell her that she is the most beautiful an' swell dame that you never saw, an' that she acts so good that you wouldn't know it was her.

By the time I arrive at this Hollywood, I have learnt all this stuff because I think maybe I will start gettin' around with my sex-appeal with some of these film stars an' for all I know Mae West is going to fall for me in a big way, which is a thing I would like. An' when I get to Hollywood I buy myself a taxicab like I was some big noise an' I get around to these film offices an' they say I should see some guy called Schrotzel.

So I go in an' I see this guy who is sittin' in a big office, an' I tell him I am Abie Valparaiso, the Swing King from Cuba, an' he says much he cares but that I am workin' with No. 5 Unit, which is starring a very temperential film actress called Magda Manyana, an' have I got any numbers that would do for her.

So I show this guy my smash hit—"You Didn't Know What Love Was Til I Come from Cuba with my Tuba," an' this guy goes blue in the face an' says that if this is a sample of my work as a song-writer then I ought to make a big success as a grave-digger. He then says that anyhow this Magda Manyana is so nuts that anything will go with her, an' that I should go along an' discuss a theme song with her.

So I get around to this dame an' she is a swell dame with very high heels an' a figure like she was a serpent with nerve troubles, an' this dame is havin' one helluva bust up with some guy called Fernandez, who is the songwriter who has got the air because I am comin' in his place to work for this dame.

So I tell this dame the paragraph outa the book which I have learnt about how lovely she is an' how she acts so marvellous that the last time I saw her I went unconscious for three days, an' she then says that she can see that I am one of the biggest smash-hit writers that ever happened around here.

I then show my song an' she says that she can see I have got a lotta genius an' she asks this guy Fernandez what is a tuba, an' he says that it is a sort of pertater, which shows you that this guy is jealous of my appeal. This film star then says that anyhow this does not matter as she does not come from Cuba anyhow, an' that I should write a song about some place she does come from, an' when I ask her where she comes from, she says I should ask the publicity man as she has forgot.

So I say good-day, an' I go off to some swell hotel where I am stayin', an' I start to write a big boop-a-doop theme song for this dame which I am goin' to call " The Birth of the Finkelstein Blues," an' next day I get around to the studio an' they say there is no work for me to do to-day, but I should go an' get my pay-cheque. So I feel very good about this an' I get a cheque for two thousand bucks, an' they tell me to take this down to the bank and cash same.

Now I am feelin' very swell, an' I am walkin' on hares to the bank, when out from some corner springs Police Captain Dooley O'Hagan an' he tells me he is lookin' for me, an' I tell him that he is a big cheese an' that I am Abie Valparaiso, the Swing King from Cuba, an' he had better watch himself before I start to get tough with him. He says O.K., he is looking for Abie Valparaiso because that guy is wanted in New York on seventy-two different charges.

I now feel very sick because it comes to me sudden that this guy who sent me to the agents in New York was Abie Valparaiso.

So I say that we should talk this thing out, an' that he knows very well that I am Abie Hymie Finkelstein who would not hurt some mice, an' he sees the cheque in my hand an' he says that maybe he can get me outa this jam

I have got myself in, but it will cost me plenty dough—about two thousand bucks—an' that I had better cash the cheque an' meet him down at the depot an' give him the dough so's he can take me back to New York an' prove that I am not Abie Valparaiso. He also says that maybe when I have got this dough he will be a good friend to me an' maybe he will be able to straighten out this business for about nineteen hundred an' fifty bucks, so that there will still be somethin' in it for me.

Now I am feelin' not so good but I see that there is nothin' to be done about this, so I go down to the bank, an' when I get there they take the cheque an' they tell me to get outa there good an' quick because this guy Fernandez has got the film company to stop payments to me, an' so they throw me outa the bank an' make a lotta rude remarks to me that I wouldn't make to some dogs.

Now I sits on a seat an' I think that I will wait until Police Captain Dooley O'Hagan, who is waitin' down at the depot, should catch his train back to New York, because I know that if I show up without this dough he will pinch me for bein' Abie Valparaiso. So after a bit when the train has gone I get a very big idea an' I find out where this film star lives an' I get around there an' I tell her how all these people are treatin' me like I was a lot of wolves, an' she draws herself up like she was an emperor an' she says that she is always the friend of the underdogs an' that she is not goin' to have me gypped by any so-and-so of a film company, an' she opens a bag an' she gives me two thousand bucks an' says that she will get this outa this guy Schrotzel at the film company.

She then does a big act an' puts her hand on my head an' says that all through my life I should remember her as a great an' lonely artist strivin' to live for her art an' to be a friend to the underdogs an' that if this guy Schrotzel does not ante up she will bust him one with a blackjack. After this she kisses me on the top of my head an' tells me to scram.

Now I am once more very pleased with myself, because it looks like this film star is falling for me in a big way, an' because I have got two thousand bucks, an' I am walking on hares an' thinkin' to myself that maybe I will open up a big store around here called Finkelstein Incorporated, when Police Captain Dooley O'Hagan jumps out at me from some corner an' says what do I think I am tryin' to get away with around here, an' that he has been around to the bank an' they have wised him up that they would not cash the cheque.

Police Captain Dooley O'Hagan now says that he is goin' to take me back to New York to stand trial because I am Abie Valparaiso the swindler, an' when I say I am not Abie Valparaiso he says he will go up to the film company an' see what has been goin' on around here an' that I had better wait for him down at the depot.

Now I am once more very sick because I know that in a minute Police Captain Dooley O'Hagan will find out that I have got some dough, an' I am right about this, because in a few minutes he comes around an' he says how this Schrotzel has told him that I have got two thousand outa the film star an' she is bawlin' him out to pay it back to her.

He also says that unless I hand over this dough for my defences fund he is goin' to get this Schrotzel to file a suit against me for false pretences by tellin' them I am Abie Valparaiso when all the time I am Abie Hymie Finkelstein, an' when I say that it does not matter who I am, because whoever I am I am always goin' to be arrested for something, he says that if he has another crack outa me he is goin' to smack me down for insultin' a police officer, an' he takes the two thousand bucks off from me an' then gets on the train an' goes off without giving me anything at all except a bust in the nose.

So I sit down an' I think that it is a terrible thing the way that everything happens to me like it does.

I find that this Fernandez has made a dirty double-

165

cross against me because he has been to the film publicity man and the publicity man says that this Magda Manyana comes from some place called Gorgonzola an' he has pinched my big idea and done a number for her called "You Didn't Know What Love Was Til I Come from Gorgonzola with my Pianola," an' she looks at me like I was a lotta rats an' says that Schrotzel won't give her the two thousand bucks an' that I should hand it over back again to her because I am an impostor, an' when I tell her that I have had this dough pinched off me by a police captain for my defences she has me thrown out on my ear.

I then think that after all Lilly Scapalensi is maybe not such a bad dame when you look at her sideways, an' that maybe she will fall for my sex-appeal an' send my car fare so I should get back to New York; but when I do the reverse-the-charges long-distances call to her she tells me that her old man has thrown away the till an' got himself an iron safe, an' that unless she can get hold of some dynamite it looks like I ain't got no prospects at all.

So I ask all youse guys if you see some big genius hitch-hikin' back to New York you will know it is me, an' if you go to the movies an' you see this Magda Manyana you will see that she is a bum actress an' that even if she does come from Gorgonzola she is still nothin' but a big cheese.

THE WEEPING LADY

From the narrative of ex-Detective-
Inspector V . . . J . . ., C.I.D.

THEY say that every crook gives himself away in the long run. I suppose the exception proves the rule; anyhow, Etienne Duchanel (that was *one* of his names), was the exception all right. During my thirty years' service as a detective officer I spent about ten years with a weather eye open just in case I *might* get something on Etienne. And so did the French police; and so did the German and the Swiss and the Italian.

But we never did.

He was a first-class crook—a perfect artist at his work. He would do, on the average, one big job a year—always successful and with never a clue to hang it on to Etienne.

Yet he slipped up on his biggest job—the Sidka rubies. The French police knew that he was responsible for the theft. So did we, but we could never prove it.

It was only three years ago that I learned the true story. He told it to me himself—sitting on the rustic seat at the end of his flower garden near Monaco.

Mr. Etienne Duchanel was in Paris resting after a little job in Berlin that necessitated a period of quiet.

Every night he would take a little walk after a visit to a theatre or a concert. He would always walk in the same direction straight past the Place de l'Opéra round to the right and back home to his *appartement*.

But on this particularly lovely night Etienne found himself feeling that there was something in the air. He had a strange sense of anticipation.

He had turned, as usual, down the rue Gavourelle when suddenly, on the other side of the street, the front door of one of the biggest houses in the fashionable quarter opened wide and, silhouetted against the light, he saw the charming figure of a woman—weeping bitterly.

If you knew anything of Etienne you would not be surprised if I told you that he pulled down his white waistcoat, gave a flip to the brim of his soft black hat, and crossed to the distressed lady.

By this time she had closed the door behind her and had walked, or rather tottered, a few steps down the street.

"Madame," said Etienne, "it seems that you are distressed. My poor services are entirely at your disposal. Can I do something? I am Garrache, Colonel of Chausseurs."

She stopped and wavered. Apparently she was so overcome that she did not know what to do. Etienne took her by the arm and led her to the step beneath the portico of the nearest house.

"Sit down and try to compose yourself, Madame," said Etienne. "It is a sin that so beautiful a woman should be reduced to tears. Tell me all about it."

She endeavoured to stifle her sobs.

"You are charming, M'sieu," she murmured brokenly, "but there is nothing to tell. My name is Heloise Sidka—that should tell you all you want to know!"

Etienne whistled to himself. Heloise Sidka! Paris had heard *that* name. Every newspaper had been filled with the story of her treatment at the hands of a husband who had reached the ultimate depths to which drugs and drink may bring a man. At the moment, three actions, brought against him by his wife—this woman who sat weeping so bitterly—for the return to her of her personal property, were pending against Sidka in the French High Courts.

She seemed to compose herself a little.

"To-night I decided to leave his house for ever," she

168

whispered. "I am penniless, but I possess a valuable ruby coronet—the Sidka coronet—my father's wedding gift to me. But *he* knew what was in my mind. A few minutes ago he tore the coronet out of my hand and locked it in the safe. He told me I could bring an action for the return of *that,* too!

"I am desperate—desperate and ashamed. I cannot bear this terrible publicity. I do not know what to do."

Etienne was affected. The proximity of this beautiful woman who wept affected him deeply. He permitted himself to put his arm about her shoulders—merely, of course, as some sort of moral support.

After a few moments' thought he spoke.

"Listen to me, Madame," he said quietly. "I have lied to you. I am not Garrache, Colonel of Chausseurs; I am far greater than that. I am Etienne Duchanel, the most accomplished cracksman in the world, if I may say so!"

She raised her head and looked at him in wonderment.

"Duchanel," she repeated. "I have heard that name."

Etienne shrugged. "Listen," he repeated. "I take it that you have the keys of the house you have just left?" She nodded. "And I take it that in, say, half an hour, your enterprising husband will be so drunk that nothing will bother him. Am I right?"

She nodded again. She was interested.

"Well, Madame," continued Etienne, "the rest is easy.

"In half an hour's time—at two o'clock, that is—you will let me into the house. You will lead me to the safe. I assure you that there is no safe made by human hands that can withstand Etienne Duchanel.

"Madame, in an hour's time the Sidka coronet shall be in your hands!"

She thought for a moment. Then she looked at him. A gleam of moonlight glinted on her wonderful auburn hair.

"M'sieu," she said brokenly, "M'sieu Duchanel, you are wonderful. You give me fresh hope. I cannot thank you sufficiently. What can I say? What can I do to show you my gratitude?"

"That is easy," said Etienne. "Shall we have supper? I must telephone and wait for one or two little instruments that will be necessary to open the safe. Your company while we eat will be sufficient reward!"

Two hours later Etienne Duchanel followed Madame Sidka up the wide staircase of the house. Occasionally, as they moved cautiously up the stairs, a suggestion of her perfume came to his nostrils.

Etienne permitted himself to dream dreams.

Five minutes later, and they were in the library with Duchanel's flashlight on the safe. Twenty minutes after that he had the safe door open.

He flashed his light upon the steel shelves within. There, before them, glittering on their velvet bed, flashed the Sidka rubies.

Etienne heard her sigh. Then, as he put out his hand to take the gems, the electric light flashed on and an acrid and cynical voice broke the silence.

Standing by the door, holding an automatic pistol, stood an insolently grim man wrapped in a silken dressing-gown.

The woman caught her breath. "My husband!"

The man in the dressing-gown grinned.

"Exactly, my dear—your husband," he repeated. "So you thought you would get the rubies, did you? You thought you could come sneaking back with some cheap crook and steal your precious gems, did you!" His voice sank to a passionate whisper.

"Get out, both of you," he hissed. "Get out before I kill the pair of you—and quickly!"

The woman turned to Etienne.

"Let us go, for heaven's sake!" she whispered.

They walked down the staircase in silence. After them came the sound of Sidka's soft laughter.

Etienne ground his teeth with rage.

Presently, as they walked slowly in silence down the street, Etienne stopped and turned to Heloise Sidka.

"Madame," he said, "this is not the end of this business. Etienne Duchanel is not to be threatened by a drunkard. Listen to me. You are to go straight to the Hotel des Milles Fleures and secure a room. Stay there to-night. To-morrow I will bring you the Sidka rubies. I, Duchanel, promise you this!"

"But, m'sieu," she whispered, "Etienne—how will you do this?"

He smiled.

"Madame," he said, "at my *appartement* I, too, have a pistol! I shall take you to your hotel, then I shall go back to the restaurant and telephone my valet to bring round my automatic; *then I shall go back and talk to Monsieur Sidka*. Do not argue, Madame. My mind is made up.

"Please give me the front-door key!"

Twenty minutes afterwards, having deposited the lady safely at the Hotel des Milles Fleures, Etienne sat and drank a cup of coffee at the restaurant where he had supped.

At any moment he expected Laparet, who was bringing his automatic. Etienne smiled to himself.

Sidka would not expect him to return. His visit would be an entire surprise. The dope fiend had forgotten that two people could play one game!

Etienne looked up as he observed Laparet coming towards him. The valet handed him a small document-case. Inside he could feel the weight of the pistol.

"I am sorry I was so long, M'sieu," said Laparet. "But the taxi was held up. There is great excitement afoot."

"What excitement?" asked Etienne.

Laparet shrugged his shoulders.

"Have you not heard, M'seiu?" he said. "The Sidka rubies have been stolen!"

"What!" Etienne almost bounced from his seat. His amazement was interrupted by a page.

"Excuse me, M'sieu," said the boy. "You are wanted urgently on the telephone—a lady desires to speak to you."

Almost in a trance, Etienne followed the boy to the telephone box. A soft and charming voice—the voice of Madame Sidka—came to his ears.

"Dear Etienne," said the voice, "you did fall for it, didn't you? You see, we—my boy friend and I—have been after the Sidka rubies for weeks. We knew you always walked past the house at night, and, although we' had the key of the front door, we knew we could never get the safe open. Only one man could open that safe— Etienne Duchanel!

"So we laid for you. Don't you think my imitation of Madame Sidka was good? Poor old silly, didn't you know she's been in Berlin for the last three weeks! And don't you think the boy friend was good? He was hiding in the library in a dressing-gown and directly you'd got the safe open he came in and did his doped husband act, then when we'd gone he just took the rubies and slipped off.

"All the time the real Sidka was asleep—upstairs. My auburn wig was rather good, too, wasn't it?

"Anyhow, I think you're a sweet. We're just leaving Paris by car, but maybe we'll meet again one day. Au revoir!"

Etienne hung up the receiver and walked slowly back to his table in the restaurant. Laparet regarded him in surprise. He had never seen Duchanel look so shocked.

Suddenly the face of Etienne Duchanel broke into a smile. It was a smile of appreciation.

The appreciation of one great artist for another. He remembered her tears—her winsomeness—her beauty.

"Well, I'm damned!" said Mr. Duchanel, and ordered a double brandy.

THE PIN

I

IF you live in the West End of London do not be surprised if on some occasion you encounter an individual whose hat, shoes and linen are perfect; but whose suit is so old that it looks as if it might fall to pieces at any moment. Looking more closely, you will realise that this suit was a very beautiful thing, the work of a master craftsman, and of a colour which, though quiet and subdued, possesses a weird and indefinable quality.

You will be more surprised if you recognise the wearer of the suit as Mr. Lewis Walford; for, if you know of him, you will know that he is sufficiently endowed with this world's goods *not* to wear such very old clothes.

And if you know him well you will know that he wears that suit on one day in the year only, the twenty-first of October, and that for the other three hundred and sixty-four days of the year it hangs in a wardrobe, covered in a silken cloth. No one ever brushes it but Mr. Walford; no one is allowed to touch it but Mr. Walford.

I am certain that the great majority of you have at some time or other witnessed a performance of Mr. Lewis Walford. At the zenith of British vaudeville he was an invariable "top-of-the-bill." Immaculately dressed in an evening suit, into which he looked as if he had been poured, and with a nice taste in waistcoat buttons and dress-studs, Mr. Walford would sing popular songs, and tell funny stories of the type beloved by music-hall audiences before they took their fickle way into the more modern cinema.

Although Mr. Walford was a music-hall artiste, he was not terribly proud of the fact. Unlike most performers, he realised that there was a world which existed outside the musty confines of " star " dressing-rooms; that there was a culture more fastidious than that indulged in by his nicest colleagues. In other words, Mr. Walford was an artiste because it was an easy way of earning a large weekly salary. He liked his profession just so much as it increased his bank balance.

And he was careful of this bank balance. He realised that the time would come when his popularity would wane, when his " friends in front " would not be quite so keen; applaud so uproariously. He was a saving man, and because he knew that the atmosphere of his profession was not conductive to thrift he banked a certain proportion of his salary each week, and allowed himself the balance for his pocket. Never, by any chance, would Mr. Walford allow himself to draw an additional cheque during the week, and it was by this rule, and sundry others, that he had managed to acquire certain property and securities which made him independent of the future and fairly good-humoured as to the present.

As the train steamed out of the long tunnel two miles from the very beautiful cathedral town of Warchester-under-Lyne, Mr. Walford, whilst appreciating the beauty of the sunset, was rather angry with himself. He was playing at the music-hall in Warchester this week, and on this journey from his last town he had broken one of his almost infallible rules, and permitted himself to play poker down the corridor with some brother Thespians. So that he now discovered that, this day being Sunday and the first day of the week, he had lost practically the whole of his allowance; and he was wondering how he would get through the week without breaking another rule— quite an infallible one, this one—and cash a cheque.

His annoyance was doubled because in Warchester there was a prince of tailors—I told you, I think, that Mr.

Walford was a very well-dressed man—and this prince of tailors, whose tiny place of business nestled almost under the shadow of Warchester cathedral, was in the habit of making two or three suits for Walford on each occasion that he visited the town. The tailor, besides being a great artist in his own particular line of business, had become, through the long acquaintanceship, almost a friend, and it seemed to Walford that if he were really to keep his rule, he would have to forgo his new clothes as well as the usual additional comforts in which he indulged when he visited Warchester.

His eyes were gladdened as the train moved round the bend which lay just before the station. Before him, to the left of the station, in a little valley bathed in the dying sunlight, lay the spires and towers of one of England's most beautiful towns. Even the music-hall, strangely enough, was a handsome building, as if the architect had endeavoured to infuse into its modernity a touch of the beauty of the surrounding buildings.

Lottie Carston, of Carston and Howles, the world-famed comedy duo, stuck her towsled brunette head round the corner of Walford's carriage.

"Well, here we are, old son," she called in that squeaky voice which drove audiences to laughter twice nightly. "Here's the old Warchester! You like it too, don't you? The place is too bloomin' slow for me. I can't get a kick out of Warchester. Give me Leeds every time!"

Walford nodded and smiled. He was glad that she took herself off. He was in no humour for Lottie.

You will think, possibly, that he had no right to be aggrieved over the fact that owing to his losses at poker he had inconvenienced himself financially, but I would again repeat that his life had been made by the keeping of rules. Mr. Walford harnessed his temperament. He made it work for him. He would not work for it. Years ago, driving a pen in a cheap lawyer's office, he had looked round for a means of escape; some avenue by which he might free himself from the soul-killing routine of a cheap room, a raucous landlady, and thirty shillings a week. He had done so. The music-halls had found him that avenue, but he was neither satisfied nor finished. He must progress; he must go on. Somewhere far ahead, possibly quite near, some new development awaited him, something for which he must be prepared. It is, therefore, more easy to understand his attitude over this financial matter, about which you or I would not waste a second thought.

Out of the train, watching his two large trunks being unshipped from the luggage-van, acknowledging the smiling cap-touchings of porters—they did touch their caps before the war—listening to a whisper from here and there . . . "Look! That's Mr. Walford . . . he's top-of-the-bill at the Empire next week" . . . he found himself becoming less unhappy each moment. He was very glad to be in Warchester; and it was, perhaps, only as his taxi drove him to the hotel wherein he usually stayed, and as they passed the little tailor's shop sandwiched in between the cathedral and the old library, that a small qualm of sadness overtook him once again.

II

THE old tailor looked up as Walford entered the shop. A straight gleam of morning sunshine fell on the old man's white hair and illuminated his smile as he recognised his customer. Outside the door sounds of the Monday morning market came quietly into the tailor's shop.

"Good-morning, Mr. Walford," said the old man. "I'm glad to see you again. Why, it must be six months since you were here last. We've all been asking when you were going to come back to us, and I'm especially glad you've come, I've got something to show you."

Walford laughed and shook hands.

"Something to show me," he repeated. "What is it?" The old man rubbed his hands.

"A piece of cloth, Mr. Walford, a wonderful piece of cloth. I don't think you've ever seen anything like it. I've handled a lot of cloth in my time—good cloth too. It *has* to be good cloth in a hunting country. Candidly, I've never seen a finer piece, or a more beautiful pattern in my life. It was an odd sample that came my way, and I kept it for you."

Walford smiled wryly.

"This is bad news," he said. "You know, Mr. Morris, that rule of mine. Everybody knows it! Well, I've been a bad boy; I gambled on the train yesterday and lost thirty pounds, so I've got to punish myself, and I'm going to punish myself by not having any clothes from you. You see, I have to be my own schoolmaster."

The tailor smiled.

"That's as it may be, Mr. Walford," he said, "but you've got to let me make you this suit. I don't care whether you pay for it or whether you don't, but you've got to have it. You see, I've saved that piece of cloth for you, and I'd be terribly disappointed if you didn't have it. Wait a minute! Let me show it to you."

He bustled off to the back of the shop, and returned in a minute carrying, almost lovingly, a bolt of cloth. Even the quiet Walford gave a little gasp as he saw is. It was a peculiar grey-blue, of very quiet tone and pattern, but there was something original, something vaguely attractive about it. He fingered it. The feel of the cloth was wonderful.

"By Jove, Morris," he said, "that's a fine piece of cloth. This looks as if it's my unlucky day. Jove! I wish I hadn't lost that money."

"Now look here, Mr. Walford," said Morris, "do let me make it. If you won't let me give it you, pay for it next time you come here. I *must* make this suit for you. I've imagined you in it for months."

The old tailor was almost fierce in his determination; as he leaned across his counter, his wide old eyes almost passionate in their intensity. Walford had to smile.

Suddenly an idea struck him.

"I've got it, Morris," he said. "I'll have that suit, and I know how I'll pay for it. Do you know what I'm going to do? I've thought of a means by which I can keep my rule, and pay you for that suit. I'm going to pawn my tie-pin."

He took the pin from his tie. It was a tiny dragon made of platinum, diamonds and rubies, small and in good taste. It was valuable.

"That's what I'll do," said Walford. "I'll borrow the thirty pounds I lost at poker on this pin. Then, on Saturday, when I get my week's salary, I'll redeem it, and the interest which I'll have to pay will constitute a fine for my weakness of yesterday. What about that?"

"Good!" said Morris. "I don't mind what you do, Mr. Walford, so long as you have the suit."

An idea came to him, and he leaned further across the counter more intense than ever.

"Mr. Walford," he said, "do something for me. Listen. Would you do this? Would you wear the suit on the stage this week? Oh, I know you always wear evening clothes, but couldn't you do your act just once in a lounge suit? I'd feel so awfully proud, somehow, if I could see you on the stage at our Empire in *my* suit. Would you?"

He gazed almost pleadingly at the artist. Walford smiled.

"Of course I will," he said, "willingly, and listen! Look here, Morris, let's make a job of this. Can you get that suit finished by to-night? If you can I'll wear it to-night at both houses."

Morris's eyes glistened.

"I think we can do it," he said. "I've made so many clothes for you, I couldn't make a mistake if I tried. One fitting will be enough. Can you come back at three o'clock this afternoon, Mr. Walford?"

"I surely can," said Walford. "Can you finish it in time?"

"We'll get it finished," said Morris. "If you try on at three o'clock I'll have it finished and sent round to the theatre at half-past seven. You're never on until about eight, and you don't know how proud I'll be to see you wear it." The old man's eyes gleamed. "What an idea," he said, "to have shown you this piece of cloth this morning, and to see you wearing it on the stage to-night. Somehow it makes me feel very happy."

Walford laughed.

"I'm certain it will make me happy too, Morris," he said. "Well, I'll wander across the road to 'uncle's' and get the wherewithal to pay you cash on delivery. Till three o'clock. *Au revoir!*"

"Good-bye for the present," said the old tailor, and he stood at the door watching the tall, well-knit figure of the music-hall artiste as it threaded its way over the cobble-stones of the square.

III

LEWIS WALFORD, standing in front of the full-length mirror in its tarnished frame in the "star" dressing-room of the Warchester Empire, experienced a new sensation as he saw himself ready for the stage dressed in a lounge suit.

But what a suit! Morris had excelled himself. It fitted as a suit should fit. It was wonderful. Mr. Walford who, like most nice men, was without any delusions with regard to himself, realised that this suit added immeasurably to his personality. He found it hard to put into words exactly what he meant by this thought, but the nearest approach was that somehow the suit made him look rather like a gentleman, and when Mr. Walford thought " rather like a gentleman," he meant like one of those exquisitely indifferent people whom one sees coming out of any really old club which fronts Piccadilly; people with tradition, who did things which were right quite automatically, and without any necessity for previous thought. This impression gave Mr. Walford a decided feeling of superiority. He knew that his act was going to be very successful. He felt that the audience would appreciate him even more than hitherto. Mixed with this feeling of superiority was a touch of humility as if he realised that the craftsmanship and the taste of the old tailor had contributed to his new personality.

His success was really rather wonderful. The audience would not let him leave the stage, and it was only after Mr. Peebles, the fat and good-humoured manager, had gone before the curtain and informed the audience that there were other turns on the bill, and that Mr. Walford had already worked twice his time, that the artiste was allowed to depart.

In his dressing-room he stood, a little flushed, certainly very happy, but with a feeling that something was in the air; that this new and wonderful atmosphere, somehow created for him on this visit to Warchester, would bring something which might be nice. These ruminations pleased Mr. Walford so much that he was almost a little annoyed when, after his customary double knock on the door, his man, Stones, put his head round and, after his usual manner, followed it with his long body. Stones had been Walford's dresser for seven years. There was very little that the two men did not know about each other. Stones respected Walford, mainly because he was *different* from the usual run of variety artiste of those days, who was a hail-fellow-well-met individual, full of good temper, and quite often of alcohol. Another thing which Stones appreciated was that Walford never lost his temper. He was naturally a rather quiet man, so quiet that the dresser

suspected that under this placid exterior there lurked
deep feeling.

Walford looked at Stones, and Stones looked back at
Walford. Walford was surprised because on Stones' face
there was a look almost of amazement, and it was not like
Stones to be amazed at anything in particular.

"Well," asked Walford, "who's dead? Have you seen
a ghost, Stones?"

The dresser gulped.

"No, Mr. Walford," he said, "but there's a lady to
see you downstairs—a real lady, Mr. Walford. I asked if
she'd give her name. She said 'No,' she wanted to speak
to you; would you please come down. She's not English,
Mr. Walford. . . ."

He broke off as if he were going to say something else
which second thoughts had shown him might be unnecessary or impertinent.

"Funny," said Walford. "Most of the people who
come to see me in Warchester are people we know, Stones.
Go down and tell her I will be down in a minute."

"Yes," said Stones, but paused at the door. "Er—Mr.
Walford," he said with some hesitation, "this lady looks
like one who wouldn't like waiting an awful lot. I
mean . . ."

Walford laughed.

"All right, Stones," he said. "You told me she was a
real lady. Are you trying to suggest that we don't often
have real ladies to see us?"

Stones disappeared round the edge of the door. Walford
took a look at the glass, straightened his tie, and prepared
to follow his dresser. At the bottom of the flight of stone
steps which led to the little passage behind the stage-
doorkeeper's cubby hole, he saw a woman; and the sight
of her made him almost gasp. Walford's quick eye, trained
by years of stage experience to note detail, took in the
perfect details of her suit, the small expensive hat, the
exquisite shoes, and those indescribable marks of breeding,

those unknown qualities which he had always admired and respected.

He knew who she was. Touring variety artistes, with long railway waits, and dull hours in the train, are avaricious readers. He had seen her photograph; that face had looked at him before out of the pages of expensive English and foreign periodicals.

He was a little shaken. He could not possibly imagine what she wanted with him, but the technique of the stage, that "other personality" which is at the command of people whose business is to pretend that they are something else, came to his aid, and it was a very suave and cool Lewis Walford who stepped towards her.

"You wanted to see me, I think," he said.

"Yes."

The word came very clearly. He realised that her voice was as beautiful as she was.

"I wanted to speak to you. I saw your performance to-night, and I wanted to tell you how very much I admired it. You are very clever."

She spoke slowly, speaking her English carefully. Walford realised how beautiful her own language—Austrian —would have sounded. He noticed, too, that her hands were trembling a little.

"That is very good of you," he said. "It is always a great pleasure to an artiste to know that his efforts are appreciated."

They stood looking at each other. Walford realised instinctively that she wanted to say something else, that she was nervous, that she was almost fighting with her desire to leave this dusty atmosphere of backstage, and get away. His sensitiveness made him want to help, but for the life of him he could think of nothing to say, so he stood quietly waiting. Eventually she spoke, rather quickly, as if she wanted to get this hard thing over.

"I wondered," she said, "I wondered, Mr. Walford, if you would care to have supper with me to-night." She went on quickly, "I have a house a few miles outside Warchester. If you would like to do this I will send my car for you after the second performance."

She stopped. Walford saw she was flushing.

To say that he was surprised would mean nothing. He was amazed, but just how amazed even he could hardly realise, but his instinct told him that he must make the whole thing seem most natural; he must deal with it as he had always imagined himself dealing with a delicate situation.

He smiled.

"I cannot tell you," he said, "how honoured I am. I should like nothing better in the world."

She drew her breath in quickly. It was almost a sigh of relief. Walford realised that she must have experienced almost a little agony whilst awaiting his reply. Then she put out her hand.

"Thank you," she said. "It will be so nice."

She shook hands quickly, turned, and passed through the open door out of Walford's sight. Somewhere outside he heard the low purr of a high-powered car as it moved away.

He turned and walked slowly up the stone stairs back to his dressing-room. He entered the room, and raising his eyes from the ground saw himself reflected in the long mirror on the opposite wall. For once he could get no cohesion into his thoughts. He could find no logical explanation for an amazing happening. In the corner, Stones, re-arranging Walford's make-up, looked up.

"Did you see the lady, Mr. Walford?" he asked.

Walford turned on him.

"Mind your own damn' business," he said.

As they faced each other over the polished oak dining-table, the antiquity of which was in keeping with the ancient room, the thought came to Mr. Walford that he had ceased to be anything except a straw carried on some current of circumstances over which he had no control.

Things which he had desired to happen seemed to be happening. On several occasions during previous visits to Warchester he had admired the exterior of the house in which he now sat; had almost wished that he had the nerve—common to most would-be sightseers—to ring the bell and ask if he might look over it.

Their meal had been just as comfortable a one as the circumstances merited; their conversation a little forced as if each were keeping up a pretence. Mr. Walford found himself intrigued as to the purpose of this invitation.

Had it been one of Warchester's "county" ladies—a member of one of those hard-riding or drinking families which had made the Warchester-under-Lyne country famous—he would have understood readily; he would have understood the sudden desire for intimacy on the part of a woman whose life is mainly made up of repressions and conventionalities, but, as he permitted himself to glance at the face of the girl who sat opposite to him, he could not bring himself to think that this could possibly be the case.

I might throw an additional light on Walford's character by saying quite frankly that had the invitation been one given by one of the aforesaid "country" ladies it would not have been accepted. Walford was no prig, and certainly not a saint, but, as he would himself have put it, "he preferred to do his own hunting," and patronising attempts at familiarity were inclined to leave him quite cold.

For the end of September the night was strangely warm,

and through the double windows, opened on to the lawn at the back of the house, came a dozen sweet mingled scents, those indescribable scents of countryside nights. Above, Walford could see in the sky groups of stars, and one bright one standing out from the rest which, he thought with a little amusement, might be his own particular star. Busily cracking walnuts for her, he wondered whether it were possible that in say twenty minutes' time he would have bidden her adieu and been preparing to drive back to the town, but he found himself believing and hoping that this would not be so; he felt instinctively that there must be something else, and he hoped that he would know soon what this something was.

He had not long to wait. She spoke quite suddenly. She seemed to think of things suddenly, and again he had the impression which he had received when he had talked to her in the stage-door of the music-hall, the feeling that she found difficulty in speaking, not because she was afraid to speak, but because she feared his reactions to what she had to say. She spoke slowly, seemingly careful of the words which, belonging to a strange language to her, should have their proper value.

"I know," she said, "that you are wondering why I have asked you to come here to-night. Possibly you have received such invitations before. If you have you will have thought that they have not been from people who are exactly like myself, so that if my explanation is a little lengthy you will understand that I make it in order that you may not misunderstand me.

"I have not bothered to tell you who I am. I think that it is possible that you know."

Walford nodded.

"I am glad," she went on, "that you do know. I do not know very much of life, having been brought up in the rather close confines of a foreign court where people's morals are of such small account that those of a few of us need careful guarding. Mine always have been. I have never known one iota of the freedom which is the common experience of your well-bred English girls. All my life I have been watched—guarded. This little oasis of freedom which has come to me now, these two months spent here in this house which I have hired, accompanied only by one intimate friend, a woman in whom my parents have complete confidence, but who, thank heaven, is human enough to allow me to do as I wish during this short period, has been bought with my life.

"You seem surprised, but it is not very surprising. If you have read your papers you will know that next month I go to my own country to be married. I do not know the man; therefore I cannot love him. It is one of those matches to which unfortunate people like myself are born, but, as far as I was able, I fought and struggled against it. Unfortunately," she smiled unhappily, "my struggles were unavailing. I believe they always are in cases like my own. There are so many very logical reasons which can be adduced as to why we should do things that we do not wish to do, reasons which our brain must see, although our heart loathes them, but I got something from my bargaining. In return for my consent to this match, my agreement to be reasonable, and not to make unnecessary trouble, I secured permission to live my own life for these two months."

Walford nodded.

"I shall always remember that," she continued. "They have been blessed with a few happy memories. I have even experienced loneliness, such a charming experience when one is not used to it. I have known the joys of walking over the countryside alone, of thinking and of saying the things I wish to think and say. I had been almost content to accept the five weeks which I have spent here as being worth a little of the years of boredom which I feel are awaiting me, but to-night I was not content. That is my explanation."

186

Lewis Walford's fingers played nervously with the engraved handle of a fruit-knife.

"I understand," he said. "In a little way I can realise how you feel, and how you think, but I still do not understand why I have been necessary to complete the little picture which you have built for yourself during these weeks of freedom, a picture which I understand will be useful to you to look upon in the time to come."

She smiled.

"Do you not understand? I will tell you why I think you were necessary. When I saw you on the stage to-night, knowing nothing of you, I believed many things about you. I think that you are a man of whom I have often thought. I believe, and I believe it more every minute, that I love you."

v

LEWIS WALFORD, walking slowly in the sunshine across the Cathedral Square, realised that life had indeed turned many pages quickly for him. The sun was shining. It had shone all through the days of this week. It seemed *natural* that it should shine. Used to analysing his impressions of life, he found that he had now no desire to analyse, that he wished only to accept unquestionably the rather wonderful things which were happening to him. Oddly enough, he did not even want to think very deeply about them in case his thoughts would end in the realisation that to-day was Friday, and that Sunday would find him with his two trunks and Stones at the railway station waiting for the train en route for his next town.

His hand, in his pocket, encountered a little roll of notes, the balance left of the money which he had secured by pledging his tie-pin. His steps had brought him outside the jeweller's shop which possessed a pledge department round the corner, and he stood vaguely looking at the assortment of jewellery in the window. His eye was taken by a little gold loving-cup which stood on a velvet cushion in the centre of the window. It was very old, and an inscription underneath said that it had been found when the foundations of the original Warchester Cathedral were excavated. The price was seventy guineas.

Quite slowly, and as if his mind were elsewhere, Walford walked round the corner and entered the pledge office. He nodded in reply to the assistant's "Good-morning"; the man remembered him.

"I pawned a pin with you on Monday, you remember," said Walford, "for £30. I want to sell it. Will you give me another seventy guineas? I paid £200 for the pin."

The assistant went off, and, after a little discussion, returned with the owner of the shop. He held the pin in his hand.

"Good-morning, Mr. Walford," he said, "excuse me saying so, but I admired your turn very much last night. I will willingly give you another seventy guineas for this pin, but—and I am not saying this in my own interest—it is really worth more. It's a very fine pin."

Walford smiled.

"I know that," he said, "but you see I want that gold cup which I see costs seventy guineas, and I have rather got an idea that I don't want any balance. I'm fond of the pin, and I'd like to give the pin up for the cup. Weird people, you know, we music-hall artistes."

The jeweller smiled and brought the cup. Fingering it, Walford knew that she would like it.

"It's very thin," said the jeweller, "but it's hundreds of years old, and it hasn't been touched at all except we've reinforced the base, but it's been done very well, and the gold exactly matches."

"Keep the pin," said Walford, "and I will take it. Will you have engraved 'From L. W.' underneath the base of the cup, and I will call for it to-morrow morning. Can you do it in the time?"

"Oh, yes, Mr. Walford," said the jeweller. "I'll have it done. If you come in to-morrow morning I'll have it packed up, and you receipt ready. Good-morning, Mr. Walford."

Outside, the artiste wandered slowly in the direction of the music-hall to see if there was any mail. He was glad about the loving-cup. Somehow, in some indefinable manner, the pawning of his pin to pay for the suit which he had worn when she had first seen him, the surrendering of the pin in order to acquire the cup to give to her as a souvenir of this wonderful week, these things seemed pre-destined by a fate which, for once, had smiled very kindly on that Lewis Walford who used to drive a pen in a cheap lawyer's office, and who now sang songs on the music-halls.

Because in Walford there was some philosophical strain, he could feel no acute disappointment that the parting must come soon. You cannot bargain with fate, but where other people would have *said* this, Walford believed and *felt it*. He must not allow himself to be disappointed. He must not meet this kindly fate with a frown because his joy could not go on for ever. He must only remember always, and remembering, count himself lucky.

He gave her the cup in the garden. The moon shed, it seemed to Walford, an extra wonderfully vivid radiance over the smooth lawn, illuminating with a thousand little diamond-like lights the edges of leaves, reflecting on the clumps of chrysanthemums and the tall heads of dahlias which, clustering together, seemed to bow their heads in acquiescence to the soft night winds. This radiance enwrapt them and their little world, this transient, wonderful world which belonged to them only, in a silver mantle. The thought brought back very vividly to Walford some words of a prayer he had heard years before when, to evade a rainstorm, he had taken shelter in a chapel in another country town—" O Blessed Virgin, wrap me in the blue mantle of thy love." He repeated them as he walked back—for somehow he could not bear the idea of driving back by himself—towards Warchester. The country road, brilliant in the moonlight, stretched like a wide ribbon before him. Standing on the top of the little hill, he looked back and saw her, tall and gracious, a slim white figure, rather lonely in the centre of a green lawn silvered by moonlight. He raised his hand in farewell. Before him, in the valley, were the twinkling lights of Warchester. Their movement reminded him of the activity, the busy-ness, of life. Behind him was that peace which is love, which comes only once to any man.

The bustle of Warchester station on Sunday morning, with the music-hall company taking its several separate routes, bidding noisy farewells, and shouting good-humoured messages to their distant members of the profession, left Walford unmoved. Standing alone on the platform, with Stones sitting on his two trunks some yards away and watching his master covertly, having come to the conclusion that " something radical had happened to Mr. Walford," Walford had succeeded in evading the too pressing attentions of Miss Lottie Carston who, he thanked his stars, was not playing on the same bill next week.

Soon after, as his train pulled slowly out of the station, and then as Warchester disappeared with the sun glinting on its spires, sitting alone in his compartment, Walford opened the little package which had been left early that morning at his hotel. He put on one side the little box, and read the note :

" MY FRIEND,—I wanted you to have something so that you might remember. This was all I could find which seemed to me to look like you. Will you wear it for me? For ever yours, A."

He knew before he opened the box that in it was his pin. Somehow, the old tailor, he and she, the suit, the loving-cup and the pin were but the happy instruments of fate.

Stones put his head round the carriage door.

"Mr. Lowell of Lowell & Harvey's on the train, and wants to know if you will join them in a game of poker."

Walford looked up with a smile. Last Sunday Stones had uttered practically the same words on the journey to Warchester . . . last Sunday . . . a thousand years ago.

"Tell Mr. Lowell I won't play, but I'll come and watch them," said Walford. He smiled more broadly. "Tell him it's against my rules. I'll be along in a minute, Stones"

Stones went off, and Walford sat gazing before him, with unseeing eyes, fingering the pin.

GUN MOLL BLUES

When there's hooch then I'll drink it to Sadie—
Just a hocha with nothin' to lose,
What a hot little stand-'em-up lady;
What a dame when she laid off the booze;
What a racketeers' high-steppin' baby,
Full of pep, dope an' what have you got,
With an eye for a guy that said maybe,
An' a raw tonge that said maybe not.
On champagne she'd hand out a fan dance,
And on rye could she chant Gun Moll Blues?
When there's hooch then I'll drink it to Sadie,
Just a hocha with nothin' to lose.

Scraut was a shyster lawyer an' he was as good as they go,
As crooked as hell, but at law he was swell, there was
    nothin' that guy didn't know.
When some mobster was pulled for a shootin', an' his pals
    heard the news of the pinch,
Then for Scraut some thug's dame would go rootin' an' by
    morn he'd be out for a cinch.
What a guy, what a law-bustin' twicer, there was no thug
    that he couldn't spring,
Why he'd got half the town in his pocket an' cops just
    meant nothin' to him.

He'd every durn thing that he wanted; he was sittin' on
    top of the game;
He'd got power an' dough stacked for burnin', but he
    wanted some other guy's dame.
An' Scraut had to have what he fancied, you see he was
    that sort of cuss,
But he liked to fix things nice an' easy—no shootin', no
    shoutin', no fuss.

Now dames is a strange proposition—contrary—are you
    tellin' me?
Listen mugs, I'll explain the position, an' it wasn't so easy
    you see;
For this dame that Ed Scraut was so stuck on—what a
    shape in a tight evenin' gown—
She was Frank Ritti's own sugar baby—the cutest gun
    moll around town.

Now was that jane Sadie a honey? Was she good? Had
    she got this an' that?
With an ankle that made guys walk backwards, an' a lot
    of brains under her hat.
She'd got charm, sex-appeal an' what have you. She'd got
    eyes like the light of the moon;
She'd a figure that caused ten divorces an' her walk made
    tired business men swoon.

Frank Ritti was sure a swell mobster; a torpedo—a death-
    dealin' wop.
The king of a dozen big rackets, an' like wops didn't
    know when to stop.
He'd been mixed in a hundred bad killin's, an' things was
    a trifle too hot,
For one day the cops called the Feds in, an' it seemed he
    was set for the spot.

G-men are a mean proposition. As coppers they're durned
    hard to beat.
They reckoned that Frank was just poison, they'd got him
    all set for the heat.
An' Frank knew he'd better be scrammin', until things
    blew over a bit,
So he went to see Scraut for the say-so, and Scraut told
    him straight he must quit.

"You don't stand a chance, Frank," he told him, "that
    last job of yours was a wham.
If they get you this time, kid, they'll burn you; here's a
    tip, take it now on the lam."

Ritti scrammed. He knew that he had to. He was hot an'
    he wasn't a sap.
He knew that the Feds burned to get him, but he thought
    he could sure beat the rap,
So he cleaned up, pulled in all his money, got his auto, a
    gun, an' pushed out.
An' believe me or not he turned the durn lot for safe
    keepin' to—who d'you think—Scraut!

Yes, he handed that shyster the kitty—well, Frank was a
    sap if you like,
An' there was Ed Scraut sittin' pretty, with the dough,
    while the wop took the hike.
The Feds an' the state cops went after, they said they'd
    run Frank to a stand;
And Washington put a reward up—some dough let me tell
    you—ten grand.

Now Sadie was left in a room-house, with no dough, she
    was feelin' right out,
But soon after some guy comes an' tells her to go round
    an' talk turkey to Scraut.

"Listen, baby," says Scraut, "here's a straight one. I'm
    tellin' you Ritti's all through,
The coppers are certain to get him, an' then what are you
    goin' to do?
Now he was all right when he had it, but he ain't goin'
    to worry for you—
Use your brains, kid, if you pull a fast one, you can get
    yourself outa the stew."

"You don't have to tell me," says Sadie. "An' believe me,
  I'm listenin', see.
I ain't no wop's run-around lady, an' Ritti means nothin'
  to me.
If you got an idea, well, just spill it, if it's good, well I'm
  here on the mat.
If it's bad, O.K., honey, I'll kill it, so shoot it from under
  your hat."

Scraut sits at his desk blowin' smoke-rings, an' the moll
  takes her powder-puff out,
An' while she is shiftin' the nose shine, her eyes, like a
  cat's, are on Scraut.

At last he says, "Kid, here's an earful. There's ten thou-
  sand reward out for Frank.
If you know where the wop's got his hideout, why the ten
  grand is right in the bank.
Let's shoot the works. You give the say so, let 'em pinch
  him, he'll sure get the heat,
While we get the jack; hit the high spots. How's it go?
  Ain't it right up your street?"

Sadie thinks, then she walks to the window, an' stands
  for a bit lookin' out.
Then she turns an' she laughs like a jackal, then she
  swings her hips over to Scraut.

"I'm sold, boy," she says, "an' I'll do it. Ritti's washed
  up. He always was slow.
I'll tell you just how they can get him, an' we'll take a
  run an' the dough.

"I've a date with the wop at a garage. It's ten miles out
  of town, just a dump.
It's a frame house that just holds a roadster, with a loft
  up above an' a pump.

It's a place Frank's been runnin' for months now, an' he'll
  meet me there now he's blown town.
Now the front of this dump is a shutter that you work
  with a switch up an' down.

"Up above there's a loft. There's a phone there, an' a
  table, there's no stair nor door.
There's only a trap an' a ladder leadin' right down on to
  the ground floor.

"Now get this, Scraut. Here's how we do it, an' it looks
  pretty easy to me.
We just have to have it all fixed up so there won't be no
  flowers for me.

"Thursday night Ritti drives to this garage, an' he'll
  drive right inside that's a cinch.
As he drives in why I pull the switch down an' scram
  outside quick—what a pinch?

"Before Ritti knows what I'm doin' or jumps out, the old
  iron shutters drops,
An' you're up above in the loft, see? An' you phone to
  town for the cops.

"He can't get at you for the trapdoor is bolted your side,
  honey, see?
Then I take a dive for my auto so the cops don't have
  nothin' on me.

"They'll be there pronto an' get him, they'll fill that wop
  right up with lead.
An' when the war's over you come down, an' claim the
  reward like you said.

"But don't forget, Scraut, that we're splittin', an' five
  grand is comin' to me.
An' when it's blown over I'll meet you; we'll go places
  together, kid, see?"

196

Scraut got up an' his pig's eyes were shinin'. "Gee,
    Sadie," he says, " you're a wow.
What a scheme, it's a cinch an' I'll do it. Then will we
    hit the high spots an' how?"

What a set-up. What a sweet pair of crossers. Well,
    dames are like that, as for Scraut,
Why, that crook would have crossed his own mother,
    and laughed when she started to shout.

So they got it all fixed on a schedule, and they soaked up
    a bottle of gin.
An' Sadie was drinkin' to Frankie, an' just what was
    comin' to him.
As for Scraut, why he thought it durn funny, for Frank
    to be crossed by a jane,
While he'd got the sucker wop's money, an' he laughed
    till it gave him a pain.

Thursday night Scraut was set in the garage, as he sat in
    the dark in the loft.
He'd made sure that the trapdoor was bolted, for he knew
    when Frank found he'd been crossed,
He'd start to raise hell, fire and murder; he'd sure try to
    shoot his way out.
But he couldn't get up to the loft floor, which was all
    Scraut had worried about.

Pretty soon his quick ears heard Frank comin'. In the
    quiet of the night country air,
The sound of a big car came hummin', an' in no time
    Frank Ritti was there.
Downstairs Scraut heard Sadie say, "Hey, Frank, drive
    her in, I've put juice in the pump."
Then he heard her run, grinned as Frank shouted, and
    the shutter came down with a bump.

He could hear Sadie laugh from the roadway, he could hear Ritti cursing like hell.
As he called Sadie all he could think of, and smashed at the shutter as well.
But the shutter was good, Frank was netted, he was caught like a rat in a trap.
He'd been fixed by his own sugar baby, Frank Ritti—the Big Shot—the sap!

Scraut grabbed up the phone, rang headquarters, an' said he'd got Frank on the beat.
The cops said they'd come around pronto, they were all set to hand Frank the heat.
They reckoned to give him a drum full, to fill him right up full of lead.
They knew if they pinched him he'd fix it, but you can't break a jail if you're dead.

Scraut put down the phone. He was grinnin', an' he smoked as he sat on the floor.
Below he could hear Frank still cursin' an' Scraut reckoned that wop must be sore.
Then suddenly—there in the darkness—the phone rang. Scraut sweated with fear.
He didn't know why, but it got him, when he heard Sadie's voice in his ear.

"Well, you cheap double-crosser—you fixer, you twicer, you double-faced clam,
I've got you on the spot, Mr. Lawyer, an' I reckon you're sure in a jam.
You thought I was playin' your game, Scraut, an' that's where you made a mistake.
I was playin' my own, how d'you like it, an' I'm sittin' in right on the take.

"Now listen. You've just got one chance, Scraut. An' it's
    six to four you'll get yours.
Cos why, well because there's a gas pipe, that runs
    through the two garage floors.
Through the pipe in the loft where you're sittin', is a hole
    that is out of your reach.
I've just turned the gas on at the main, kid. How d'you
    like it? Can you smell it? Well, screech.
You poor fish . . . so you're frightened. Take it easy, you
    don't have to shout.
Just control yourself, baby, an' listen, an' maybe there is a
    way out."

Scraut sweated. The gas gettin' stronger, made his nostrils
    distend wide with fear.
He could feel the dark air gettin' thicker, his brain
    wouldn't work—he felt queer.
Then through the phone he heard Sadie, she was laughin'
    an' it sounded like ice.
Then she stopped an' he heard her start talkin'. "Listen,
    Scraut, you can win . . . at a price.

"In the garage Frank's waitin' the coppers, he'll wait
    with a gun in his mitt.
He'll shoot it out—die like a mobster, not a weak-kneed
    law-snivellin' nit.
Now up in that loft is a pistol. Go get it . . . do you think
    that sounds grim?
Then go down the trapdoor, fight Ritti. You've got just
    one chance . . . you or him.
But if you stay there you're a goner, for that gas must
    be lousy by now.
An' another ten minutes will find you, as dead as
    Maloney's old cow.
There's your choice . . . you two-faced crook shyster, you
    never thought you could be wrong.
Well, have you thought what you're askin'? Is it gas or
    a bullet? So long!"

Scraut found the gun, slouched to the trapdoor, half
  asleep from 'he gas-tainted air;
Then he breathed as he flung it wide open, and he crept
  down the rickety sair,
To the garage beneath. . . . When he made it, he cursed
  and he raged at the sight,
For the shutter was up . . . Ritti vanished . . . and Scraut
  gazed straight into the night.

He cursed and he raved like a madman, at the game the
  cute Sadie had played.
Then he sucked in the air, threw the gun down, and out
  into the darkness he swayed.

Well, 'hey found him next morning in tatters. He was
  just like that—tatters and tags.
For the coppers who waited for Frankie had blasted
  Scraut right into rags.

When there's hooch then I'll drink it to Sadie—
Just a hocha with nothin' to lose,
What a hot little stand-'em up lady;
What a dame when she laid off the booze;
What a racketeers' high-steppin' baby,
Full of pep, dope an' what have you got,
With an eye for a guy that said maybe,
An' a raw tongue that said maybe not.
On champagne she'd hand out a fan dance,
An' on rye could she chant Gun Moll Blues?
When there's hooch then I'll drink it to Sadie,
Just a hocha with nothin' to lose.

HONOUR AMONG THIEVES

WHEN Detective-Inspector Mardy Brown was assigned to the Palmont platinum case he sent Sergeant Heathers to look over the ground first.

This was his invariable rule, for Heathers, a young and efficient detective, would come back filled with theories, which Mardy Brown used or discarded as he found necessary.

The outline of the case which the Detective-Inspector had received from the Assistant Commissioner was as follows:

Some time between six and eight o'clock on the morning of Monday, June 20th, twelve large diamonds, which were temporarily set in a platinum casting, had been stolen from the safe of Geoffrey Palmont, a dealer in precious stones. The safe was let into the wall in the dining-room, and had been opened in the ordinary way by someone who, by some means, had secured the combination of the safe lock. Other articles of value in the safe were untouched.

Mardy Brown was assigned to the case at ten o'clock on the morning after the discovery of the robbery, the local police having failed to find any clue on which they could adequately work. He sent off Heathers immediately, and at twelve-thirty that worthy returned, threw his hat in the corner, and plumped himself into a seat opposite his chief's desk.

"This mystery is over, Chief," he said.

Mardy Brown looked up. As usual, he was busily engaged in chewing gum.

"That's quick work, Heathers," he said, "but as usual, I expect you're wrong. Who did it?"

Heathers grinned. "Listen here," he said, "supposing I were to tell you that at half-past seven on the morning of the robbery The Floater—supposed to be a very respectable workman employed by a firm which had contracted to vacuum-clean the morning room at the Palmont's—spent three-quarters of an hour in that room. Well?"

Mardy Brown whistled. "The Floater!"

He thought for a moment. "That's all very well, Heathers," he said, "but I don't see anything wrong in The Floater doing an honest job of work. You know, he told me he was going straight when he came out five months ago, and I felt rather inclined to believe him. Another thing, have you ever known The Floater to open a safe by means of the combination? He's a blow-pipe expert. Give him an oxy-acetylene apparatus, and he'll open anything including a battleship. But if you mean to tell me that The Floater would open a safe with his finger-tips or that he fluked a knowledge of the combination, well, I don't believe you."

"Just a minute," said Heathers, "there's more to this. Supposing there was somebody in the flat who could have given him the combination—somebody who had overheard it or watched Mr. Palmont opening the safe, what would you say then?"

Mardy Brown considered, chewing voraciously.

"Well, then I might start believing it," he said.

Heathers drew his chair a little closer.

"All right then," he said. "Well, listen to this. Do you remember that swell-looking girl—the one we used to call The Countess—the girl that The Floater was so sweet on?"

Mardy Brown nodded.

"All right," the other continued. "Well, she's the housemaid at the Palmont flat. Now, what do you think?"

Mardy Brown scratched the side of his nose reflectively.

"I still don't think The Floater did it," he said. "He's an independent cuss. I can't see him putting in his girl as a housemaid in order to find out the combination of a flat, getting himself a job with a company that's going to vacuum-clean it, and sitting down and waiting until the time was ripe to pull the job. He hasn't got the patience, and he hasn't got the brains."

Heathers' face expressed amazement.

"You beat me, Chief," he said. "The evidence in this case is sticking out a foot. You've got two crooks inside the flat—The Floater and The Countess. The Floater walks out at seven-thirty and at nine-ten the robbery is discovered, and you say that he isn't in it."

"I don't say anything," said Mardy Brown. "Maybe he is the man, but, if so, he's changed his methods. Where's the girl now?"

"She's still there," answered Heathers. "She's done her hair differently and dyed it, but I recognised her in a minute. I wasn't fool enough to let her see, though. She thinks she's got away with it, and that I don't know who she is."

Mardy Brown grunted. "Where's The Floater?" he said.

"At his usual address," said Mardy Brown. "On what charge are you going to arrest him? Suspicion? I didn't know you could arrest a man for that. And, even supposing he did pull that job, do you think he's going to have those diamonds hanging round just where you can see 'em? They'd be miles away by this time. You've got a couple of good pointers, but that's all you have got."

The Detective-Inspector inserted another slab of chewing gum into his mouth.

"You lay off this, Heathers," he said, "and hand me my hat."

He rose to his feet, a short, chubby man of five feet five, with a round, placid face and a bland and innocent ex-

203

pression which had been the undoing of many very clever criminals. He put on his bowler hat slightly over one eye, and left the office, still chewing.

Heathers regarded his retreating figure with amazement.

A half an hour afterwards Mardy Brown, having taken a taxi, knocked at the door of the ramshackle building which housed The Floater, otherwise Mr. William O'Hagan Gollett, a large and powerful gentleman of Irish ancestry, who had made the acquaintance at different times of most of his Majesty's prisons, usually on a charge of safe-blowing.

He greeted Mardy Brown with a smile.

"Mornin', Chief," said The Floater.

"Morning, Floater," said Mardy Brown.

He sat down, and put his hat under the chair. Then he produced another packet of chewing-gum, and, after offering it to the other, selected a slab, and continued chewing. He came to the point at once.

"Know anything about this business at the Palmonts' flat, Floater?" he asked.

The Floater looked thoroughly grieved.

"Oh, go on, now, go on," he said. "I s'pose you're going to tell me I did it! First thin' I knew about it was when I saw it in the paper this mornin'. I said to meself, I said, if that safe 'ad been bust open instid o' bein' opened gentlemanly like in the proper way, they'd 'ave said it was me."

Mardy Brown nodded. "You know, Floater," he said, "it doesn't look so good for you."

"What d'yer mean?" said The Floater.

"Just this," said Mardy Brown. "You were at that place at seven-thirty yesterday morning working a vacuum-cleaner in the room where the safe was, and your girl— The Countess—has been employed there for some months as a housemaid. Well, it doesn't look so good, does it? A lot of people might think that you two had got some game on together. A lot of people might think that The

204

Countess had found out the safe combination; easy enough for a quick-eyed woman like her to watch Mr. Palmont when he opened the safe and to see what the figures were. It would be easy enough for her to slip that information to you, and you get away with the stuff, now, wouldn't it, Floater?"

The face of the cracksman registered deep disgust.

"Well, I thought you knew me better, Chief," he said. "Jist imagine that, now, as if I'd do a job like that now. Listen 'ere."

He drew his chair closer to the other.

"When I came out after that last stretch five months ago didn't I tell yer I was goin' straight?"

Mardy Brown nodded. "You did," he said, "and I believed you."

"All right," said the other. "I got that job with the vacuum-cleanin' company two weeks afterwards, and I've 'ad it ever since. Now, when I went to work there they'd never done any work for the Palmonts, so you can't say I got that job for the purpose o' gettin' inter the Palmonts' flat. An' another thin', what's all this stuff about The Countess bein' my girl? She ain't my girl. She used to be my girl."

Here the face of The Floater registered infinite sadness.

"But she ain't now. She did the dirty on me when I was in quod las' time. She lef' me. Women are like that."

Mardy Brown nodded.

"Not so good, that, Floater," he said. "You know," continued the detective, "I have always had a soft spot for you, and whilst English law presumes that a man is innocent until he's found guilty, with a record like yours things don't look too good for you."

"Oh, really," said The Floater, "don't they? I should worry. Yer know very well yer can't prove anythin'. I've never seen the blooming diamonds. I've never 'ad 'em, and I don't want to."

"All right," said Mardy Brown. "Now, tell me, what time did you leave that flat?"

"I lef' at eight o'clock," said The Floater.

"And what did you do then?" asked the detective.

"I put the vacuum-cleaner an' all the paraphernalia on the van," he said, "an' sent it back to the office."

"I see," said Mardy Brown. "Why didn't you go back with it?"

"'Cause I wanted to 'ave me breakfast," said The Floater, "that's why."

"I see," said Mardy Brown. "Don't you usually go back to the office with the stuff?"

"Yes, I do," said The Floater, "but I didn't feel like it yesterday mornin'."

Mardy Brown looked sad. "That doesn't look so good, does it?" he said. "You know what the ordinary flatfoot would say. He would say you'd passed that stuff to somebody when you got outside that flat, and that's why you didn't go back to the office with the van."

"I don't care what any flatfoot says," said The Floater. "I never took any diamonds. I know when I've took somethin'."

"Do you wear a watch?" asked Mardy Brown suddenly.

The Floater expressed supreme contempt.

"Do I look like the sort of bloke what wears a watch?"

Mardy Brown nodded. "All right, then, how did you know it was eight o'clock when you came out?" he said.

"I'll tell yer," said The Floater. "I thought yer'd be asking me that in a minute. When I got out I was 'ungry, and I made up me mind I'd 'ave some breakfast, so I sent the van off with the stuff, and I started to walk down the road. About fifteen yards away from the Palmonts' there's some offices, and a feller was just goin' inter one of 'em. 'E asked me if I could oblige 'im with a match. I give 'im a match, an' I asked 'im what the time was. 'E tol' me it was five-past eight. That's 'ow I knew."

"I see," said Mardy Brown. "What was he like?"

"'E was a tall, well set up feller," said The Floater, "an' 'e must 'ave worked in these offices 'cause 'e 'adn't got a hat on; looked as if 'e 'ad just been out get somethin'."

"Pretty early to be working in an office," said Mardy Brown. "They don't usually open at eight o'clock."

He leaned towards the other.

"So you think that this fellow who told you the time worked in those offices, do you, Floater?"

"Yes, I do," said The Floater.

"All right," said Mardy Brown. "Do me a favour. Just get your hat and come along with me now. Let's see if we can find this fellow who told you what the time was."

The Floater sniffed. "Think I'm tellin' yer a packet of lies, don't yer?" he said. "I think it's a bit odd when I got to go trapsin' about the place with p'licemen all day. This is my day off, too."

"Never mind, Floater," said Mardy Brown. "If it wasn't you, for once in your life you're on the side of law and order. And, mark you," he continued, "I believe it was."

The Floater grunted in disgust, but said nothing.

Three-quarters of an hour later Mardy Brown and The Floater walked slowly towards the block of offices which lay just past the Palmont flat. Suddenly The Floater put his hand on Mardy Brown's arm.

"There you are, Chief," he said. "There 'e is, the very feller. Now go an' ask 'im."

Mardy Brown looked up. Sure enough, a tall, well set up young man, with a large and Hebraic nose, was just leaving the offices and crossing the road.

"Good enough," said Mardy Brown. "I believe you, Floater."

"Well, why don't yer go an' ask 'im?" said The Floater.

"I don't have to," said Mardy Brown. "You're not such a fool as to tell me he was the man if he wasn't."

He felt in his pocket, and produced a half-crown.

"There's your fare home and a drink, Floater," he said. "Go on."

The other spat on the coin, and pocketed it.

"So I ain't goin' to be pinched to-day, Chief?" he said.

"Not to-day, Floater," said Mardy Brown. "Maybe to-morrow. We'll see. So long."

Mardy Brown, still chewing gum, hailed a taxi-cab and was driven back to the Yard. Arrived there, he sent for Heathers, and gave that worthy instructions that The Countess was to be kept under close observation, shadowed everywhere, and a description of anybody she might meet carefully taken.

Heathers grinned. "So you're coming round to my way of thinking, Chief," he said.

"Coming round to nothing," said Mardy Brown. "Get on with it."

After that he wandered along to the photographic room, and spent a long time going through lists of photographs. When he came to that of The Countess he spent quite some time gazing at the picture of the good-looking girl. She was good-looking! In his heart Mardy Brown felt a little bit sorry for The Floater. It must be hard for a slow and bovine mentality such as that of the cracksman to be left in the lurch by a pretty girl like The Countess.

Eventually he left the photo gallery, and went out to lunch, this being the only time when he ceased chewing gum.

At two o'clock he returned to his room, and at three o'clock his telephone-bell rang.

"That the Chief?" asked a voice. "This is Detective Bayford, No. 4726, speaking. Sergeant Heathers instructed me to pick up the housemaid at the Palmont flat. She was given a day off to-day, and left the flat at half-past twelve. She went to a little café near Victoria, and met a man there—tall, good-looking young fellow with a Jewish nose. They had lunch together. Then he returned to a set of offices in Victoria Street, and she went back to the flat. That's all, sir."

"Thank you very much," said Mardy Brown. "That's all right. You can come off that job now. I know all I want to. Meet me outside those offices in twenty minutes."

He replaced the receiver, picked up the office phone and got Heathers' room.

"That you, Heathers?" he said. "Meet me at the entrance, will you, and take a pair of handcuffs with you."

"You bet, Chief," said Heathers. "You going to 'pinch' The Floater?"

"I'll 'pinch' you in a minute," said Mardy Brown, picking up his hat.

The two officers took a taxi-cab, and drove to the offices in Victoria Street. Here Bayford met them, and together the three men entered the building.

Five minutes later in an office on the second floor Mardy Brown faced a tall, good-looking young man.

"Hullo, laddie," he said. "We want you."

The young man stiffened. "May I ask what for?" he asked insolently.

"You may," said Mardy Brown. "The Palmont diamonds job."

"I don't know what you're talking about," said the other.

Mardy Brown inserted another piece of chewing-gum into his mouth.

"Heathers," he said, "go round to the Palmont flat and arrest The Countess."

He turned to the young man. "You're a slick pair," he said, "but the little job didn't come off. Mark you, it was one of the cleverest ideas I've ever struck in my life. Whilst The Floater was in prison, The Countess gave him the chuck, and joined up with you, but, you know, our records at the Yard are pretty good. You're both of you experienced pickpockets. I expect it was your idea to lift the Palmont diamonds, and that's why she got that job in the flat. She had plenty of opportunities for seeing what the combination on the safe was.

"But wasn't it a wonderful idea that you had when you heard that the poor old Floater, who was going straight, was the man who was coming round to do the vacuum-cleaning? Which of you was it got that big idea?"

Mardy Brown's blue eyes bored into those of the young man.

Heathers, who had not yet gone, and Bayford, looked at their Chief in amazement.

"It was a big idea," continued Mardy Brown. "Shall I tell you what you did? Knowing that The Floater was going to be at the flat at seven-thirty, The Countess opened the safe and took the diamonds at seven o'clock. I expect the poor old Floater was pretty surprised to see her there, and as he was going out, probably asked her to return to him. Whilst he was talking she slipped the diamonds into the pocket of his coat. When he came out you were waiting for him. You went up to him, and asked him for a match, and, whilst he was fumbling in one pocket, you picked the diamonds out of the other. And if it hadn't been for the fact that The Floater had asked you what the time was, and, if I hadn't disbelieved him and made him take me along to show me where he met you, and, if you hadn't been coming out of the offices at that very moment, I expect your little plot would have succeeded and we should have 'pinched' The Floater. But when I saw you," said Mardy Brown, with a grin, "I remembered you. Take him along, boys."

THE MAN WITH THE EYEGLASS

From the narrative of Helena Barckham—
Private Detective

I AM not a private detective in the ordinary sense of the word. I have always specialised in tracing missing, or stolen, works of art, checking up on art counterfeiting, tracing originals of antiques and other business of this sort.

The strangest case in which I ever found myself concerned was that of the Massaq Corot. This priceless picture—an invaluable work of art—was stolen from Leplow House, a north country mansion which was then rented by the Graf von Massaq, the German collector.

After some investigation I got into touch with Gerda ——, a very beautiful Swedish woman who had been mixed up in several businesses of a like sort. Through her I saw the famous (or infamous) and charming Gerard Darracqual, probably the first picture thief in the world, commonly known as The Man With The Eyeglass.

We found the picture, but the story of the theft is more than interesting. Here it is:

One evening as Darracqual was arranging to his fastidious satisfaction his white tie before going out to dinner, Valatz, his valet—and accomplice—informed him that no less a person than Gerda —— was waiting downstairs to see him.

Darracqual smiled. He expected trouble with Gerda.

A few minutes later he went down.

She was, as usual, exquisitely dressed, and looked more beautiful than ever. Darracqual gave her a cigarette.

"What is it, my dear?" he asked. "What's the job this time?"

She smiled, showing her lovely teeth.

"I come to see you about two things," she said in her soft, broken English. "First, don't you remember that once you said you would like to marry me? Well—I am ready!"

Darracqual laughed.

"But you didn't take me seriously, did you?" he said. "And haven't you heard that I am going to be married soon?"

Her eyes narrowed.

"So it is true," she murmured. "Very well, Gerard, but remember that no woman could make you as happy as I could. But enough of this—let me talk to you about the second thing, since I no longer appeal to you."

She told him her plan. It was nothing less than the stealing of the Massaq Corot from Leplow House. The picture, part of Massaq's collection, was easy to get. There was no watchman. Gerda had a marvellous copy of the picture in her possession that could take the place of the original and that would deceive a casual inspection long enough for the original to be got into Belgium, where she had a purchaser who would pay a good price and resell in America.

She thought it would be the perfect ending for Gerard's career and he was inclined to agree.

She had photographs and plans of the house; the picture gallery, the grounds—everything. All the spade work had been done. All that remained was for Darracqual and Valatz to get into the house, cut out the picture, and get it out to the car that would be waiting near by, putting the copy in its place.

Darracqual thought for a while and then agreed to do the job. He was to go fifty-fifty with her.

They arranged details and then he helped her into her

furs. She looked out of the window at the thick London fog and made a grimace.

"I do not like this country and its fogs," she said. "I had hoped that you and I—" she shrugged her shoulders.

"Au revoir, my friend," she said.

When she had gone, Darracqual rang the bell for Valatz.

That worthy grinned.

"What is it, boss?" he asked. "What's Beautiful got for us this time?"

Darracqual lit a cigar and readjusted his eyeglass.

"I don't know," he murmured. "I don't trust her. And this job looks easy, Valatz—*too* easy. But we'll do it, in our own way."

Four weeks later the theft of the Corot was discovered. The copy, so beautifully done that it had even deceived von Massaq's first casual glance, had been fitted into the original frame.

Scotland Yard was called in and, after three weeks of fruitless investigation, von Massaq offered a reward of two thousand pounds. Two days after this he received an anonymous letter suggesting that if the reward were increased to three thousand "there might be something doing." The increased reward was advertised, and very promptly a letter was received from Gerda ——, who was staying at a London hotel.

I went to see her.

She promptly "sold out" on Darracqual. She gave the date and details as to how the theft had been carried out; informed me that the Corot was, at the moment, in the hands of a receiver in Brussels, where Darracqual was also to be found, and hoped sincerely that her beloved Gerard would get five years!

A wonderful example of "hell having no fury like a woman scorned!"

I went back and reported to von Massaq. Obviously

the woman desired revenge on Darracqual as much as the reward, but the thing was to get the picture back.

Next day I went over to Brussels with a detective-sergeant from Scotland Yard, who was to bring back Darracqual. The Belgian police had been advised of the circumstances and we were met in Brussels by two detectives, who promptly took us round to the receiver indicated by Gerda ——, and who kept a small antique-shop. There I got my first surprise. The Belgian policeman arrested the man on suspicion and then demanded production of the picture. He produced it.

It was also a fake!

I began to be worried and felt that the time had come to use a little tact. We got rid of the Belgian detectives for the moment, and went round to Darracqual's hotel.

He was, as usual, quite charming.

I came to the point quickly. I suggested that if he liked to make it his business to see that the Corot was returned immediately, it was quite possible that he would not be prosecuted.

His smile deepened.

"Miss Barckham," he said, "let me assure you that any prosecution against me would fail; however, as I am always glad to be of use to you I will certainly return to England and interview the Graf von Massaq.

"*Perhaps* I may be of use—who knows?"

I thought that his insolence was superb.

We returned to England the next day and immediately took train for Leplow House. When we arrived there Darracqual proceeded, in his usual suave manner, to talk to von Massaq.

"Let us understand each other, Graf," he said. "You believe that I have stolen your Corot and that you can prosecute me. I shall proceed, in due course, to prove to you that no prosecution could possibly succeed; but before I do this it is essential that I know I shall receive the

214

reward if, through my information, the Corot is recovered.

"*I therefore suggest that you place the sum of three thousand pounds in the hands of Miss Barckham here, with instructions that she is to hand that sum to me when I have done two things—first, showed you how you can recover the Corot, and secondly proved to you that I have never stolen it.*"

After some talk von Massaq agreed.

Darracqual smiled and pointed to the fake Corot hanging on the wall.

"Now, Graf," he said, "if you will remove the very thin stretcher of canvas on which that copy is painted you will find beneath the original Corot.

"*It was never removed from this gallery!*"

Von Massaq gasped.

"I guessed that Gerda —— was out for revenge on me," continued Darracqual, "as well as the reward which she knew would be offered, so instead of removing the picture I merely stretched the copy over it.

"I had caused a second copy to be made and this was the one I took with me to Belgium. I knew that you would chase after that!

"*So you will see that it is impossible to prosecute me for stealing a picture that has never been removed from your house!*

"And, as I think you will agree that you would never have *seen* your Corot again without my assistance, I think that I am entitled to the reward."

Von Massaq walked over to the picture, removed the frame and, with Darracqual's assistance, took off the top stretch of canvas.

Underneath was the real Corot.

After a great deal of argument Darracqual was given a thousand pounds, von Massaq got his picture and everyone was satisfied—except the detective-sergeant, who was annoyed at seeing Darracqual slip through his fingers, and Gerda, who was furious at the failure of her plot against Darracqual.

But, as Darracqual pointed out as he pocketed the £1,000, it is almost impossible to please everyone!

INFORMATION RECEIVED

It is not often that one meets a French detective officer with a sense of humour; but Emile Gaucharde, of the Sûreté Générale, is an exception to this rule. Hence this story:

One evening, in 1927, he and I were sitting outside the Café de la Paix, drinking vermouth and watching the crowds pass. Suddenly, Gaucharde growled and, looking up, I saw that his attention was concentrated on a tall, immaculately dressed and extremely attractive man who was passing near our table.

The man saw Gaucharde, checked, and turned towards us. He was smiling and his aquiline features radiated a wicked good humour.

"Ah, my dear Inspector, it is good to see you again," he said, with a little bow. "Often I have thought of you with the greatest kindness!"

Gaucharde was so furious that he could hardly speak.

"Look here, Kalienski," he spluttered, "don't you dare to speak to me! And watch your step. I've still got my eye on you, my friend!"

The other shrugged and his smile broadened.

"Dear Inspector," he said, speaking excellent French with a Russian accent, "do not mistake me. I do nothing that is wrong. I am always a gentleman; always I remember that I was an officer in the Czar's Imperial Sharpshooters. I would not stoop to anything which might result in my apprehension by you, dear friend!"

He turned away, waved airily to my friend and, still smiling, disappeared into the crowd.

I ordered some more vermouth. Gaucharde drank it and then began to grin.

"I'll tell you about it," he said. "I know you are curious, and you know that it is not often that I tell stories against myself; but that man is one of the few people who have ever had the laugh of me.

"In 1924," he continued, "Paris as you know was filled with Russian *emigrés*. Amongst them was the man who has just passed. He had no passport—few of them had—but it was believed that he was a Russian officer of aristocratic birth; and he called himself Count Feodor Kalienski.

"We were not particularly interested in the gentleman until, after some months, we were informed that he had departed from the paths of virtue and was indulging in a little quiet burglary. All the indications pointed to this information being true. Unfortunately for ourselves, we could never get anything on him.

"Eventually, a robbery occurred at Auteuil. It was carried out in the most superb manner, and it looked very much like Kalienski's work. My chief was livid with rage. He sent for me and told me I was to get the Count somehow; that I was to have him watched night and day. He was to be kept under observation until we got sufficient evidence of some sort or another to arrest him, and if he attempted to leave Paris we were to arrest him on suspicion at the railway station.

"The idea in not arresting him on suspicion immediately was because we hoped that if we allowed him his freedom he might possibly give something away, or do something that would give us a line on which we could get the necessary evidence. He did nothing suspicious, and it looked as if he had done us in the eye again.

"Then, one day a Russian came to see me at the Sûreté Générale. He was a nasty little fellow, a waiter, employed

217

in one of the cheap cafés in Montmartre. He told me he had some rather interesting information about Kalienski.

"His story was this. The Count was at one time very fond of a woman, a Russian, a Madame Stephanie Varovnova. These two, it seemed, had been greatly in love with each other until quite recently, when, apparently, the Count had succumbed to the charms of another lady, and Madame Stephanie was aching for revenge.

"The waiter suggested that a visit to the lady in question might be greatly worth while, as she was in a frame of mind to sink Kalienski.

"I went and saw her, and I must say I was very pleased with the result of my visit. I found her a very beautiful and charming woman—tall, slim, a characteristic Russian lady of the type that refuses to be scorned in love without doing something about it—and if you know anything about Russian women, you know what that means!

"She was unable to give me any information about the Count's past misdeeds, but, and this was very much more important, she was able to give me the exact details of the next coup which he had planned, and which, in a moment of confidence, he had divulged to her.

"Briefly his scheme was as follows. Near the Faubourg St. Antoine was a very large newly-built block of mansion flats. It was an expensive place, replete with every comfort and luxury; and on the fourth floor there was living another Russian known to Kalienski, an *emigré* by the name of Alexandrovitch, who possessed some very fine jewellery, which he had succeeded in getting out of Russia.

"Alexandrovitch had been living on this jewellery, selling it a little at a time. He kept it securely in a wall safe in his sitting-room.

"One of the pieces was a flat platinum and diamond plaque, which was reputed to be worth a couple of hundred thousand francs.

"Some time before, when the Count had been on his beam ends, Alexandrovitch had got him a situation as a valet at this block of flats, and the Count, said Madame, had made good use of his time by making keys to Alexandrovitch's flat and, by a very close observation, learning the combination of the safe.

"Alexandrovitch was leaving Paris, and the Count proposed to walk round one evening to the house, at a time when most of the servants were out of the way, let himself into the flat, take the diamond plaque, and go off with it.

"It was quite a simple business. Even if anyone saw him, they would know that he had been an acquaintance of Alexandrovitch's and would suspect nothing.

"The lady also informed me that the robbery was to take place in a week's time.

"Needless to say, I was delighted, because it looked just the sort of thing that the Count would do. And inquiries which I made the next day showed that he had actually worked at the block of flats.

"I was delighted. I felt that at last I was really going to get my man, and I tell you I had a certain feeling of personal satisfaction at the thought of laying the enterprising Count Feodor Kalienski by the heels.

"So on the night which Madame Varovnova had informed us the robbery was to take place I had the block of mansion flats surrounded. Every entrance was watched. I placed no men inside the place because I wanted Kalienski to carry out the robbery in peace, and it was my intention to arrest him as he left the place afterwards.

"Sure as a gun, at eleven o'clock, immaculately dressed, the Count appeared and sauntered into the apartment house. I gave him time to get upstairs and do the job and then, with Ferrassi and Dupont I walked over and waited inside the entrance.

"Five minutes afterwards Kalienski came down. As he approached the doorway I walked forward to meet him. He gave me a charming smile.

"'Good-evening, Inspector,' he said. 'I am delighted to see you. How do you do?'

"'You can cut all that out, Kalienski,' I told him. 'I am going to arrest you on a charge of burglary and I should advise you to say as little as possible!'

"He raised his eyebrows.

"'Dear Inspector,' he said airily, 'I think you must be a little mad. I do not know what you are talking about. I have just paid a little visit to see my friend Alexandrovitch and discovered that he is out. I would also like you to know that I resent your insulting suggestion and I insist that I be taken to the nearest police station and searched, and that afterwards you make a proper formal apology for your rudeness!'

"I must say I was astonished. However we took him to the nearest police station and searched him and he had nothing on him at all. There was not so much as a smell of a platinum and diamond plaque on the man.

"And, I had to say that I was sorry and let him go! What else could I do?"

"Next evening I was sitting in my office when a letter was brought in to me. I opened it. It was from Kalienski. He said:

"'MY DEAR INSPECTOR,—I regret very much that I have taken the advantage of the present situation in order to shake the dust of Paris from my feet. Much as I hate to leave your so charming city, I considered the process—having regard to all things—necessary.

"'But now let us get down to the business of this platinum and diamond plaque. I know that you will be very surprised to hear that this valuable piece of jewellery will, when my good friend Alexandrovitch returns, be discovered to be missing. Madame Varovnova has been having you on a little piece of string. It was she who was responsible for the robbery, and she, like the clever little woman she is, made you think I was going to do it, detracting attention from her own plot to get it. It was stolen for her by an accomplice.

"'But, because I think you should be compensated for your trouble last night, if you will go round to Madame Varovnova's, I am perfectly certain that you will find the jewellery there. It was sent to her, and arrived at her house this afternoon, in a stout manilla envelope.

"'And you should hurry, because I have reason to believe that she is about to go off to Spain with a new gentleman friend of hers, and I do not think that you should allow it. *Au revoir,* dear Inspector. Feodor Kalienski.'

"I went round immediately to Varovnova's house. She was not in, but on the hall table was the brown manilla envelope which the Count had described.

"We waited for her to return, and asked her to open it. Inside was the plaque.

"Again we were in a difficult position. Madame Varovnova was livid with rage. She said that Kalienski's letter was just a lie; that she had nothing to do with the scheme, except that she had been informed of the plan by Kalienski, and that when we came round to see her she had told us the truth.

"We had nothing against the woman, and yet I could not for the life of me understand why the Count, having got away with the plaque—for I was certain that he had stolen it somehow—should have sent it to her of all people.

"However, I could not explain this situation; therefore I informed Madame Varovnova that—for the moment, anyhow, certainly until the return of Alexandrovitch—she would not be allowed to leave Paris and that she must regard herself as a suspected person until the matter was cleared up.

"This infuriated the lady still more for, as Kalienski had said, she had planned to go off to Spain with a rich gentleman whose acquaintance she had just made.

"A week afterwards, Alexandrovitch returned. We made some more discoveries. The first one was that the diamond plaque which had been sent to Madame Varovnova was an almost perfect imitation of the true one—a fake. The real plaque was gone!"

"So the Count had it after all, Inspector?" I said.

"Oh, no," he said, with an almost piteous expression. "Nobody knew where it was."

"About a fortnight later, Alexandrovitch's insurance company, who was being pressed by him to make good the loss, received a letter from the Count informing them that if they would send twenty thousand francs in a registered envelope to the address in Holland which he gave them, ten days after the receipt of the money, he would tell them where the plaque was.

"As it looked as if they were going to lose two hundred thousand francs, they thought they might as well take another chance. They sent him the twenty thousand francs, and ten days afterwards—for he kept his word—he wrote and told them where the plaque was.

"It was under the carpet in Alexandrovitch's own sitting-room, where Kalienski had put it. It was a diabolically clever bit of business. He knew Varovnova knew of his affair with the other woman, and he realised that she would most certainly give away to us the plan which he had unfolded to her some time before. So he proceeded to turn the whole situation to his own advantage. It was he who sent the Russian waiter to us in the first place, knowing perfectly well that we should go to Varovnova.

"He knew, too, that we should wait downstairs on the night of the robbery. So he had prepared a facsimile of the diamond plaque and arranged for it to be sent round to Varovnova on the afternoon after the burglary.

"When he went upstairs to Alexandrovitch's flat, he opened the safe, took the real plaque, and simply put it under the carpet. No one would look for it there! And he knew that when we stopped him and found nothing on him we should let him go, and also take off our men who were watching him. That gave him his chance to make his getaway from Paris."

"That's all very well, Inspector," I said, "but he passed by here and spoke to you a few minutes ago. Why didn't you arrest him?"

He looked at me wryly.

"On what charge could I arrest him?" he asked. "He never stole the plaque. He simply took it from the safe and put it under the carpet, and on the day that the insurance company sent him the money he wrote a long and affectionate letter to Alexandrovitch, telling him that on the night in question he had gone round to the flat to see Alexandrovitch; that when he arrived there he found the safe open; that it was obvious that someone who knew the safe combination was after the plaque; so he hid the piece of jewellery under the carpet before closing the safe. He also told Alexandrovitch that he was sure that we were trying to hang the burglary on to him, and that he was certain that some friend of Varovnova's had done it!

"Alexandrovitch insisted on believing this, and actually reported me to my chief for trying to hound an honest man!"

Gaucharde gritted his teeth. Then suddenly he broke into laughter.

"The Czar's Imperial Sharpshooters!" he said. "*Mon Dieu*, what a nerve!"

THE GIGOLO

Muskat stood on the corner of Brook Street and Bond Street, waiting for the girl. There was a slight drizzle of rain and he was forced to stand close to the edge of the pavement in order to avoid the hurrying crowd of people who were leaving their work and dashing for buses.

He did not mind waiting. He was feeling pleased with himself, as if he had done something worth while, as if he had, at last, justified his existence.

Lots of women looked at him. He was aware of this fact and regarded it as his due. He was so used to it that he took little notice unless the woman was very attractive or very expensively dressed. Then Muskat would give her a short, sharp look—a practised look—more from habit than actual intent.

He was good-looking. He had a good figure and knew how to hold himself. He was handsome in a peculiarly feminine manner. His skin was good and his mouth well-shaped; but his eyes were too close together.

His clothes were too well cut. His shoes a trifle too pointed. His shirt and collar were of silk and his tie was expensive. He wore a signet ring on the little finger of each hand.

He was a gigolo and had done fairly at his profession. Like most people of his class he was able to find an excuse for his manner of existence. He had tried everything else first, he thought. In fact he had not tried at all. He had slacked and fallen down on every job he had ever had; or he had given it up in order to "find something better." Finding something better meant finding something easier to Muskat.

He might have been a crook but he had not the necessary courage. The idea of going to prison frightened him. He did not like work, or getting up early, or concentrated effort. So he became a gigolo.

But he was sick of it. He was tired of the continuous naggings and pettinesses and instructions and pesterings of the woman who kept him. At first it had seemed not so bad. True she was twenty years older than he was, but at the beginning she had been generous.

Muskat had not feathered his nest sufficiently during the first year of his association with her. He had realised that months ago.

Now she was beginning to economise. Like everyone else her income was depleted. She had reduced expenditure as much as possible. It was true that she had left Muskat to the last. She had not cut his allowance until she had cut everything else. But eventually, as she explained, it had become necessary, and she did it.

He grinned as he thought how very surprised the old girl would be when she came out of the bathroom and found his note. She would be furious—livid—with rage. She would probably have hysterics and curse and shriek and swear like a trooper. Well . . . much he cared.

She could not go to the police. Muskat was certain of that. He knew too much, and some of the letters she had written him would make good reading in a police court. She just daren't do it. He knew that.

He took his platinum cigarette-case out of his pocket and lit a cigarette. He was free! Wonderful thought! To-morrow he would be in Paris with Myra. Maybe he would marry her. Maybe not. But they would have a great time.

And Primpeau would be delighted at getting the bracelet. Muskat knew that the French Jew would pay three thousand pounds for it.

He remembered the night when Primpeau had first seen the bracelet.

Muskat and the old girl had been at a night club on the

Place Pigalle. Primpeau had come in and nodded to Muskat who had met him in a bar a day or two before. Primpeau knew that Muskat was a gigolo. He liked knowing gigolos. He often got very cheaply pieces of jewellery which they had stolen from their women. He sold them in his shop.

Sometimes a woman would recognise her own ring or necklace or whatever it was, and she would come in and buy it back. Primpeau always grinned to himself on these occasions. They seldom asked any questions. They just paid up and took the piece away.

Muskat had joined Primpeau at the American bar. They had cocktails together.

"That's a fine bracelet she's wearing," Primpeau had said. "If they're diamonds it is worth a lot."

"They're diamonds all right," Muskat had answered.

Primpeau had looked at him with a grin.

"I'd pay three thousand for it," he said.

"Perhaps she'll give it to you one day. . . ."

Muskat threw the cigarette away. Primpeau would pay three thousand for it—maybe a bit more.

He looked at his watch. It was nearly half-past seven. Myra was late. He wished she would hurry up.

Somehow Muskat did not dislike the idea of waiting for Myra. She was about the only thing in the world that was worth waiting for, he thought. Yet at the same time if anyone had suggested that his method of living was not one that would commend itself to any woman who called herself " nice," Muskat would have been vaguely annoyed. He was not particularly ashamed of being a gigolo simply because he had never, during the whole course of his life, worried about being mean or petty or dishonest. He was all of those things and thought that everyone else was too, therefore his own peculiar business seemed to be quite an ordinary one to him.

And Myra was possessed of the same weird mentality. She thought that Muskat was a nice man! She was quite unable to see through him and his lies and pretences. She thought that he had just had "hard luck" and was getting along as best he could, and the fact that he "got along" very comfortably by the worst possible means in the world never seemed to trouble her in the slightest degree.

Really she was an empty-headed little thing with hardly any standards but with an apparent fondness and admiration for Muskat.

He lit another cigarette and looked at his watch. He was beginning to get tired of waiting.

He thought about her. The idea of her thrilled him. She was young, so virile, and she thought so much of him. There was no doubt that she loved him passionately. She had always believed in him too. He wondered what she would have thought if she had known how he made his money. . . .

But he knew that she would never have promised to. go with him unless he had money. She worshipped money. Most girls of her sort did. Quite a lot of the mannequins who worked with her were kept, or had an eye on some old gentleman whom they intended to marry. They all wanted what they called "good times."

Well, he had money—or would have to-morrow after he had sold the bracelet to Primpeau. He felt rather pleased at the manner in which he had got it. There was rather an Arsene Lupin touch about the whole business he thought.

He had noticed that the old girl always wore the bracelet when she went out to a cocktail party. When she returned, she would take it off and throw it on to her dressing-table, before she went to bathe and dress for dinner. She left most of her jewellery lying about on the dressing-table, but she always locked the bedroom door after her on her way to the bathroom, and kept the key looped over her finger with a piece of string.

Muskat had waited three weeks to get a chance to take

an impression of that key. He had walked about with a piece of wax in his pocket all that while. At last opportunity came his way.

On her way to the bathroom one night she had met him in the passage and had stopped to kiss him. The key had fallen off her finger and over the balustrade on to the stair-landing below.

He had gone down for it; had pretended to accidentally kick it even further down. Bringing it back to her he had pressed it against the wax cake in the palm of his hand and had got the impression. Getting the key made was easy.

Three-quarters of an hour ago he had got the bracelet. She had gone to a cocktail party wearing it, and also had told him that she would be back again at a quarter to seven and would want him to take her out to dine at eight o'clock. He was to come and pick her up at seven-thirty.

He went back to the house at seven o'clock. He knew that she always spent half an hour in the bathroom with her maid, fussing about with creams and lotions. He let himself quietly into the house with his own key with which she had supplied him; ran quickly up the stairs; listened for a moment at her bedroom door, then unlocked it, entered, picked up the bracelet and walked out of the house. No one had seen him. No one had been about.

Then he had had a quick whisky and soda, just to wish himself good luck, and had gone to meet Myra.

He grinned to himself as he thought of the old girl's face when she went back to the bedroom and found the bracelet gone and, in its place, the note he had left. He imagined her tearing open the envelope with her plump be-ringed fingers and reading what he had written:

"I'm sick of you. I've had enough of you. It was bad enough when you let me have enough money, but since you've been mean it's unbearable. I'm off for good. Of course, you can go to the police but you won't. I've too many letters of yours."

He lit another cigarette.
Where the devil was Myra? It was nearly a quarter to eight. Coming towards him he saw Freda Ballaston—one of the mannequins at Myra's place. He walked towards her.
"Hello, Freda, where the deuce has Myra got to?"
She looked at him with a sly smile.
"Don't you know?" she asked, smirking. "Surely she would have told you. She was married this morning. She married that fellow from the Argentine—the dago. . . . I am surprised that she didn't tell you about it. It's been on for a long time. . . . Well. . . . Good-night. . . ."
She smiled at him again maliciously, and walked off.
Muskat stood transfixed. Then he thought that Freda must be fooling. He dashed up to Bond Street tube station and telephoned Myra's flat.
It was true enough. The housekeeper confirmed it. She had been married that morning. All along she had been making a fool of him. Stringing him . . . laughing at him.
He came out of the telephone booth and walked down Oxford Street cursing. He was livid with rage. To be made a fool of by a girl like Myra!
Soon his anger began to abate. Muskat had not enough character to be angry for long. Anyhow he had the bracelet. He would go over to Paris to-morrow and fix things with Primpeau. There were lots of other girls in the world, just as attractive and young and vital as Myra.
He hailed a taxi and drove to his rooms in Knightsbridge. His disappointment over Myra was, in some measure, appeased by his thoughts of the old girl's fury over the loss of her bracelet. This idea amused him. He was glad that someone else was hurt.
By the time he arrived at his rooms he was almost in

good humour. Life was not so bad and it was going to be better. He would set himself up in Paris. Maybe he would start some business—or better still, find some fool woman—there were lots of them about.

He put his key into the door and opened it. As he switched on the light he noticed an envelope in the letter-box. He picked out the letter and glanced at the handwriting.

It was from the old girl. . . .

He tore open the envelope and read :

"Monkey Dear,

"I know you're fed up with me and I know I've been keeping you short of money, but I haven't been able to help it. Dividends have been bad and it would have been criminal to sell stock with the market like it is.

"But I want to give you a chance and I realise that I'm just an old woman who ought to be through with love, so I've sold my best bracelet this morning. I've had a paste imitation made that looks very good so no one will ever guess.

"And when you come to dine with me to-night I'm going to give you the money and your freedom. Don't be late, dear."

Muskat tore the bracelet-case from his hip pocket and opened it. He took it under the light and stood looking at the worthless imitation.

Outside a taxi-cab hooted.

THE LAST STRAW

From the narrative of Samuel —— of Chicago,
ex-racketeer

"IN my experience guys don't reform until they have to; and they have to when things gets a bit too hot for 'em—see?

"I ain't no moralist. I been paid to bump off guys an' I've bumped 'em off an' slept the same night just like I did when I was a kid. Still, that don't prove nothin'. Maybe other fellers would have kept awake.

"The whole thing is that any guy is liable to go soft; an' if a guy goes soft there's only one reason—a woman. But when a sap in my late profession goes soft it ain't likely to be so good for him. See? Somebody is sure goin' to get him an' there ain't goin' to be any Victoria Cross issued to him after he's dead. *No, Sir!*

"I can tell you a story. It happened in Chicago. Maybe you'll find a moral in it. Some of you writin' guys 'd find a moral even if there wasn't one. Well—here goes."

Charles Letten was all right until he linked up with Hymie Characq—commonly known as "French," and Rosanna was all right until she linked up with Charles. Then the trouble started.

Charles was all right. He was working for a big firm of wholesale stationers, and everything was going well until he started to poke his nose into things that didn't concern him. That's when he got up against French. French gave him the opportunity of being "taken for a ride," right away, or joining up with the gang.

Charles didn't want to die, so he joined up.

A year or so ago bad men in Chicago used to be pretty bad, believe me, and French was probably the worst of them. He was just as evil as he could be. There wasn't a thing that he would boggle at. He was just as tough as hell; and there was only one person who was a bit tougher than French, and that was his wife—commonly known as The Boss. She was good-looking, cruel, and generally awful.

Even French was afraid of her.

Charles went on working for the firm of stationers, for French liked his people to have the cover of a real job. It was about three months after he had started in with the gang that Charles—who, by the way, was inclined to be a decent kid—met Rosanna.

He fell in love with Rosanna. She was slim and lovely and was secretary to a banker. She believed in Charles. He said nothing of his connection with the French crowd. He was hoping, rather desperately, to break away from it. He had a hope!

Then French's wife found out about Rosanna, and that just tickled her silly. The idea of busting up a romance looked swell to her. So she had an anonymous note sent to Rosanna telling her that Charles was a crook. Rosanna tackled Charles about it and he spilled the beans. He told her what had happened to him.

Rosanna was angry. She had lots of grit. She found out The Boss and told her just what she thought of her. That wasn't a very wise thing to do. She made an enemy who would stop at nothing.

The Boss got annoyed. So she had a little conversation with her husband and fixed things for the girl. Nothing would content that tough, blonde wife of French's but that she must ring Rosanna into the gang too—and she did.

French had influence with all sorts of people in Chicago, and the police " pulled in " Charles on a charge framed up by a friend of French's. Then French gave Rosanna the chance of either joining up and working with the crowd or seeing Charles sent up the river for a five-year stretch. Rosanna was in love with Charles, as I have said, so she chose the gang.

They had a bad time, those two, when Charles was released. The Boss and her husband went out of their respective ways to make life generally awful for them, and they succeeded.

Every bit of dirty work that had to be done was just another job for Rosanna and Charles. French's chief lieutenant—a terrible fellow, a Swede named Gorltz—managed to make life appalling for them.

You may wonder why they didn't try to make a get-away, but if you had known Chicago in those days you wouldn't wonder. A man like French was a big shot, and he could pull anything he liked. If those two had tried to escape they would have been pulled in on something or other before they had got ten miles.

Then the funny thing happened.

French's gang pulled a job. They held up a motor-car and took a diamond necklace off the dame that was in it. That wasn't so good, because the dame happened to be the wife of a U.S. senator and there are limits to things that you can do even in Chicago. The police began to get busy and French was tipped off that it was an established fact that his gang had pulled the job and that somebody had got to get "sent up" for it, and pretty quick, too!

Then French's wife had a funny idea. She thought it would be a good joke to plant the necklace on Rosanna and send her off out of Chicago accompanied by Charles. Then the police could be tipped off and the pair of them arrested.

Everybody would then be happy, thought The Boss. The senator's wife would have her necklace back; Charles and Rosanna would go "up the river"; the police would be satisfied and French's gang would be well rid of a pair

233

of puling infants whose hearts had never been in their "work" anyway, and who, she thought, were a pair of sick headaches.

A nice woman, The Boss——!

French thought it was a great idea and sent for Gorltz. Gorltz suggested that Charles and Rosanna should be sent to New York on a pretended job; that the necklace should be slipped into Rosanna's dressing-case while it was being taken to the railroad station, and that when they had started, somebody could telephone the detective bureau who could then "wipe-up" Charles and Rosanna at the station. After a bit he decided that he didn't like the dressing-case idea and would think up something a bit better.

So that was that!

Gorltz went on to suggest that French and his wife should themselves "blow" out of it to their house in Pennsylvania at the same time, so that they should be out of Chicago while Charles and Rosanna were being tried.

It was all fixed up. Gorltz went round and saw Charles, and told him that he had to go to New York with Rosanna and explained what he had to do there; then he went along and saw Rosanna and gave *her* instructions. He was always very nice and polite to her, was Gorltz, with a sneer in his voice and an evil grin on his face.

He was still grinning when, that evening, he gave Charles a beautiful fur coat to give to Rosanna.

"The kid'll wanna look swell in New York on this job," he said. "And besides, Charlie, she'll just love you for that coat—eh, boy?"

Next evening they all met in French's flat. French and his wife were leaving on a train half an hour before the New York Flyer was supposed to be taking Charles and Rosanna.

It was a bitterly cold evening and the five of them sat around drinking coffee.

Then Gorltz got up.

"I'll get your luggage taken down to the station," he said to Charles, and the boy came up and took off Charles's kit-bag and Rosanna's dressing-case.

Gorltz spoke to French.

"Chief, you gotta be movin' too," he said. "Your train's due in any minute now——" He proceeded to help French's wife into her fur coat. A grin came over his face. He whispered in her ear.

She took the hint.

"Say, baby-face, just hand over to me that fur coat you're wearin'," she said to Rosanna with a smirk. "It's better than mine. You don't think you're goin' to wear a better coat than me—do you? Strip it off, you silly-lookin' so-and-so!"

Rosanna said nothing. Her spirit was pretty well broken. She just handed over her new coat and took The Boss's fur coat for herself.

French and his wife prepared to go. They said good-bye to Charles and Rosanna and they were both grinning like fiends. It was a good joke.

When they'd gone Gorltz spoke to Charles.

"Here's a note for you," he said. "It's some further dope on what you gotta do in New York. Read it when you get to the station."

He wished them good-bye. He was grinning too!

French and his wife were arrested on the Pennsylvania railroad station. The senator's wife's necklace was found sewn into the lining of The Boss's fur coat—*Rosanna's fur coat, that was*!

Even they couldn't pull themselves out of *that* break. That night found them in jail.

When they arrived at the station Charles opened Gorltz's note. He read this:

"Listen, you pair of pikers. When you get to New York take the first boat and get out of U.S. Give yourself a break. You're not fit to be gangsters—you haven't got the heart.

"I'm fixing French. I gave them a chance. I suggested to her that she should take your girl's fur coat. *If she hadn't done it she'd have been all right*. As it is, I had the necklace that you two were going to be planted with sewn up in the lining. I never did like The Boss, and I wanted to see if she'd be mean enough to take the coat off your girl.

"You see, I had a girl once, and The Boss fixed her—too!

"Well—she took the coat, and it was your break.

"I always did like a joke.

"Well—so long.

"GORLTZ."

Charles and Rosanna are in Belgium to-day. Yeah—they got a shop there. Doin' well.

Gorltz? He was bumped off three weeks later on the corner of the Gregory Boulevard in Chicago.

He always did like a joke.

A LIFE FOR A LAMP

From the story of Charles H—, ex-night watchman, Manhattan Docks

"THERE's always stories where there's docks. I reckon I've listened to more stories than most fellers.

"Ef you're one of these guys that believes in romance you can't do better than hang around Manhattan Docks ef you wanna get stories.

"The boats come in an' go out; an' every boat carries a load of tragedies an' comedies—but the comedies don't matter much. There ain't so many of them——

236

"My strangest story? Yeah—I got one. Who ain't? But this story is a real good 'un. It happened when I was a junior watchman twelve years ago, when I was doin' the midnight to four a.m. stretch.

"I'll tell it to you, an' you kin judge for yourself. I reckon it's good. . . ."

"It sounds funny for a guy to be a junior night-watch when he's forty-three, but that's how old I was when this happened.

"The night-watch in charge was a feller named Ollsen. He was a Norwegian, I guess, an' a good feller too. He was a regular guy.

"Our job was patrollin' round No. 4 Dock, an' also keepin' an eye on the surrounding neighbourhood. We was supposed to tip off anything funny to the Customs men. At this time there was a lot of smugglin' of one sort an' another goin' on.

"An' Manhattan was a bit funny in those days, y'know. Lots of strange guys hangin' around. Fellers who'd come back from the war and who wasn't very pertickler about bein' quick with a shootin' rod. They was up to anything, and was they tough? They was the sort of guys who'd use manhole covers to play draughts with.

"One night Ollsen and me went to a speak-easy just off Mangrove Court—a place not half so nice as it sounds —and whilst we was there some swell guy comes in. He was buyin' drinks for everybody and doin' himself well. I didn't like the look of him much.

"Ollsen told me to keep clear of this guy. He was a big-time racketeer in the days when a racket was a racket, believe me.

"Apparently this guy's main stunt was dope-runnin'; Ollsen told me that nobody ever knew how they got the stuff off the boats—but they got it all right. This feller did all the business with the Bowery an' Chinatown, where he sold the real stuff. As well he used to water cocaine down too, with boracic powder, and sell that to the smart guys who liked to look for new thrills on Broadway. You know 'em!

"I watched out for this feller. He sort of interested me. I like sittin' back and watchin' things quietly. Bein' a night-watchman gets you that way. I suppose it's walkin' about by yourself most of the night—thinkin'.

"An' it was easy for me to keep an eye on him. Everybody was used to see me hangin' around the place, and as my beat often took me around the streets alongside the No. 4 Dock neighbourhood, a district where the feller used to operate—his name was Tony ——, he was an Irish-Italian, if you please!—nobody ever took any notice of me.

"An' what a feller he was for swell dames. You oughta seen some of the dames who used to come down to the lousy speak-easies around there to meet Mr. Tony ——. They used to look like a million dollars, and he treated 'em just like dirt. Ollsen said he used to do a bit of blackmail as a sorta sideline. A nice guy, I reckon. Anyhow, he certainly had some of those dames where he wanted 'em. They seemed to stand for anything.

"I used to wonder about some of them women. They looked as if they'd been pretty nice at some time or other—before they met Tony ——, I mean. Somehow they made me think of my own girl—she got a job with some travellin' show way back fifteen years ago when she was eighteen years, an' we ain't never seen her to speak to since—an' I hoped that wherever she was she'd never run into a guy like Tony ——.

"One night Ollsen and me got an evenin' off, an' we went to a Broadway show. It was a good show, I reckon. Afterwards, some cop, who was a friend of Ollsen's, put us on to a speak-easy near the Forties, an' we went along there. Presently in comes Tony —— with a swell dame. She had been a good-looker once, I guess.

"Some guy who we got talkin' to told us that this woman was the one who looked after Tony ——'s Broadway racket. She used to do the dope-placin' around that neighbourhood for him. I sorta felt sorry for her.

"Somehow I got particularly interested in this Tony —— guy about this time, and I started doin' a bit of inquirin' round about the docks. I've said that people didn't take much notice of me around there, and it wasn't difficult to find out what Tony —— was at.

"Apparently he had a good scheme for gettin' hold of the dope. It seems that it used to be floated off the big boats by people aboard who was in his pay. They used to drop it overboard in a floating box with a small motor propeller, an' when the box was driven in to the dockside somebody picked it up. I got to hear that Tony —— was expectin' a big cargo an' that he didn't quite know how to get it landed, so I thought that I might give him a hand.

"I went an' saw him. I told him I was hard up an' needed some jack, an' that if there was a big box of the stuff to be landed it could be done easy. I said that if he liked to drive down himself in his car I would let the car into No. 4 Dock. I said he had better get used to drivin' down and parkin' the car inside the dock, an' I would tell Ollsen that he was payin' me a few dollars for lookin' after it. So that when the night came to put the stuff on the car nobody would notice it. I said that I would pull out to the boat myself and they could let the box down to me over the stern. I would use one of the port dinghies so everything would look all right, especially as we night-watchmen was supposed to row around the dock basins occasionally.

"He thought the idea was good an' gave me fifty dollars for myself. Then every night when he came down I used to let his car inside No. 4 Dock gates. I used to make him drive it along the stone pier and stop just on the left of the pier lamp that we lit at dusk. I made him stop there because, except for a foot or two on each side of the lamp, the place was pitch dark.

239

"A week or so afterwards the boat came in that had the stuff aboard. Tony —— tipped me off that he would drive down to his usual speak-easy an' then say he was goin' straight back to Broadway. Instead of that he would turn off, an' I would have the gate opened for him at twelve o'clock. He would drive right down the pier and pull up as usual by the lamp. I would close the gate behind him, run off to the dinghy and pull out to the boat, get the stuff, pull back to No. 4 pier, where he would come down the side steps and help me get it into the car, then he could drive off with it.

"At five minutes to twelve I went down to the engine-house an' started up the suction pump workin' in No. 4 Dock Small Basin. I had previously done something else I wanted to do. Then I went down to the gate an' waited for Tony ——. He was punctual. He saw me opening the gate and he trod on the gas an' shot down the pier just like he had got in the habit of doin'.

"I just hadn't told him that I had moved the lamp twelve feet off the end of the pier on a long iron rail I had got.

"He naturally miscalculated, and when he saw what had happened it was too late. He went clean over the end of the pier, and the No. 4 suction pump that I had set workin' did the rest. The suction pump sucks off the water at the bottom of the basin out of inlets in the cement sides, and the pump just sucked Tony —— down an' through the inlet, an' that was the end of him.

"And if ever they empty No. 4 Dock Basin they'll find his two-seater on the bottom!

"Nobody ever seemed to even miss him. He had a lot of enemies, and the authorities thought naturally that somebody had taken him for a ride. Anyhow, they were glad to be rid of him.

"An' that was the end of Tony . . .

"Why did I do it? Well—I just didn't like him very much—see? An' there was another thing. You remember that swell dame I told you about—the one we saw him with in the Broadway speak-easy?

"Well, that was my daughter, see? The one that went off when she was eighteen—the one who was doin' Tony ——'s dope-runnin'.

"That sorta got me annoyed, an' I thought I'd fix Tony ——.

"An' I fixed him."

DEATH IN THE LIFT

From the Narrative of Señor Enrico ——, one time Junior Secretary at the —— Legation

"LIFE and death sometimes depend upon a hair, señor? No one should know that better than I. But if you ask me whether it is permissible to kill a man, then I must say that the answer must depend upon circumstances.

"I myself have killed a man; but the fact does not perturb me at all. I feel that, in the particular circumstances, I was quite justified.

"The amusing part of the business was, however, that in considering myself entitled to kill this man I was acting under a belief that was entirely incorrect.

"You would like to hear the story? But, of course, I shall be delighted to tell you.

"Thank you. I will have coffee—black—and a cigar—a long Bolivar.

"Ten years ago I was junior secretary at the —— Legation in London. I was ten years younger than I am now, passably good-looking, and possessed of—I hope—the good manners for which my country is not unjustifiably noted.

"It was my habit to go to the theatre every Friday

night and after the play was over I used to return to Queen's Gate—in the vicinity of which I lived—and take a stroll.

"It was pleasing to walk along your wide, clean streets in the cool night air, and, just before retracing my steps homeward, I would invariably visit a coffee-stall in that district and drink a cup of tea, not so much for the tea but in order to study the interesting English types that would foregather at this particular coffee-stall after midnight.

"One night, as I stood there drinking my tea out of those so very thick cups for which your coffee-stall-keepers have such an amazing attachment, I was startled by the sudden appearance out of the darkness of one of the most lovely women that I have ever seen in my life.

"You will understand that being attached to a Legation I was used to meeting many beautiful women; yet this particular one was possessed of a wonderful grace of figure and a beauty quite ravishing.

"It was also quite obvious that she was very, very frightened.

"She would glance over her shoulder every now and then almost as if she feared that someone would attack her. Her oval face was very white, and about her beautiful violet eyes there were the shadows that indicate nervous strain.

"Even the long white fingers that held her cup were trembling.

"I suppose that if I had been an Englishman I should have done nothing; but I am not an Englishman, and I am not possessed of that marvellous coolness of temperament which I admire so very much in your countrymen. I cannot bear to see a beautiful woman troubled, and, therefore, I approached her quietly and asked her if I could be of service to her in any way.

"At first she appeared to be even more nervous than

ever, but eventually she regained some control of herself and thanked me for my offer of service. I advised her to drink her tea quietly and then to tell me what was troubling her.

"We walked round the quiet square, and, in a trembling voice, she told me her story. She could no longer keep silent. She was desperate.

"It appeared that she had been living in America for some time, and, owing to circumstances which do not matter in my tale, she had become 'mixed up,' I think you call it, with a man who was nothing less than a criminal. This man had some hold over her, and she was unable to escape from his clutches for a long time.

"But at last her opportunity came and she was able to disclose the story of this man's nefarious activities to the police. Even his influence could not save him, and he was sentenced to seven years' imprisonment, and she escaped to England.

"But he swore that directly he came out of prison he would kill her, and she knew that he would carry out his threat.

"On this particular day she had heard of his arrival in England, accompanied by two of his confederates, and she believed that her end was near.

"I pointed out to her that England was not America; that he would not be allowed to murder people as he liked in this country, but it was of no avail.

"She was terrified. She was afraid to return to her flat, which, she said, had been under the observation of two strange men all day.

"Señor, I was affected. I was, as I have said, ten years younger than I am now and my heart was touched. Also, I found myself more than attracted to this most beautiful woman, whose exquisite evening gown set off a beauty more radiant than I had ever seen.

"I had an idea. I told her that I would take her back
243

to my legation offices; that she might rest in safety on the couch in the rest-room, and that next morning I would take further steps to ensure her safety.

"After a long discussion she agreed. I called a cab, and we drove to the Legation. I opened the front door with my key and led her to the rest-room, which was in the rear of the ground floor. I switched on the light and drew up the couch in front of the electric fire. I wished her good-night and was about to leave her when the thing happened.

"As we stood in the middle of the room there was a sudden crack, the window at the back of the room was shattered and a bullet embedded itself in the wall. It had missed her by inches.

"I acted promptly. I switched off the light, took her by the hand, dashed out of the building, and, taking a cab that was passing, took her to the house of a woman relative.

"On the way she sobbed bitterly.

"'You see, it is useless,' she said. 'He will get me. That bullet missed me by inches. If it is not to-night it will be to-morrow night.'

"'Nonsense, señora,' I said. 'Have courage. You are safe now. Do you know where this man lives? If so, tell me. I will deal with him.'

"At first she refused, but after we had arrived at my cousin's house and she felt more safe she told me the name of the hotel where the desperado was living. She had learned it only that evening. He had a suite on the second floor, No. 15, and she entreated me to keep away from him.

"But my blood was up. I left her, telling her that I would return immediately, and I drove straight to the hotel where this villain was staying.

"It was an hotel of good class, but of the smaller sort, situated in the centre of London. I pushed through the swing-doors and looked round for the night-porter, but the hall was empty, the man was elsewhere—a lucky coincidence.

"But at the side of the hall stood the lift. I stepped into it, pressed the second-floor button, and rose.

"Arrived at the second floor, I opened the lift gate. As I did so a door in the corridor immediately opposite the lift opened. On the door was the number—15. A man stepped out.

"He was in evening clothes, tall and dark, and one look at the villainy written on his face told me that he was the man I sought.

"I struck him in the face, and, as he staggered back, against the wall, I seized him by the throat. Holding him against the wall, I called him by every foul name I could think of in your language, and I told him that if he continued to persecute the lady who had asked my aid I would kill him like a rat.

"Then I released him.

"He pulled himself together; then, with a sudden movement, he sprang into the lift. At the same moment he flung-to the outer lift gate and stood inside grinning at me, protected from me by the steel grille.

"'Say, you think you're clever, don't you—you wop!' he hissed at me. 'All right, waal, you can get back to your girl friend and you can tell her that I'm goin' to get her—see? *I'm goin' to get her, an' just when I want to!* Maybe to-morrow, maybe the next day, maybe next month. Wherever she runs I'll follow her. She'll never know when it's goin' to happen . . . but it will happen. Goodnight, wop!'

"He laughed in my face and began to close the inside gate. Then, mad with rage, I did something instinctively. I thrust my walking-stick through the steel grille at his face, missed him, *but I got the crooked end of my stick round his neck,* and, as he pressed the button to make the lift descend, I pulled his head forward.

"His neck was caught between the lift floor and the

245

floor of the corridor. The descending lift broke it like a reed, splintering my stick at the same moment.

"My spine turned to ice. I ran quickly down the stairs. The hall was still empty, and at the side stood the lift with its cargo of death.

"I passed quickly through the swing-doors of the hotel. No one saw me.

"I walked quietly home and went to bed.

"Next morning I read in the newspapers of the 'accident' that had occurred and later of the coroner's warning to people to close both doors of a lift before descending.

"I smiled to myself.

"And now, señor, observe the strangeness of fate! *Next morning the very old and charming gentleman who occupied the house opposite the back of the Legation came round to apologise for having accidentally discharged his sporting rifle while cleaning it the night before.*

"*This was the bullet that shattered the window. The bullet which so enraged me.*

"A coincidence—is it not so—señor?"

CHICAGO PAY-OFF

You can't beat the rap. I've met guys who thought they could miss the pay-off; but they was always unlucky.

Remember Two-time Caselli. I worked for him once. He was a great guy—sometimes.

Well, one night Two-time is sitting in his swell penthouse apartment doin' a bit of quiet thinkin'. He is figurin' out that the rackets is all gettin' washed up; that it is time he pulled somethin' really big an' got out of it. Chicago is not so good for him. Why? 'Cause Snetkin, the straight cop, who's runnin' the Homicide Squad at police headquarters, has got an idea in his head that he's goin' to pull in Two-time. He reckons that Two-time has been gettin' away with a durn sight too much for the last seven years, an' he's just waitin' for a chance to get the hooks on the big boy. See?

Two-time walks over an' has a look at himself in the mirror over the fireplace. He looks good to him. He's a bit jowly, maybe, an' a little bit fat, but he's still got that "come-on" look that the dames fall for, an' his hair is still nice an' wavy, even if it is a bit thin on the dome. He stands there lookin' at himself, admirin' his five-dollar tie, his thirty-dollar silk shirt, an' wonderin' just what it is he's goin' to make the big clean-up over. You got to understand his main racket was liquor, an' the liquor racket ain't been so good since they pulled Capone in.

Comin' up in the elevator is Jenny, an' does she look swell? There ain't no doubt that Jenny is easy to look at. Her clothes is all Fifth Avenue, an' she's wearin' a Persian lamb coat an' muff. Parked inside the muff is a .38 colt automatic.

Her face is nice an' kind an' pretty an' smilin', just like the cat what swallowed the canary. Believe it or not, that girl, Jenny, on this particular night, looked swell. And how!

Jenny is the wise baby. Five years ago she comes in to New York from a Connecticut farm. She was twenty-two an' had a hundred an' fifty dollars an' a lotta hope. After kickin' around New York, wearin' out her Oxfords on the streets that ain't paved with gold so that you'd notice it, the money goes an' the hope gets part worn.

Then she runs into Two-time. He gives her the once-over an' fixes her up with a job at the Green Parrot night club which, as you know, is a pretty good place for girls that ain't so good, an' six months after that Jenny knows all the answers.

She sticks along with Two-time for a year, an' when Jimmy Pereira, who is a real booze boss, puts a couple of slugs into Two-time one night for old times' sake an'

Two-Time goes to hospital, Jenny decides she'll change partners.

She goes along with Pereira, an' what Two-time forgot to teach her Pereira starts to hand out with both hands. So, by this time, she's pretty good. What she knows would fill a Carnegie library, an' what she don't know is what stamp collectors could stick under the stamp an' still not miss.

Jenny pushes open the door of Two-time's apartment an' walks straight in. He just grins.

"Well, fancy seein' you, Jenny," says Two-time. "My, but you're lookin' swell. Whata you doin' in Chicago?"

She sits down.

"I'll tell you in a minute, Two-time," she says.

He gives her a straight gin an' he stands in front of the fire, fingerin' his tie an' lookin' at her. Two-time is feelin' pretty good. You gotta know that he got the name "Two-time" 'cause he said the dames always came back twice. An' he's standin' up there, thinkin' that it's the old story with Jenny, an' that she just couldn't keep away from him. After a minute he says to her:

"Well, babe, what's the riot?"

She finishes her drink an' she looks up. Two-time is thinkin' that she's still a mighty pretty woman.

"Here's the latest, Two-time," she says. "They're springin' Pereira to-day——"

Two-time whistles.

"You don't say?" he says. "The dirty rat. So they're goin' to let him out, are they? Go on, Jenny."

"It's this way," she says. "He phoned me this mornin' an' told me that he was comin' to Chicago to-night an' I was to get a quiet room for him in a quiet hotel so's he could do a little bit of business before he scrammed out of it. You see, Jimmy ain't feelin' so good. First of all, gettin' sent up was a surprise to him when he thought he had everybody nicely fixed an' secondly, he's got an idea that there are one or two guys, includin' yourself, Two-

248

time, round this burg who'd be only too glad to take a pot at him."

Two-time nods.

"Well, what's he comin' here for?" he asks.

Jenny grins.

"He's comin' here for the dough, Two-time," she says. "It might surprise you to hear that he's got 200,000 dollars United States currency stacked in the safe deposit right here."

Two-time whistles an' starts to do some quick thinkin'. Jenny goes on:

"This mornin' on the phone Jimmy gives me the layout. When he gets here, which will be at seven o'clock, he's goin' straight to the hotel. I'm goin' round there to meet him an' he's goin' to give me the key of the safe deposit box. Then I'm supposed to go round an' get the money. Then I give him the tip-off that all's clear an' that there ain't any guys watchin' round on the entrance to the hotel, an' then he figures we're goin' to scram up to New York."

"So what?" says Two-time.

Jenny smiles.

"Well, that's where he's makin' the one big mistake," she says, an' her voice is grim. "Here's how I've got it fixed. I've got him a room, No. 73, at Mitzler's Hotel on Grape Street. This room is at the back of the hotel an' looks out over the Barrel Street alley, an' on the other side of that alley is the back of the Penfold Hotel.

"At seven o'clock to-night I'm goin' round to Mitzler's to meet him an' get the key. Then I'm supposed to go off to the safe deposit to get the satchel, but I ain't goin' to. I'm goin' to slip round the corner into the Penfold an' I'm goin' to meet you in the long bar, an' I'm goin' to slip you the safe deposit key. All you do is to jump a cab, go round to the safe deposit an' get the satchel with the dough. Directly you go I go upstairs to the third floor.

"There's a bathroom there an' the window looks right

249

across the alley, right into the window of room No. 73. I fixed with Jimmy that I'll signal him that all's clear from that window after I've got back with the money, but I ain't. The only all clear I'm goin' to give him when he comes to the window of No. 73 is with this!"

An' she tips her muff an' shoots out the .38 colt.

Two-time whistles.

"Gee, kid, so you're goin' to shoot him across the alley. What a swell idea! What an alibi!"

"O.K.," she says. "Now directly you've got the satchel you take another cab an' you go straight off to the railway depot an' book a compartment on the New York Flyer. Directly I've done the job I get into a cab an' meet you down there. We open the satchel an' split the dough. You go your way an' I go mine. How's it go, Two-time?"

Two-time stands in front of the fire, fingerin' his tie an' lookin' down at her. Then he just smiles an' he says:

"It's a great idea, kid. I'm sold on it. I'll be waitin' for you in the long bar at the Penfold at seven-fifteen. How's that?"

She gets up.

"O.K., Two-time," she says, "let's have a drink on that."

An' they stand there drinkin' gin straights an' smilin'.

At seven-fifteen Two-time's standin' round in the bar at the Penfold, drinkin' highballs an' feelin' pretty good with himself. All the time he's got one eye on the door.

Then Jenny blows in. She walks straight up to him an' she slips him the key with her right hand. The left is busy inside her muff.

"Go to it, Two-time," she whispers, "an' be quick. I'm goin' to hang round here for ten minutes an' then I'm goin' to bump him. See you down at the depot."

Two-time cocks his hat an' puts the key into his waist-coat pocket.

"O.K., babe," he says. "I'll be there with bells!"

An' he scrams. Outside he gets a yellow cab an' drives good an' fast round to the safe deposit. Everythin' is fine. Three minutes later, with the satchel in his hand, he gets back into the cab an' he drives down to the depot, but he don't book any compartment on the New York Flyer as arranged. He just buys a single ticket to New York. Then he waits around.

Pretty soon along comes Jenny. She's still smilin', but she's got a little bit of a strained look around the mouth, Two-time thinks. She comes up to him.

"Well, Two-time," she says. "Here we go."

He looks down at her an' he grins.

"You know, Jenny," he says, "you're a fool dame. You don't ever learn nothin'. You don't really think I'm goin' to give you any of this dough, do you? You know," he goes on, "you break my heart sometimes. You're just as big a mug as when I first picked you up in New York. You was a big blue-eyed babe, an' that's what you still are. Didn't you learn nothin' from me or Pereira? Ain't the rackets taught you nothin'?"

He hands her the ticket.

"There you are, kid," he says. "There's your railway ticket an' now scram out of it an' think yourself durn lucky to make a get-away."

Jenny looks at him. Her eyes are blue an' wide.

"Do you mean to tell me you ain't givin' me my share of the jack?" she says, pointin' to the satchel.

Two-time grins at her.

"Not a cent, baby," he says. "Now scram out of it!"

She scrams.

Two-time stands watchin' the train steam out. Then he turns an' walks away. He's feelin' pretty good. Here's the big clean-up he's been lookin' for. Two hundred thousan' an' all the better 'cause it's Pereira's. Two-time grins as he thinks to himself that it's durn funny that the girl who he threw over before she went to Pereira should

251

be the one who bumps off Pereira an' hands Two-time all this dough. Outside the station he calls a cab an' drives round to his apartment. He gets in the elevator an' goes up. Things is pretty good. He's plannin' a big night.

He gets out of the elevator an' opens his apartment door. Opposite, on the other side of the room in the darkness he sees a spot of light. He snaps on the electricity.

The spot of light is the end of the cigar stuck in the mouth of Snetkin, Chief of the Homicide Squad, who's sittin' in the corner with a couple of his boys.

Snetkin grins.

"Hallo, Two-time," he says. "How're you goin'? I wanna talk to you."

Two-time throws the satchel on the table.

"Say, Snetkin," he says, "you got your nerve, comin' into my place like this. This ain't a waitin'-room. What's eatin' you?"

Snetkin knocks the ash off the end of his cigar.

"Somebody bumped Jimmy Pereira to-night, Two-time," he says. "He was shot in front of a window in room 73 at Mitzler's an' that window looks across to a bathroom at the back of the Penfold Hotel, an' you was seen in the Penfold bar to-night at seven-fifteen. Well, what about it, baby?"

"What about what?" says Two-time. "Are you suggestin' that I bumped Pereira?"

Snetkin grins.

"I ain't suggestin', I'm tellin' you," he says. "You shot him from the bathroom in Penfold across the alley."

"Yeah," says Two-time. "Ain't you the funny bozo? So I killed Jimmy Pereira, did I? Say, where do you get that stuff, Snetkin? I ain't even seen Pereira."

Snetkin grins again.

"Listen, kiddo," he says. "Pereira's girl, Jenny-the-Red, phoned us to-night at 7.20 that she had seen you in the long bar at the Penfold an' that you told her that you was goin' upstairs to bump Jimmy Pereira. Well? You went up an' you done it, didn't you?"

Two-time does some quick thinkin'. He's rememberin' Jenny's wide blue eyes. He comes to the conclusion that he's in dutch an' that he'd better spill the whole works. So he tells Snetkin all about it.

Snetkin just laughs some more.

"It's a great story, Two-time," he says, "but it just don't wash. First of all let me tell you this. Pereira arrived at Mitzler's Hotel at *six* o'clock to-night, not seven, an' he sent the girl round to the safe deposit for the money right away, an' she took it back to him. We found the bag with the dough in by the side of his body. By the way, what have you got in that satchel?" asks Snetkin, grinnin'.

He gets up an' walks across to the table an' he picks up the satchel. He takes out a penknife an' he cuts the lock off, an' he tips the satchel up an' there falls out on the table two .38 colt automatics.

Snetkin picks one up an' smells it. Then he picks the other one up an' pulls out the magazine.

"Well, baby," he says to Two-time, "look at this. Two shots fired out of this gun an' we found two in Pereira. Big boy, you're headin' straight for the chair. We got you this time!"

Two-time don't say nothin'. He's just thinkin'. He's just rememberin' what he said to Jenny down at the depot, that she was still a mug.

He gets it. He looks at Snetkin an' he grins.

"It's a pinch, Snetkin," he says. "Say, I reckon that whoever christened me Two-time was right. I been clever once too often!"

He puts out his hands for the handcuffs that Snetkin is fingerin'.

"Let's be goin', boys," says Two-time.

THE END

HICKORY DICKORY DOCK

Agatha Christie

Hercule Poirot is called in when strange things begin to happen in a student's hostel: a rucksack is slashed, a silk scarf cut up, objects disappear . . . until finally murder is done.

BURKE'S LAW

Roger Fuller

Millionaire cop Captain Amos Burke steps out of his Rolls-Royce into a high society party—and a baffling murder. A fast-moving novel based on the top-rating Granada TV series.

FINAL CURTAIN

Ngaio Marsh

Vicious practical jokes stalk a famous actor. Roderick Alleyn is called in: but he is too late to prevent a particularly nasty murder. " She's one of the best three detective story writers in the world." BIRMINGHAM POST.

THE SUNKEN SAILOR

Patricia Moyes

A sailing idyll turns into a nightmare of violence and murder. " A new Queen of Crime . . . can be mentioned in the same breath as Christie and Marsh." DAILY HERALD. " She has put the 'who' back in whodunit!" ANTHONY BOUCHER.